ACKNOWLEDGEMENTS

WORDS CANNOT adequately express my thanks to Doyl Peck, for his extra effort, support and patience on my behalf. I feel very fortunate to be associated with him and all of the wonderful people at Sounds of Zion. I owe a special thanks to my mother, Cheryl Storrs, for her constant faith in me, never ending-encouragement and boundless supply of ideas. Thanks, Mom, for continually being there for me. As always, a heartfelt thanks to my sister, best friend and editor, Suzette Jensen. She always finds a way to fit me in to her busy schedule. Thanks, Suzette, I appreciate all of your efforts. Finally, to my wonderful family, Kreg, Carson, Carter, Sierra and Bristol—thank you for believing in me. Your excitement for my books makes writing fun.

CHAPTER ONE

"HANNAH, HANNAH! Are you okay?" called Hunter, searching nervously in the darkness for his sister. "Where are you?"

"I can't find her anywhere," squealed Hayden.

"What about Alli? Can you see her?" asked Hunter frantically.

"No, I can't see much of anything. It's too dark in this cave!" Hayden snapped in frustration. "I can't get my eyes to focus yet!"

"Man, Hayden, I really hate these caves!" exclaimed Hunter.

"I'm not loving the whole cave thing either, Hunter!" agreed Hayden. "You know how much I like small, dark places. The main cave was small enough for me."

"This cave isn't that big. Where did those two girls disappear to?" growled Hunter as he ran his fingers across the rough rocks, feeling for an opening.

"Do you see anywhere they could have fallen or

climbed into?" asked Hayden, looking nervously at the ground.

"The cave's too dark to see much. I'm not sure there's anything for them to fall into," replied Hunter. "So, I guess the only way I'll know if she fell is to find the same hole and fall in myself!"

"Then, where in the world did they go?" questioned Hayden. "They couldn't get too far."

"Hannah!" screamed Hunter. "Where are you?" Not hearing a reply, he got down on his hands and knees and started crawling on the floor.

"Hannah, Alli, where are you?" yelled Hayden, stumbling through the cave. "Hunter, could they be hurt?"

"I sure hope not," Hunter replied.

"Then where are they?" asked Hayden worriedly.

"I can't believe this!" Hunter growled angrily. "I don't know where they could...Ouch! Ouch! That hurt!" he exclaimed.

"What's the matter?" asked Hayden. "Are you hurt?"

"There's a gigantic rock over here, and I hit it with my chin," he exclaimed, rubbing his chin as he whined. "Yes, I'm hurt!"

"Quiet a minute, Hunter," insisted Hayden. "I think I hear something."

"Where? What do you hear? Where are they?" asked Hunter, clumsily shuffling toward Hayden. "What can you hear?"

"Ssshhh, will ya, please!" insisted Hayden, trying to listen. "I'm not even sure the noise I hear is the girls. Maybe all this yelling has warned one of the tribes from this cave that we are here, and now they're on their way to find us."

"Oh, great! I hadn't thought about that!" exclaimed Hunter. "What will happen if they come out here?"

"That would be interesting, wouldn't it?" replied Hayden. "How would we explain all of this to them?"

A slight sound rattled again in the cave, causing an echo to bounce back and forth against the walls.

"I can't tell for sure where the noise is coming from. Can you, Hunter?" asked Hayden, straining to hear and unsure where to look.

"Come on, Hannah. This isn't a joke anymore! Where are you?" Hunter shouted angrily.

"We've got to get out of here. If one of the lost tribes comes to protect the cave and we're in here, there could be serious problems," warned Hayden, nervously scanning the cave.

"We can't leave the girls!" exclaimed Hunter. "What do we do about the girls?"

"We might have to...," started Hayden.

"You don't have to do anything about the girls!" shrieked Hannah, frightening Hunter as she jumped into the open. "I'm right here!"

"I'm right here, too," squealed Alli excitedly, as she jumped from behind the large rock Hunter had just hit his chin on.

"Hannah? Alli?" shrieked Hunter, shocked at their sudden appearance. "Is that you?"

"Surprise!" Hannah called.

"Surprise?! Surprise?! What do you mean surprise?"

demanded Hunter. "Oh, you can't be serious. You didn't just pretend to be lost, did you?"

Hannah smiled, "We're only playing with you!"

"We'll, that wasn't very funny," screeched Hayden, as he dropped his head into his hands. "You scared us to death! We thought you were hurt - or worse!"

"We thought members from the lost tribes were on their way to get us!" growled Hayden. "We thought we were in big trouble."

Angry at the situation, Hayden moved out of the small cave into the light of the big cave. He was followed closely by Hunter. Hayden took a deep breath, leaned back against the wall, then slid to the ground and sat down.

"You know what, guys? That really wasn't funny," declared Hunter, as he sat on the ground next to Hayden. "My heart was racing. If we let you two girls get hurt, Dad would never forgive us."

"Come on, Hunter. You have to know we truly weren't trying to scare you. We were only playing with you two," insisted Alli, hoping to console her friends. "Please, don't be mad at us."

"Well, maybe only scare you a little!" added Hannah, grinning nervously at her brothers.

"We've wasted half an hour looking for you two, rather than figuring out exactly what we need to do to bring back the ten lost tribes," Hunter scolded, scowling at his sister. "I'm a little mad at you, Hannah. This wasn't really the best time for jokes."

"You're not just mad that we tricked you, are ya?" asked Hannah, smiling.

"Yes, I am mad that you tricked us!" replied Hunter. "But I'm more upset that you picked the wrong time to mess around."

"Okay, you're right. This probably wasn't the best time for jokes or playing. I promise it won't happen again, Hunter," Hannah assured him. "Now, before Mom and Dad have a total melt down because we've been gone so long, where do we start?"

"Alli, please get the letter off the desk that Joseph Smith left for us, and let's see what it says again," suggested Hayden.

Alli nodded, turned without a word and hurried to the table. Collecting the note, she quickly rushed back toward the boys and handed the letter to Hayden.

CHAPTER TWO

AS HAYDEN TOOK the letter, he shook his head and grinned. "Who would have ever thought the Kimball family legend was true? How could it be? When Grandpa Kimball had showed us kids the lamp and told us about the legend, we were sure it wasn't real. But as we traveled with Mom and Aunt Shirley on what was supposed to be a boring church history road trip, at every landmark Hunter, Hannah, Alli, and I visited, we mysteriously solved another clue. Clues us kids were sure had been solved years earlier. One by one we discovered a host of mysterious secrets left specifically for us, by prophets of old.

After solving the last clue and aware of being followed we found the entrance into the Hill Cumorah and suddenly find ourselves surrounded by the lost treasures of the Book of Mormon. And now to be directed by the prophet Joseph Smith in a letter to find and bring home the lost tribes, how does life get better than this?" Hayden thought as he stared at the hand written note.

"Hello, Hayden. Come on, Buddy. Why don't you read that letter out loud so all of us can hear?" called Hunter.

Hayden looked up, peered over the edge of the note and asked, "Do you want me to read the letter out loud?"

Hunter raised his eyebrows, puckered his lips, smirked at his brother and then silently nodded his head.

Hayden, watching Hunter's reaction, smiled and shrugged his shoulders. Then he quickly began to read.

"*Hunter, Hannah, Hayden and Allison,*

As I sit alone inside the Hill Cumorah, secluded from the eyes of any mortal, I contemplate the feelings of my heart in meditation. I am overjoyed to write this letter to you. Much favored of the Lord, I have been allowed to see, in vision, the things, which are to come. As I watch the hardships that you face each day in the world in which you live, I feel encouraged to know the true conviction of your hearts is to build up Christ's Kingdom on the earth.

"*I feel as though I have known you all my life, and I look forward to the day when I will be able to throw my arms around you. Remain steadfast in your commitment to the Lord. Endeavor to fulfill His every commandment, and the Comforter will always be at your side.*

"*With that said, your immediate assistance is required. The world has been waiting for you to wax strong in your testimonies of the gospel, and that day has finally arrived. As you* look about your surroundings, you will see many treasures. Many of the treasures that lie hidden in this room are the treasures spoken of by prophets of old. But they are of no importance at this time, and they are not the true treasures hidden in or spoken of with regard to the Hill Cumorah. They are not to be removed from this room for any reason. Should you attempt to do so, your punishment would be severe. The Lord would most surely erase your memory of this place and how to return here. You are also forbidden to reveal this location or speak of the treasures inside - unfortunately, even to your grandfather at this time.

"As you look upon this room, you will notice ten separate openings scattered about the walls. Each opening is marked with a small, gold plate engraved with the name of the tribe that resides deep within the cave. Your task will be one of peril - surely full of hardships should you choose to endure it. Yet, each house must be returned for the fullness of the Lord to continue.

"Therefore, your charge, should you choose by your own free will to accept it, is to return to your day the Scattered and Lost Tribes of Israel from the four corners of the earth. Bring at least two - one man and one woman - who may show the path to their people. Be aware as you make your decision that the adversary will do everything within his power to stop you from completing the tasks, which the Lord hath placed before you.

"Your lives may be in grave danger on many occasions. Know also that if your trust is placed in the Lord, righteousness will prevail. Whatever your choice, I cannot wait until *such time that I have the opportunity to shake your hands and reside in the company of such worthy Sons and Daughters of God. You are those that He has sent forth — His most noble and valiant soldiers — to reside on the earth during these last days.*

"'I know you will fulfill the mission you were sent to earth to accomplish. Humble yourselves before the Lord, that He may guide you in your journey to return our lost brothers. May the Comforter always remain at your side. Remember to keep your eyes single to the glory of our God.

Your eternal brother,
Joseph Smith, Jr.'"

"I still can't believe that I'm being asked to help the lost tribes return," said Hunter. "I've never done anything spectacular like this before. I don't know what I could have possibly done in my life that would justify the Lord believing in me this much."

"Who are you kidding, Hunter? In the pre-mortal existence, when you chose to be on the Lord's side, even though it was going to be harder than Satan's way, you chose it," said Hannah. "To me, that means that you do something spectacular every day of your life."

Hunter shrugged his shoulders at Hannah, grinned slightly, and replied, "Thanks, Hannah. But, I'm still kinda mad at you!"

"Sorry, Hunter. But you do have to admit, we got you two!" Hannah exclaimed, giggling.

"Come on, guys. We've got to get down to business. According to the letter, we need to help the lost tribes find their way here. Did you two girls see any way for us to find a lost city when you were messing around in the cave?" Hayden asked sternly.

"What do you mean?" asked Alli, unsure what Hayden was asking.

"An opening or entrance to another cave, did you see anything like that?" replied Hayden.

"I crawled on my hands and knees the entire time I was in there, and I didn't see or feel anything that might lead us anywhere," replied Alli. "Did you, Hannah?"

"I ran my hands across every wall and behind every rock looking for a place to hide, and I didn't feel or see anything either," added Hannah.

"Then how are we supposed to find anything, especially people?" Hayden questioned, irritated he did not know what to do. "The cave is more like a room, not a tunnel that leads somewhere."

"We must be missing something," reasoned Alli. "We've overlooked something, I know it!"

"Like what?" asked Hannah.

"I don't know. What about the plaques over the caves? What do they mean?" questioned Alli, pointing to a plaque.

"I wish I could read reformed Egyptian, 'cause then I might have an answer. But, I don't have any idea what these mean," said Hayden.

"What about a Book of Mormon. There has to be one in here, don't you think?" asked Hunter. He jumped to his feet and looked around the room.

"How will the Book of Mormon help us?" questioned Alli.

"I was hoping there might be a reference or something," Hunter replied, searching around the room.

"A reference to what?" she quizzed.

"A reference or any information that would help us with the lost tribes," Hunter replied.

"You mean a clue?" asked Hannah.

"Yeah, I mean anything that might lead us in the right direction," Hunter replied, still searching for the book.

Hayden slowly climbed to his feet and scanned the room. With nothing in sight, he called, "Hunter, I bet the only copy of the Book of Mormon in here are the actual Golden Plates. And as hard as we try, I don't think we're going to be able to translate any of those pages."

"You know what guys?" asked Hannah softly.

"No! What?" replied Hayden smiling.

"You know how cool it is that the Lord trusted us enough to be in this very cave with the golden plates of The Book of Mormon?" she replied, grinning from ear to ear. "It doesn't get any better than this!"

"Yes it will!" exclaimed Alli excitedly.

"When we bring the ten tribes home, now that will be cool!" interrupted Hayden.

"No, when we meet Joseph Smith and the Lord, now that will be really cool!" added Alli.

"You know what would be totally cool right now?" asked Hunter as he stared at Hannah.

"What?" questioned Hannah, sure he would say something they hadn't thought of yet.

"If you guys would help me so that those things you just talked about could really happen!" he exclaimed sarcastically.

Hannah smiled a crooked smile, scrunched her nose and shrugged her shoulders at Hunter and replied, "We were just dreamin' for a minute. You know it might be good for you to dream with us!"

Hunter twisted his lips to the right and then back to the left as he thought. Nearly three full minutes passed before he finally replied. Ignoring Hannah's statement, he asked, "Do any of you remember the names of the ten tribes?"

Hannah studied the plaques carefully, looking for any indication as to which tribe they represented. "I can't remember all of them, but I do remember a few of them from Brother Hutcheon's Seminary class. Let's see...I can remember the name, *Issachar*, and *Gad*, 'cause I always thought they were funny."

"I can remember *Simeon* and *Levi*," added Hayden.

"What about you, Hunter? Can you remember any of them?" asked Hannah.

"I'm thinking," he snapped, angry he couldn't remember any of the names.

"What about you, Alli? Can you remember any?" asked Hannah.

"I had to memorize them for church once. But that was a long time ago. Give me a second, I'm trying to remember what they are," she replied softly, deep in thought. "Okay, I think I can remember...My mom would NAG me until I was DIZzy, then I would Jumble and SLuR my words. That's it!" she exclaimed, excited to have remembered.

"What's it?" questioned Hunter, confused by Alli's riddle. "What do you mean your mom would NAG you?"

Alli, hardly able to contain her excitement, replied, "That is the sentence I came up with so I could remember the tribe names. My mom would NAG – Naphtali, Asher, Gad, until I was DIZzy – Dan, Issachar, Zabulun. Then I would Jumble – Judah – and SLuR – Simeon, Levi and Reuben – my words."

"Alright. What a great way to remember, Alli," exclaimed Hunter.

"Yeah, good job, Alli," agreed Hannah. "I never would have thought of that!"

"So what now?" Alli asked proudly.

"I thought we might be able to match the number of letters in each tribe name, with the number of letters engraved in the plaques over the cave. Then we'll know which cave belongs to which tribe," Hayden explained.

"Good idea! Okay, the first cave has three letters," said Hannah quickly, as she pointed to the plaque, ready to get started.

"So that cave belongs to either Dan or Gad," replied Hayden.

"And the second cave has six letters," called Hunter anxious to help.

"Okay that cave belongs to either Simeon or Reuben," answered Hayden.

"The third cave has three letters again," added Alli, wanting to help.

"Okay, we know that cave belongs to either Gad or Dan," replied Hayden.

Hannah hurried to the plaque above the fourth cave and yelled, "This cave has five letters, Hayden."

"That cave belongs to either Asher or Judah," Hayden replied excitedly.

"The fifth cave has eight letters," called Hunter, carefully counting every symbol on the plaque.

"Then that cave belongs to the tribe of Naphtali or Issachar," replied Hayden.

"The sixth cave has five letters," hollered Alli, pointing to the plaque as she counted.

"And the seventh cave has seven letters," called Hannah.

"Okay, wait a minute. I'm trying to keep everything in order," said Hayden. "If you've counted the letters correctly that means the sixth cave belongs to either Asher or Judah, and the seventh cave belongs to Zebulun."

Hayden continued to scribble in the dirt on the cave floor for several moments before he looked up at the girls and asked, "How many letters in the plaque above the next cave?"

Hunter hurriedly counted the letters. "The eighth cave has eight letters," responded Hunter, in a low mysterious voice.

Hayden laughed as he again scribbled in the dirt. "Okay, the ninth cave?"

"I'm not sure," replied Alli. "This one is different."

"What do you mean it's different?" questioned Hannah, as she walked toward Alli.

"Well, look. This plaque has two words. One with four letters and one with six letters," she replied, pointing at the plaque.

"What?" questioned Hunter. "What do you mean?"

"Seriously, look. This cave is marked with two words," Hannah insisted.

"How many letters are on the next plaque?" called Hayden. "Maybe that will help us figure this out."

"Well, the plaque over the tenth cave has several words written in English," replied Hunter.

"What does it say? What does it say?" Hannah asked impatiently. "Read it out loud!"

"And a highway shall be cast up in the midst of the great deep," read Hunter, trying to act mysteriously.

"What does that mean?" asked Alli.

Hayden jumped to his feet and rushed to the entrance of the tenth cave. "What's going on, Hunter, any ideas?"

"I'm not sure," Hunter quietly replied.

"Oh, I know that voice. What aren't you telling me?" demanded Hayden suspiciously.

"Seriously, I'm not sure," Hunter replied, smiling.

"Come on, boys. What's up?" Hannah asked nervously.

"Hunter!" called Hayden, irritated. "Tell us! What do you think the writing means?"

"Well," Hunter started, "the only thing I can think of is that these other caves aren't how we find the lost tribes. I think the caves are where the tribes will wait once we bring them back."

"What makes you think that?" asked Hannah.

"When I was crawling around in the cave, it felt more

like a room to me. There were no tunnels, no openings, nothing. Right?" he asked.

"Not that I found," Hannah replied.

"That's just it. I bet if we check all the other caves, they won't have any openings either," said Hunter.

"Then how do we find the lost tribes? The letter from Joseph Smith said we would find them in the caves," replied Hayden, a little confused.

"No, the letter said, 'each house must be returned for the fullness of the Lord to continue'," replied Hunter.

"Doesn't the letter say that each tribe resides deep within the caves?" asked Alli. She walked toward Hayden and the letter from Joseph Smith.

"No, the letter actually states that each tribe resides deep within the cave—singular not plural," replied Hayden, as he read and re-read the letter.

"So, what is the deal with the ninth cave?" asked Hayden. "Why are there two lines of letters?"

"My guess is that Levi and Simeon will both reside in that cave when the tribes are returned," answered Hunter. "And the tenth cave is where we go to find them."

"So what exactly does the writing on the plaque mean?" questioned Alli. "What makes you think that this is the cave we're supposed to start searching in?"

"Well, I read in one of Grandpa's books about Orson Pratt. In the article, Elder Pratt talked about the returning of the Ten Tribes. He referenced Section 133 of the Doctrine and Covenants, and he quoted the sentence that is engraved on the plaque," replied Hunter.

"Really?" asked Alli.

"Yes, really. 'And a highway shall be cast up in the midst of the great deep'," Hunter read again.

"Are you sure, Hunter?" questioned Hannah.

"Yes, I'm sure," Hunter replied confidently.

"Alright, we know where we have to go, so let's get moving," insisted Hannah, heading toward the entrance to the cave.

"Oh, no. Don't you dare do that again," Hayden warned. "You two wait right there for us. We'll walk into the cave together!"

"Let me remind you that I am older than you are, Hayden. And I will be doing whatever I choose," Hannah snapped angrily. She didn't like being told what to do. "Come on, Alli, let's get moving."

"Wait a minute, Hannah," insisted Hunter. "There's no light in the cave. This could be dangerous, and we don't want to go searching in the cave until we're all ready to go."

"Hunter, it's not like I'm going to go anywhere," complained Hannah. "I just want to look and see if there's an opening or something inside. Besides, I'm ready now!"

"Well, to use the same argument that you did, I am older than you are, and I'm asking you to wait until we're all ready to go," he calmly replied.

"Why?" argued Hannah. "Why aren't you ready, now?"

"I was hoping there might be some tools or supplies in here—something we could take with us on our journey that might help us," Hunter replied, as he quickly turned and started looking through the cave.

"Would it be alright if Alli and I just stepped inside and let our eyes adjust to the darkness?" Hannah asked mischievously.

"I would prefer you didn't," replied Hunter, not even looking up. "Hayden, will you please help me look for supplies."

"What do you have in mind?" questioned Hayden, unsure what supplies could possibly be inside the cave.

"Maybe an old lantern that Joseph left behind, or even something that could mark our trail—like ink or yarn. A pocketknife or gun, on the chance that we might need them. I don't know what exactly, just anything that could be useful," Hunter replied, as he maneuvered quickly around the room.

"Hunter, look at the entrance to the cave," said Hayden, pointing. "The girls are gone again!"

"Great! Hannah, Alli. Would you two please get back here?" Hunter shouted loudly.

"Hunter, help!" Alli called frantically.

"Aaaaaaaahhhhhhhhhhh, aaaaaaaaahhhhhhhhhhhhh!" screamed Hannah.

"Yeah, sure. This time, I'm not falling for their tricks," whispered Hayden. "Let's ignore them. They'll get bored and come out in a minute. Besides, I've done all the searching for them today that I care to do."

"Yeah, I'm not falling for their tricks either," agreed Hunter, ignoring the screams and continuing his search for supplies.

"Hunter, Hayden, Hannah needs help!" Alli screamed in a high, shrill voice. "Hurry! Please, hurry!"

"Sure, she does," replied Hayden, smiling at Hunter.

"Aaaaaaaaaaaaahhhhhhhhhhhh!" screamed Alli. "Aaaaaaaaaaaahhhhhhhhhhhh!"

"Funny, girls. I'm not amused. You can come out now. We're not going to run in there after you!" called Hayden. "We're not falling for your tricks!"

"They're really trying hard this time to get us to fall for their jokes," whispered Hunter.

"Yeah, real hard," replied Hayden as he shook his head.

"They're almost funny to listen to," replied Hunter softly. "Come on, girls. Get out here and help us make our plans. We've got to get moving. We've got so much to do today. No more wasting time," insisted Hunter as he headed back toward the cave's opening.

"Hannah, Alli, the fun's over. Get out here!" called Hayden, as he peeked his head inside the dark cave, trying to locate the hiding girls.

CHAPTER THREE

THE WIND TORE frantically through Hannah's long, blond hair, which stung her face as it whipped back and forth. Unsure where she was or what was happening, and unable to see her surroundings as she rapidly slid through twists and turns on the mysterious rock slide, she wildly grabbed and kicked at anything that might help her to stop falling. With nothing but slippery stone within her grasp, she continued to slide deeper and deeper into the darkness below; terrified she could be killed at any moment from the fall. Hannah screamed with all her might, stopping only long enough to gasp for a breath, before she continued screaming again. As she slid, the tunnel shifted suddenly, dropping Hannah three feet straight down. She landed with a thud, stopping only momentarily before she again fell out of control on her endless ride of terror. The tunnel seemed to widen suddenly as Hannah fell uncontrollably, slamming her back and forth against the sides of the tunnel, bruising every part of her body. Exhausted from grabbing and kicking at the rocks, and in pain from the hard fall, Hannah was ready to give up, when suddenly her body jolted to an abrupt stop.

Surprised to no longer be falling, Hannah reached her hand nervously toward her face, pulled her hair away from her eyes so that she could see, and quickly looked down toward her feet. Startled at the dark emptiness below her, she quickly closed her eyelids, squeezing them tightly together, hoping everything that was happening was all a terrible dream. Hannah slowly pulled her eyelids open and again looked down toward her feet. Several seconds passed before her eyes finally focused, revealing a small crack in the rock. She blinked her eyes twice, hoping her eyes were playing tricks on her, and again looked down toward her feet. Finding everything the same, she quickly studied the crack in the rock. She was relieved to see that the front edge of her tennis shoe was caught on an edge slightly protruding from the rock.

Afraid she could slip at any moment, she carefully searched for anything to help support her weight. All she could find was the smooth, cold rock wall of the cave. Frustrated with the situation, and afraid of what was below her, Hannah looked up toward the top of the cave and screamed. "Hunter! Hunterrrrr! Where are you?! Please! Please help me! You know I'm claustrophobic. I really need your help! I can't do this!"

Positive that she had screamed loud enough for Hunter to hear her, Hannah listened carefully, hoping he would respond at any moment. Several anxious seconds passed, but Hannah could hear nothing. No reply from Hunter or Hayden. An eerie silence was all that could be heard in the cave. She softly laid her head on the rock wall, closed her eyes, and whispered to herself as a tear rolled down her cheek. "Why am I always so impatient? If I'd only waited a few more minutes, Hunter would have walked into the cave with me, and he would've been the one to fall. Instead, it's me barely hanging on here, and it's me with my life teetering on a tiny ledge!"

She grinned to herself as she pictured Hunter, all six feet two inches and one hundred eighty pounds of him, awkwardly trying to balance on the small ledge in the rock. Hannah smirked while she momentarily daydreamed about Hunter precariously hanging onto the ledge. Unexpectedly struck by falling dirt and pebbles, she was quickly brought back to the present and the dangerous situation she was faced with. Holding her hand up to shield her eyes, she quickly looked into the darkness above, hoping the falling debris meant someone was trying to rescue her. Excitedly, she called, "Hunter! Hunter! Is that you? Hunter, save me! I need your help, come on, answer me!"

Hannah again listened intently, hoping for the slightest indication that someone would soon be there to rescue her. Concentrating on the vibrations in the wall, she was sure she heard the faint sounds of Hunter's voice calling to her.

Thrilled to have heard a voice, she pulled her head away from the growing vibrations in the wall, looked anxiously into the darkness and yelled, hoping her voice would help Hunter to find her.

"Hunter, is that you? I'm right here, and I'm ready to be saved! The muscles in my legs are really burning. I can't hold on much longer. Would you please hurry up?" She paused momentarily to listen, and then started calling again. "Hunter? Hayden? Anyone? Someone, please answer me!"

Pausing to breathe, she waited anxiously to hear a voice, any voice. Several nervous seconds passed before she again heard muffled noises not too far in the distance.

"Finally!" she exclaimed out loud to herself. "I knew Hunter would figure out a way to rescue me from this crazy slide of terror." Nervously, Hannah waited for Hunter to appear above her in the tunnel and carry her back to safety, or at least throw her a rope and pull her back up to the cave.

As the sounds and vibrations in the cave grew louder and louder, Hannah's heart began to race in nervous anticipation of her rescue. As her knees started to shake and quiver from fatigue, she struggled to keep a steady grip on the wall. The shaking and burning in Hannah's muscles intensified as every second passed, until she could no longer keep her footing on the ledge. As her muscles gave way under the stress, she slipped.

Fearful of what was below, she frantically reached for the rock's edge, praying she would be able to grasp it and hold on tight. Her body bounced abruptly as the small fingers on her right hand caught the tiny ledge and brought her body to an immediate stop. Surprised to have actually caught the edge where she had just spent several minutes teetering precariously, she struggled to hold her weight with one arm as her body swayed back and forth. Scrambling to find something to help her hang on, Hannah looked up toward the ledge and hurriedly reached her left arm over her head.

The fingers on her right hand suddenly started slipping off the small ledge in the rock. Afraid she would start falling again, Hannah quickly tried to secure her grip. Struggling to reach the ledge with her left hand, she swung her legs to the left, hoping that would help her reach a little higher. Finally, she was able to reach her fingers over the edge.

Unable to keep her grip, Hannah watched nervously as the fingers on her left hand slipped one at a time from the edge, until she was hanging by only her right hand. Hannah swung her body again, stretching her arm as far above her head as she could, waiting patiently until the last moment before her body started to swing back to the right. Straining, she reached her hand out and unexpectedly caught the edge. She scrambled to secure her fingers to support her body's weight.

With an unsteady grip, her fingers started to slip. Only this time it was the fingers on both hands. Her heart pounded as she strained to keep her feeble grip on the edge.

"Ask for help," she heard a voice say.

"Ask for help?" she repeated silently to herself. "Who's out there?" she nervously called.

"Yes! Ask for help!" the voice again repeated.

Hannah thought about what the voice said. She quickly closed her eyes and said a prayer, asking Heavenly Father for strength and help. As soon as she was finished, her nerves were rapidly calmed, leaving her with a peace that everything would be okay.

With only the first knuckle of her fingers still holding on, her adrenalin surged, giving her the power she needed to secure a solid grip. With both hands now firmly holding onto the tiny ledge, Hannah was finally able to take a deep, cautious breath. She slowly let it out, still nervous that at any moment her strength would give out and she could again be falling to her death.

Several anxious seconds passed. Then suddenly Hannah was sure she saw something moving toward her. Excited to be rescued, she grinned from ear to ear and yelled, "Hunter, Hunter, you found me! I knew you would come for me. You're such a great brother!"

Hannah continued to watch the faint shadow move toward her. Several small pebbles fell ahead of the shadow she saw sliding through the cave. Instinctively, she ducked her head and closed her eyes, as the small rocks and dirt pelted her body. She struggled to keep her grip on the tiny ledge that kept her from falling further through the dark cave.

"Oh, no," she whispered to her herself, as she cautiously tightened her grip.

"Hold on, Hannah. Don't give up now. Only one more minute until you're rescued," she said to herself loudly. "Come on, you can do it!"

Relieved to have steadied her grip momentarily,

Hannah focused on keeping it tight. She peered cautiously up into the tunnel, squinting her eyes as she did. Shocked at what she thought she saw not far in the distance, she closed her eyes, shook her head, and again looked up into the tunnel.

Suddenly, a shrill scream echoed through the tunnel, shattering the eerie silence and startling Hannah. With her eyes still squinting tightly, she stared into the shadowy darkness above her.

"Why would Hunter be screaming like that?" she questioned, puzzled by the sound.

Hannah listened as the sound grew louder and louder, hoping at any moment she would be able to see who was there to save her. Less than thirty seconds had passed when she realized the sound was not Hunter sliding through the tunnel, it was her best friend Alli.

The thought, "Why did they send Alli?" quickly flashed through her mind. Then suddenly, she realized that Alli was on a collision course, headed directly for her.

"Maybe they have her tied to a rope and she is actually coming to save me," she wishfully hoped, praying that somehow her thoughts would come true. Only a fleeting second passed before Alli, sliding uncontrollably with no rope tied around her, slammed into Hannah's arms and knocked loose the fragile grip that she had on the small, rock ledge. Hannah was petrified as she again started sliding through more twists and turns of the mysterious tunnel. But this time, Alli was holding onto her, causing them both to fall out of control.

"What is the matter with you?" Hannah screamed

angrily, as she tried to pull Alli's hands away from her shirt. "You saw me fall into the opening back in the cave. Why did you follow me?"

"Hannah, it was dark in the cave. I didn't know that you had fallen," Alli yelled tearfully, straining to keep her grip on Hannah's shirt. "Don't push me away. I don't want to be alone anymore."

"I was hoping you had gone to tell Hunter and Hayden," said Hannah, her heart racing with fear.

"No, I didn't tell the boys! I called after you, I begged for you to stop. But when you didn't answer, I got nervous and thought you might be hurt. I had stepped only a few feet further into the cave trying to find you, when I started sliding down this rock tunnel," Alli replied, as tears started flowing down her cheeks. "Do you think we're going to die?"

"I hope not!" Hannah snapped.

Hannah's heart began racing faster and faster, and her fear of falling caused her heart to pound uncontrollably. As she watched Alli crying, tears started to stream down her own face as well. All of a sudden, Hannah became hysterical and started fighting to release herself from the tight grip of Alli's hand.

"Hannah! Hannah, it's me Alli. You know, your friend," she screamed, as Hannah almost pulled free. "Stop trying to push me away. I'm scared. I don't want to lose you again."

"I'm not trying to push away, Alli," replied Hannah. "But you've got to let go of my arms. If I'm going to find a way to stop us, I need to be able to use my arms."

Alli hesitantly released the grip on Hannah's arms and quickly grabbed hold of her waist. As Alli freed Hannah to move her arms, she yelled angrily, "You...scared...me, Hannah! I don't like the feeling of falling."

"I don't like it either," snapped Hannah, as she searched anxiously for anything that might stop them from tumbling further through the tunnel.

"What's happening, Hannah?" squeaked Alli. "Where are we falling to?"

"I don't have a clue!" barked Hannah, as she crashed into the side of the tunnel and loudly grunted in pain. "I don't know what's happening, or where we're falling, or why," she replied, through gasps of air.

Alli wrapped both of her arms around Hannah's waist, ducked her head into Hannah's shoulder and whispered, "I didn't expect to encounter a slippery tunnel today. I don't want to die here."

"Wherever here is," replied Hannah sarcastically. She couldn't see anything with her hair whipping around her face. So she was unsuccessful at finding anything that could slow their fall. "I don't want to die here either."

Hannah unexpectedly slammed into the side of the tunnel as it made a sharp S turn without warning. It quickly leveled off for several seconds before the girls suddenly shot out of the end of the slippery rock tunnel. Hannah gasped for breath from the hard hit against the wall and struggled for several seconds before she could take a deep breath. The girls found themselves outside the small tunnel, but still falling rapidly toward the ground and certain death. Hannah let go of Alli, and both girls screamed at the top of their lungs. The two girls cried in unison as they swung their arms and wildly kicked their legs, hoping to come in contact with anything that would help them stop falling. Then without warning, they landed with a hard thump into a large mound of thick, gooey mud.

"Oh, gross. What is this stuff?" asked Alli, as she tried to pull her arms free from the goo.

"I don't know," Hannah replied, unable to move, but relieved they were no longer sliding. "I don't care what this stuff is! At least I'm not confined in a small tunnel or falling into the darkness anymore!"

"Where are we, Hannah?" Alli whispered nervously, as she sat up and tried to shake the black, tar-like mud from her arms. "Do you think we're in any danger?"

"I don't have any idea where we are, Alli," Hannah replied sharply. "I only wish I had a clue. All I know is that somewhere around here, there are supposed to be people from one of the ten lost tribes, and somehow we have to convince two of them into going home with us. But after falling for the last few minutes, minutes that seemed like hours, I have no idea how we're ever going to get back to the Hill Cumorah or find Hunter and Hayden. And I really have no idea if we're in trouble. If I had to guess, I would most definitely say we're in a ton of danger."

"Do you think Hunter and Hayden will try to find us?" Alli asked hopefully, looking up toward the opening they had just shot through. "They wouldn't just leave us here to find the lost tribes without their help, would they?"

"Of course they will come for us, Alli," barked Hannah, as she scrunched her eyebrows and scowled at her friend, even though she was not really sure if her brothers would find them. "Hunter would never leave us down here. Besides, how would they explain that we're missing to my mom and dad?"

Alli looked at Hannah worriedly, and her voice squeaked as she said, "I wanna go home! This is way too scary for me. I wasn't sure I wanted to go with you three in the first place. You know I'm afraid of everything."

"I know you don't like anything scary, Alli. And I would like to go home, too. But we have a mission to complete before we can go home, and your name was on that letter from Joseph Smith, too," replied Hannah. She tried again to sit up, struggling to maneuver her way off the fifteen-foot-tall mound of gooey mud. "You know the main thing I haven't figured out yet, is how we're going to get back to the Hill Cumorah after we complete the mission. I know we can't climb back up the tunnel we just fell through."

"You're right. What are we going to do?" Alli squeaked nervously, tears again starting to well up in her eyes.

"Hopefully we'll be able to figure that out after we get a good look around here," Hannah replied, almost to the bottom of the mud pile.

"Can you see anything, Hannah?" asked Alli, as she peered over the edge of the mud, afraid to climb down to the ground below.

"Not much. Now get down here with me," demanded Hannah. "And hurry up! We need to find a place to hide in case the people here are not friendly."

"What if there are deadly animals or bugs and stuff down there?" asked Alli, still peering over the edge.

"Then we'll both get eaten, but you're not gonna leave me down here alone. Now hurry up, and get down here with me," replied Hannah.

"What about dinosaurs? You can't see any, can you?" asked Alli.

"Alli, come on!" snapped Hannah as she looked up toward Alli and motioned for her to climb down. "This is not Jurassic Park!"

"How do you know that?" asked Alli.

Purposely annoying Alli by not answering, Hannah quietly looked around the area.

"Hannah, do you think the people that live around here are dangerous?" Alli nervously asked, as she finally started to cautiously climb down toward Hannah.

"I don't know, but we're better safe than sorry," Hannah answered. She quickly scanned the surrounding area for a safe place to hide. "If we find somewhere safe, we'll at least have a chance to check out the area and hopefully have time to make a plan before we are seen."

Alli finally reached the bottom of the goo pile and walked to where Hannah was standing. She quickly joined Hannah's search for a safe place to hide. Several frustrating minutes passed and still the two girls were not having much luck. They struggled to see through the shadows in the small valley as the darkness of night filtered in, making everything around them almost impossible to see. Even the stars in the sky were barely visible through the strange, wispy clouds. The girls, afraid something was watching them in the darkness, searched for any sort of shelter.

"Alli," Hannah called nervously.

"Yeah?" she replied.

"Stay close. I don't want to lose you in the mist, something doesn't feel right out here," insisted Hannah.

"I'm right behind you, Hannah," whispered Alli as she took a hold of her shirtsleeve. "What is it, that doesn't feel right?"

"I'm not sure, so we better be quiet. Someone might be out here," Hannah replied.

"Oh, great! We're probably gonna be kidnapped or something terrible like that," said Alli.

"Give me a break, will ya, Alli? You know that I don't like the dark," Hannah said nervously. "You don't need to try and scare me."

"Sorry, Hannah," replied Alli, grinning mischievously to herself. She unexpectedly bumped into Hannah, who had stopped ahead of her. She asked anxiously, "Do you see something? Are there dinosaurs waiting to eat us?"

"Yeah, I think so," Hannah replied, smiling as she shook her head. "In fact, I think I can see a Pterodactyl up in the sky!"

"What?" screamed Alli, rapidly scanning the area above her head. "Really?"

"No, Alli. I'm only joking," snickered Hannah. "But I do think I've found us a place to hide."

"Where?" Alli asked impatiently, ready to climb into bed and fall asleep, only to wake up from this terrible nightmare in the morning.

"Look, the mountain we slid through, for extra fun today, has a ridge just under where we flew out. The ridge juts out about three feet near the bottom, by those bushes ahead of us. I think if we hide underneath the ridge and behind those bushes, we could easily scan the area without being seen by anyone," she explained.

Hannah led the way, as the two girls quickly crawled into the safety of the bushes.

"This isn't exactly what I had in mind for shelter, Hannah," declared Alli as she shivered from the chill in the air.

"What did you have in mind?" asked Hannah.

"Oh, let's see. A warm blanket, a cozy bed, a soft pillow, you know, silly things like that," Alli replied smiling.

"I guess this is better than nothing!" replied Hannah, as she rubbed her hands up and down her arms trying to warm them.

Not sure what to do next, and unable to see most of the area, the girls sat quietly and motionless for nearly twenty minutes.

Suddenly, Hannah noticed a strange smell filtering through the air. The odd smell was one neither girl had ever encountered before. Nervously, Hannah sat up on her knees and slid the leaves in front of her to the side.

"Can you see anything, Hannah?" asked Alli, as she pinched her nose closed, hoping to avoid the foul smell invading the entire area. "Any ideas where this terrible smell is coming from?"

Hannah held her hand to her mouth and placed one finger across her lips, signaling for Alli to be quiet. Alli recognized the signal and waited quietly several frantic seconds.

Hannah finally turned toward her friend and softly replied, "There's something in the distance, but I'm not sure what it is. Come here and take a look," she instructed, as she pulled the leaves apart so Alli could see. "Can you tell what it is?" Hannah asked.

Alli looked intently into the darkness trying to see what Hannah saw, but all she could see were the movements of the wispy clouds as they moved through the sky. They quickly disappeared, and were followed closely by fast-moving, dark clouds. The dark clouds were not like any the girls had ever seen back home. They were fluffy like a big marshmallow, only black in color, and very thick. They looked so ominous, Alli was sure something was hiding inside them, waiting for the right moment to jump out and attack the girls. As they watched, the clouds rolled mysteriously across the ground, quickly filling the entire valley. After they rolled in, the clouds seemed to start from the ground and rapidly work their way up to the sky, filling it with a thick, black, wet mist. Only a few seconds passed before visibility in the area was next to impossible.

Alli watched as the clouds behaved differently than she had ever seen before. Afraid of being separated from Hannah in the darkness, she quickly grabbed her friend's arm and whispered, "Hannah, what in the world is happening here?"

"I don't know, Alli," Hannah replied, as she raised up on her toes and anxiously watched the unusual weather.

"I don't know anything more than you do. I've never seen anything like this."

Without warning, a shockingly-loud boom blasted across the area, knocking Hannah forcefully to the ground. Startled by the noise and the blast, Alli screamed with all her might. Then she fell to her knees and frantically searched in the darkness for her friend.

"I wish Hunter was here," Alli said fearfully, as she reached into the darkness searching for Hannah's hand. "Don't worry, Alli. I'm right here," reassured Hannah.

Hannah, relieved to hear Alli's voice, replied, "I wish Hunter was here, too. I'm kinda scared."

"I can't figure out what's going on around here, do you know?" asked Alli.

"I don't know, but I really think we need to move further underneath the ledge. I think there's going to be a storm, and we're gonna need as much protection as we can get," suggested Hannah, as she pulled Alli to the most protected location under the mountain's ridge.

"I've never seen anything like this before," Alli said nervously. "What are the clouds doing?"

"I don't know for sure, but something doesn't feel quite right," Hannah whispered.

The girls inched closer together, positive that would be safer for both of them. They watched as the dark clouds mysteriously filled the valley, curiously billowing up from the ground to the sky. As soon as every last inch of the valley was covered in a dark grey mist, a series of bright lights started to flash along the ground.

"Lightning on the ground?" Hannah asked suspiciously. "Nothing about this storm seems to be like back home. We're in real danger here."

"Yeah, I agree. We could be in real trouble, especially if we're struck by lightning. It seems to me like the storm is happening upside down," added Alli. "The way the clouds filled the valley and now the lightning—I wonder what's coming next?"

"Don't say stuff like that, Alli," Hannah insisted. "Something bad is bound to happen if you talk like that."

Hannah had barely finished speaking, when a loud rumble started vibrating the ground around her. The rumble seemed to grow louder and stronger with every passing second, until it finally shook the ground with such force that it knocked several large rocks free from the mountainside over their heads. The girls listened in shock to the rumbling over their heads, and then watched in horror as the falling boulders shook the ground even more violently than before.

As the ground continued shaking, Hannah and Alli crouched together as low as they could underneath the rock ledge. They waited and hoped the curious storm would soon come to an end.

"Was that thunder that knocked the boulders free to roll down the hill, Hannah?" whispered Alli. "Or could the rumbling have been an earthquake?"

"With the weird clouds and lightning, I would proba-bly guess thunder. That makes the most sense to me," replied Hannah, grateful the rumbling had stopped momentarily. "But, I'm only guessing. I can't know that for sure."

The girls breathed a cautious sigh of relief, and watched as the lightning began to display a brilliant-white light show throughout the valley.

"If that was thunder, the shaking was way too strong," replied Alli, grateful not to be shaking any more. "I've never felt anything like it before."

"Me neither. Everything about this storm has been a little off," replied Hannah, nervously surveying their surroundings.

"A little off?!" snapped Alli. "Look at the clouds. They're about four feet off the ground, in a straight line," said Alli, pointing. "That's really off."

"Did you see that, Alli?" Hannah asked excitedly, pointing straight into the darkness.

"Come on, Hannah, you know I can't see anything," replied Alli, as she shook her head. "It's too dark."

"Look, in the distance, directly in front of us," Hannah replied anxiously, inching closer toward the bushes in front of them. "When the lightning flashed, I thought I saw some sort of lights or something. Maybe there's a city or village close by. I'm sure I saw something out there."

"Really? A city?" asked Alli, as she excitedly antici-pated the next lightning strike. "That would be great! Maybe we could still get a shower and possibly a warm bed to sleep in tonight?"

Hannah smiled, "Alli, even if there is a city, I don't think we'll be checkin' it out in the dark."

"Oh, that's probably true," she somberly replied. "But then again, there's always hope, right?"

"I'm not sure, but maybe," Hannah replied in a shaky voice. The ground began to rumble underneath their feet again. "If it is a city, that could either be good or bad."

"Oh, come on, not again," whined Alli, as she scooted back against the wall. She was afraid the rumbling would send rocks rolling down the mountain again, and possibly break the small ledge that the girls were hiding underneath.

This time the rumbling lasted only a minute. It was followed by several quick flashes that filled the valley with light. Alli peered cautiously into the distance, squinting her eyes tightly to help her see. The light faded as quickly as it flashed, and the girls were again left in the frightening darkness.

"Did you see the lights out in the distance, Alli?" Hannah quizzed, excited for her friend to see what she had.

"I saw where the rocks that fell down the mountain ran into a tree," Alli replied. "Did you see how close that was to us? We could be in serious trouble if the thunder continues."

"Come on, Alli. Focus for me. Look further into the distance. I'm almost positive something is out there," insisted Hannah. "We really need to know for sure if it is a city. That might be where we start to look for one of the members of the ten tribes."

Lightning flashed again, and Alli strained to see the lights Hannah was talking about.

"Hey! I think you're right, Hannah. I saw something, too!" shouted Alli, waiting excitedly for the next flash of light.

"Should we go see for sure what they are?" asked Hannah. She crouched on her hands and knees and prepared to climb out from underneath the mountain ledge.

"Wait a minute. Are you crazy? That is how we got into this mess in the first place," Alli answered heatedly.

"What do you mean *this mess*?" Hannah snapped, suddenly annoyed by her friends comment.

"I mean, if you would've had any patience and let Hunter and Hayden go first into the cave, we wouldn't be down here in this gigantic mess," Alli angrily replied. "Besides, I'm not going to go wandering around in some strange city, in the middle of a crazy storm, in total darkness. We'd probably die."

"Come on, Alli. Where's you sense of adventure?" teased Hannah, as she leaned back against the rock wall next to her friend, hoping to encourage Alli to continue.

"Sense of adventure?" Alli repeated slowly, as she contemplated her response. "Oh, I know where it is. I left it in the United States—New York, no, Palmyra to be more exact!"

"You mean back at the Hill Cumorah?" teased Hannah, smiling widely.

"Yep! That's the place. My sense of adventure stopped when we left there," replied Alli.

"How do you know we're not still in the United States?" demanded Hannah, now trying to annoy her friend.

"Well, I don't know," Alli replied sharply. "We've fallen into a land that has upside down thunder and lightning storms. I don't know about you, but where I live, the clouds cover the sky, lightning starts up in the clouds and the thunder rolls through the clouds, not on the ground!"

"Maybe we fell to the other side of the world," added Hannah, smiling. "And thunder storms are upside down here."

"Then either way, I'm right. Even if we're on the other side of the earth, we're no longer in the United States, Hannah. And my sense of adventure is all adventured out," Alli answered. "Now quit teasing me. This really isn't funny. We don't know where we are, and it's nearly pitch black here. We have no idea how we're gonna do whatever we're here to do, and we don't know how we're gonna get back to the Hill Cumorah. I can only imagine how freaked out your parents are right now."

"Yeah, but we've had a lot of fun so far!" replied Hannah. "And our journey has just begun!"

Alli knew Hannah was teasing her. She knew Hannah was trying to be strong. But Alli could hear how nervous Hannah was by the tone of her voice. Hoping to console her friend, Alli said, "Hannah, why don't we try to get some rest. As soon as there's some light, we'll get up and check out the area."

"That's probably a better idea," answered Hannah. "And who knows? Hunter and Hayden might come to look for us. If we left tonight, they would never be able to find us."

CHAPTER FOUR

HUNTER, ANNOYED that Hannah had not listened when he asked her to wait, looked at Hayden who was standing at the entrance to the cave. He held up his hands in front of him and shrugged his shoulders. "Why'd she go without me again?"

"Where'd they go, Hunter?" asked Hayden, as he cautiously leaned further inside, trying to watch Hunter search. "They couldn't have just disappeared, could they?"

"Man if they're really lost or hurt, Dad's gonna kill me," Hunter replied, puckering his lips and shaking his head, annoyed he had to search for the girls again. "I sure wish Hannah would've waited for me. But you know with Hannah, everything has to be done her way!"

"It's pitch black in there. I can't see anything at all. Can you, Hunter?" asked Hayden. He was still standing outside the cave's entrance, leaning inside, straining to see beyond the first five feet or so. "I think it's even darker than in the first cave."

"I think you're right. It is darker in this cave," replied Hunter, as he looked up at Hayden. He reached his hand out carefully, searching for the cave wall. "But what choice do I have? I've got to find them." As he kept one hand on the wall to guide him deeper into the tunnel, he continued, "You know what, Hayden? I really wish I had a flashlight or even a match. Finding those girls would be a whole lot easier if I had one."

"I wish Joseph would have left us a lantern. That would've been nice," replied Hayden.

Hayden watched as Hunter continued to search, becoming more and more frantic with every passing minute that they could not find the girls. Moving faster through the cave, Hunter stumbled over rocks and landed on the ground with a thud.

"Ouch!" Hunter exclaimed. "That hurt. This is the second time today I have stubbed my toe looking for Hannah!"

"You okay, Hunter?" asked Hayden.

"No, I'm not okay! When I find her, for the first time in her spoiled-rotten life, she's really gonna get yelled at," Hunter huffed angrily. He picked himself up from the ground and continued searching in the darkness. Heatedly, he called their names, hoping by some miracle the girls would answer. Several minutes passed, but not even a tiny squeak was heard.

"You know, Hayden, this might be easier if you would get in here and help me look!" Hunter snapped sharply, as he noticed Hayden still standing safely at the cave's entrance. "If we don't find them, we're gonna be in tons of serious trouble, and that doesn't mean only me! Dad's gonna be mad at you, too."

"You're older. The girls are your responsibility, not mine," Hayden retorted. "Besides, I've already searched in the small, dark, claustrophobic cave for the girls today."

"And I haven't?" shouted Hunter.

"You know, I bet they're tricking us again. In a minute, they're going to jump out from behind the rocks and scare me to death again," Hayden said.

"Yeah right, and Dad's gonna accept that as your excuse!" chuckled Hunter. "You're kidding yourself."

"You know I hate the dark, Hunter!" yelled Hayden, as he scowled at his brother. "You know I'd be more help if the cave was lit."

"And that's no excuse either, Hayden," yelled Hunter. "Dad's not gonna care what you're afraid of if Hannah and Alli are lost."

Hayden thought quietly about Hunter's remarks, then replied, "I suppose you're right, Hunter. But, unlike Hannah, I don't like walking into unknown and unsafe places. And I like to see where I'm going when I enter dark places," Hayden said. He took a deep breath and let it out quickly, as he hesitantly stepped one foot inside the cave. "Hunter, where do you think they've gone? It's not like they could simply disappear?" reasoned Hayden, slowly maneuvering further into the cave toward the sound of Hunter's voice.

"You're right, Hayden. They couldn't have simply disappeared. But somehow that is exactly what they've done. I can't find one single sign of the girls anywhere— not one," Hunter replied nervously. "I don't know where else I can possibly look for them. I know that I will continue to look until I find them, because I'm not going back to dad until I do. I can't believe this!" he said angrily.

"Do you think Hannah's hiding in here to trick us again?" asked Hayden, suddenly suspicious of every little noise inside the cave.

"Oh...if she is...she's gonna be...I'm gonna be so mad!" muttered Hunter, angry at the thought. "Hannah! Alli! Where are you two? You better not be hiding from us again!" he called in a stern voice. "Hannah, I am not very happy. This is no joke! I am totally serious."

The boys listened for a response, but they still heard nothing.

"The cave's not as big as I thought, Hunter," said Hayden. He had worked his way completely around the interior and was again standing at the cave's opening. "We should be able to find them in here. What's the problem?"

"I'm sure I don't know! I can't imagine what they did to get lost in here. This cave is almost the same size as the other cave, so I can't figure out what I'm missing. Finding them would be a lot easier if we could see in here," Hunter answered. "I'm really not sure what to do next. I don't have anything with me that can help us— absolutely nothing—unless the compass on my key chain will help," he joked, rattling his keys for Hayden to see.

"Don't worry, Hunter. I know the Lord wouldn't send

us on a mission and have half of us get lost forever," replied Hayden.

"If that's true, then we should find them easily," snapped Hunter. "And if you haven't noticed. We aren't finding them easily."

"Why do you say that, Hunter?" asked Hayden innocently.

"Because the girls aren't in here!" shouted Hunter, annoyed by the question.

"Well, where are they then?" asked Hayden. "They've got to be here somewhere!"

"Hayden, you know, I don't have the slightest clue! What's wrong with you today? That was a really dumb question," said Hunter, shaking his bead.

"Do you think we might have better luck if we asked Heavenly Father for some help?" asked Hayden.

"Pray? Now?" shrieked Hunter.

"Sure. Why not?" replied Hayden. "Now's as good a time as any, don't you think?"

Hunter shook his head, paused several seconds and replied, "Fine. Saying a prayer is probably a great idea. You better say it, though. I have a pretty bad attitude right now, and I'm not sure He would answer me!"

Hayden smiled at his brother and agreed. He knelt down and motioned for Hunter to do the same. Hunter rolled his eyes at Hayden, but did as Hayden suggested. Hayden looked momentarily at Hunter and then started. "Dear Heavenly Father…"

Hunter listened for nearly five minutes as Hayden blessed everything and everybody. He was sure Hayden would soon be blessing all the animals on the earth, when he finally heard Hayden mention Hannah and Alli's names. Suddenly, a calming sensation filled his entire body, and he glanced at Hayden. As Hunter stared at his brother, he was surprised to see Hayden reverently folding his arms and faithfully asking for Hunter to have patience as they learned of Heavenly Father's plan for them. Hunter smiled softly, closed his eyes and continued to listen to Hayden's faithful prayer. As Hayden finally completed his prayer, Hunter's demeanor had changed, and he quickly thanked his brother for having more faith than he did.

"Oh, you have more faith than I do. You just misplaced yours for a minute," Hayden replied, as he smiled and patted his brother on the back.

"Hey, can you hear something, Hayden?" interrupted Hunter. Closing his eyes tightly, trying to concentrate on the sound.

"Like what? Did you hear the girls?" Hayden asked excitedly.

"I heard something!" replied Hunter.

Hayden listened intently for several seconds. "I'm not sure. What am I listening for?" he asked.

"The noise is dull—almost like a rumble or something. Listen again," replied Hunter.

Hayden listened again, trying to hear the dull rumble Hunter described. Only a moment passed before Hayden elatedly said, "You're right. I can hear a rumble or something," as he held his finger to his mouth, signaling Hunter to be quiet. "It sounds almost like someone is screaming in a really low voice," he whispered.

"Where's it coming from?" Hunter asked excitedly, listening intently. "Can you tell where it's coming from?"

"Well, if you'd be quiet for a second, maybe I could pinpoint the sound," teased Hayden.

"Oh, sorry," whispered Hunter. "I'm excited. This is the first sign of the girls we've had. I'm sure the Lord answered your prayer. So, can you locate the sound?" he asked anxiously.

"Ssshhhh, Hunter. Be quiet for a minute, will ya?" begged Hayden.

Hayden closed his eyes and tried to focus on the sounds he could hear. Nearly a full minute passed before he looked up at Hunter and asked, "You can really hear the screams can't you?"

"Yes, I can," Hunter answered worriedly. "But they're really faint. I'm having a hard time determining where they're coming from," he added. He pressed his ear to the ground, hoping the vibrations in the stone would carry the sound and help him to hear the voices better.

"Do you think the noise is from the girls screaming?" Hayden asked worriedly, as he looked over to where Hunter was lying on the floor.

"Screams of them yelling for our help, not screaming in pain," replied Hunter, trying not to show his fear. "We've got to get some light in here. There has to be a secret opening or something that we can't see in the dark."

"Hunter, where are we going to find light?" asked Hayden.

Suddenly, remembering the main cave was light inside, Hunter asked. "What is lighting the cave where all the records are?" as he looked at the cave's entrance. "Why is there light in there?" He jumped to his feet and hurried back to the records room.

"I don't know. I don't remember noticing how the cave was lit," Hayden replied, hurrying to catch up with Hunter.

"Well, something in here is lighting the room," insisted Hunter, as he searched. "Come on, help me look for where the light is coming from"

"What exactly am I looking for, Hunter?" questioned Hayden. "I don't even know where to start."

"Anything that looks like it gives off light. Maybe we'll see a candle or torch. Or maybe we'll find a stone like the brother of Jared used in the boats," answered Hunter. "Look for anything."

The boys searched diligently the cave for nearly five minutes before Hayden made an incredible discovery. Shocked by what he saw, he silently crouched down on one knee and carefully pulled a small pile of brass plates away from the wall. He shook his head and closed his eyes tightly, then quickly reopened them again, looking at the object at the base of the wall.

"This can't be right," he whispered softly to himself. "Hunter, come look at this. Could this be how the room is bright enough for us to see?" Hayden called, pointing to a small, bright, greenish-blue light on the wall.

Hunter looked at Hayden and saw him motioning toward the floor. Anxious to see what Hayden had found, he quickly rushed to see what his brother was pointing towards. As he reached the wall, Hunter leaned over the pile of records on the floor. He looked at the small object glowing at the base of the wall and was mystified by what he saw.

"Do you know what this is?" asked Hayden. "Have you ever seen anything like this?"

"I have seen something like this," replied Hunter excitedly, as he looked at Hayden. "I think I've seen a plant like this before."

"Where? When? What is it?" asked Hayden.

"During Mr. Bromley's biology class last term, he showed the class several pictures of plants that looked like this one," replied Hunter. "I'm almost positive this is the same type of plant."

"What is it?" questioned Hayden.

"I'm not certain, but I think Mr. Bromley called them...uummm," Hunter paused and rubbed his chin in deep contemplation for several seconds, then looked over at Hayden, smiled and answered, "uummm, I think he called them bioluminescence or something like that."

"Bio what? What's that?" Hayden asked.

"If I'm remembering correctly, bioluminescence is a process in which certain types of fungus, mushrooms and even worms emit light. Mr. Bromley showed the class several pictures of this happening. Some of the pictures were taken under water, and several others were on land near trees. This is great! Mr. Bromley would be so excited to see these plants in real life," said Hunter, as he stared at the small, plant-like area of fungus. "I wonder if there are more plants like this around the cave?"

"Yeah, there are!" Hayden replied excitedly, as he

walked around the room. "Look, they're everywhere. They're all over the floor and they're even growing on the walls and ceiling of the cave."

"No wonder it's so light in here," added Hunter. "This is so great. I can't believe this. I'm so excited!"

"How exactly do they work? I mean, how are the plants able to survive living in here, Hunter?" asked Hayden, as he watched Hunter walk around touching every plant he found in the cave.

"I don't know for sure. Now I wish I'd paid more attention when we were learning about them in class. I can't believe how cool this is," Hunter said excitedly, as he continued to move around the cave, locating all the plants he could.

"All of these plants are a type of fungus?" asked Hayden.

"They sure are," replied Hunter.

"Well, just so you know, I think you've touched almost all of them so far. Now your hands are covered in fungus. Do you think the plants could make you sick?" Hayden asked.

"I hope not!" replied Hunter, as he momentarily stared at his hands and then shrugged his shoulder.

"I have a question, Hunter. Do you think these plants could light up the other cave?" asked Hayden. "I haven't heard the girls screaming for a little while now, and I'm getting worried. They could be in real trouble."

"That's a good idea. We could try pulling up one of the plants and see what happens," suggested Hunter, shrugging his shoulders. "I don't know if they will still emit light, but I don't see how it would hurt to try."

Hunter found a plant with several quarter-sized, mushroom-like fungus leaves. The plant was only about three inches tall and sticky from top to bottom. The fungus seemed to grow in small clusters of three to four plants all around the cave, but this mushroom was growing alone and emitting light that was bright enough to read a book in the dark.

Hunter cautiously took hold of a sticky leaf near the base and carefully plucked it from the plant. The boys watched eagerly to see how the small leaf reacted. The leaf glowed brightly for nearly one full minute before the light suddenly faded and the small piece rapidly shriveled into a tiny brown ball.

"WOW!" exclaimed Hayden. "What just happened? I've never seen a plant curl up and die that fast!"

"I guess that answers our question. We can't pull off one of the leaves and have it continue to work. We're going to have to dig out an entire plant or two," reasoned Hunter. "And we really need to hurry. You're right about the girls possibly being in real danger, and I'm sure they're scared to death."

"Which plant should we try to dig out?" asked Hayden, as he looked around the room at all the plants.

"I think we should dig out two of the biggest in the room. That way we can really light up the other cave," replied Hunter.

Hunter soon found a large plant and used his hands to remove the dirt and rocks that covered the roots. The hard dirt made the digging slow and tedious. The small, sharp rocks tore at Hunter's fingers until the tips were covered in small cuts and scrapes. Hayden watched as Hunter grimaced each time he scraped his fingers across the dirt, knowing his brother was determined to remove the plant and find the girls, no matter what.

Scanning the room for anything that could be used for digging in place of Hunter' hands, Hayden could find nothing but ancient records and treasures—nothing that he dared use to dig up the plant. He patted the pockets of his pants, hoping to find something useful. He suddenly remembered he had brought his Swiss Army Knife with him, "In case of emergencies," he thought to himself. Hayden quickly fished the knife out of his pants pocket and hurried over to where Hunter was still struggling to dig the small plant out with his fingers.

"This might work better, Hunter," he said, proudly holding up the knife.

"Oh, yes! Perfect. That will work a lot better," replied Hunter, as he took the knife from Hayden's hand. He pulled several of the switches out and continued digging the dirt away from the plant. "Where did you find the knife?"

"I forgot I put it in my pocket this morning. I wanted to have it with me, just in case we needed the knife for something today," Hayden answered.

"Nice going, Hayden! Good thinking!" replied Hunter.

The dirt and rocks around the plant seemed more like concrete as Hunter worked to remove the small plant. He chipped at the dirt with the knife for nearly five minutes before he had a one-inch area dug completely around the plant. Warily, he slid the knife underneath the plant as far as he could. Then he carefully worked the knife back and forth until he had completely encircled the plant. Not wanting to damage the plant, or tear off any of the glowing leaves, he again slid the knife as far under the plant as he could and started to pry the plant from the ground. As Hunter placed more and more pressure on the handle, the knife's blade bent nearly in half. Suddenly, the pressure from the blade was more than Hunter could hold and the knife slipped out of his hand, flipped end over end, flying eighteen inches into the air, turned blade-side down, and headed straight for the plant. Hunter's heart raced frantically, beating faster than he had ever felt before. Without thinking, he reached for the knife and snatched the handle just before the blade sliced into the plant below.

"Careful, Hunter!" called Hayden, surprised by the knife's sudden flight.

"I'm trying, Hayden!" barked Hunter. He placed his hand on his chest, trying to stop his heart from pounding so fast. Brushing the loose dirt away from the roots of the plant, Hunter pushed the tip of the knife into the dirt underneath the plant as far as he could. He carefully wiggled the handle back and forth until he was sure he had broken most of the dirt away from the plant's roots. He brushed the small pile of dirt away from the plant and pushed the knife as far under it as he could. Nervously he began applying pressure, hoping he could get the plant to finally release from the ground. Only seconds passed before the knife began to lift the plant from the ground.

"It's moving, Hunter!" exclaimed Hayden.

"I can see that," he retorted as he quickly slid his hand underneath the small plant.

"Do you think we have time to dig up another one?" asked Hayden.

"I don't know. This one took so long, I'm afraid the girls are going to be so far away from us we'll never find them," replied Hunter.

"So, what do you suggest?" questioned Hayden.

"We've got to go with what we have," replied Hunter. He stood and quickly moved toward the cave where the girls had suddenly vanished, hopeful the small plant would provide enough light to find them.

CHAPTER FIVE

AFTER THE LONG, sleepless, and frightening night, Alli awoke to the soft sounds of birds singing. Unsure where she was, her heart raced wildly. She frantically scanned the area and noticed Hannah asleep, snuggled close to the mountain wall. As the memories from the day before suddenly flooded back into her mind, a tear trickled down Alli's cheek.

"I sure wish I was back home, safe and sound in my own warm bed," she sadly thought to herself. "At least Mom doesn't know I'm missing!"

Rubbing the sleep from her eyes, she stretched her arms out the best she could under the mountain ledge, leaned up on her hands and knees and crawled toward the edge of the bushes. As she reached the bushes, she peered cautiously around the side of them, nervous about what she would find.

"So, what do you see, Alli?" asked Hannah, in a groggy voice.

Alli shuddered in fear and retreated under the protection of the ledge. She placed her hand on her chest, visibly scared, gritted her teeth and tried to hold her shaking body still.

"What's the matter? Is something wrong?" asked Hannah, sitting up and quickly crawling toward her friend. "Did you see something?"

"No, Hannah! I didn't see anything. You scared me before I could!" she replied. She took a deep breath, clenched her fists together and shook them angrily in the air.

"Oh! Sorry, Alli. I didn't mean to scare you," responded Hannah. "I saw you looking around the bushes, and I thought you might have seen something or somebody."

Alli leaned back against the rock wall, closed her eyes and took another deep breath. "It's okay. I just thought you were asleep. After the night we had, I didn't want to wake you."

"So, did you figure out where we are?" questioned Hannah.

"I didn't even get a chance to look yet," replied Alli.

"Well, let's go find out together," suggested Hannah. She crawled out from behind the bushes into the bright, beautiful, warm sunlight.

"Look, Hannah, the sun is rising over the mountain. It's beautiful! The sun is...well its bright yellow with orange and pink!"

Alli crawled cautiously toward Hannah, but was afraid to completely divulge herself from behind the bushes.

"I've never seen a sun that is that color, or a more perfect deep-blue sky!"

"After the storm last night, I can't believe there's not a cloud in the sky," replied Hannah.

"There doesn't seem to be any sign of the crazy storm last night. I can't believe how beautiful everything is around here," Alli added.

"Any idea where we are, Hannah?" asked Alli, finally climbing out from underneath the ledge, around the bushes, and sitting next to Hannah.

Hannah looked around the area, intently surveying their surroundings. "Look, Alli, we're on a ledge!" she squeaked nervously.

"What?" asked Alli.

"A ledge? We're so lucky we didn't fall last night! If we would have tried to start searching the area last night, we could have fallen and been killed," replied Hannah.

As Alli scanned the area, she found the edge only ten feet from the mountain wall. Looking to her right and then to her left, she saw that the ledge seemed to circle the entire mountain as far as she could see.

Hannah crawled across the rocky dirt to the edge of the mountain, excited to see everything in the valley. Afraid she might be seen, she carefully scanned the area for any signs of life. As she looked, she noticed an odd-shaped plateau about a hundred yards in the distance. The plateau was covered with the most beautiful green trees she had ever seen before. There were several differ-ent kinds of trees, all with different shapes and sizes of leaves. She noticed that each of the trees also had beautiful bright colored flowers. Some flowers hung down two or three feet, while others grew watermelon-sized flowers and still others had flowers of interesting shapes and sizes. As she looked at each of the trees carefully, none of them looked like any she had ever seen before.

As Hannah continued scanning the area for signs of life, she saw an enormous wall hidden under the cover of leaves and flowers provided by the many trees. Hannah was unable to distinguish what was behind the wall for sure, but hoped to find a magnificent city filled with people waiting to return with her. As she studied the area she imagined a beautiful Mayan or Egyptian Temple right in the middle of the city, surrounded by quaint little homes and people rushing all over, just like they do back home. A sudden gust of wind caused the leaves to move rapidly snapping Hannah out of her trance. Blinking twice, she noticed that the entire plateau was covered by enormous trees, bushes and thick foliage. Turquoise-blue water fell off the side of the plateau, forming a beautiful flowing waterfall.

Surprised by all the water, Hannah scoured the area, but could not tell where the water came from. As she watched it pouring over the edge of the plateau, she was amazed at the amount of water.

Astounded by the beauty of the water, she was mesmerized as she watched it gracefully fall over the edge of the plateau. Hannah followed the water all the way down the side of the mountain where it disappeared behind a soft, white, billowing cloud of steam.

Floating toward the sky rose a warm mist, leaving

small droplets all over Hannah's arms. Intrigued by the mist, Hannah looked over the edge and tightly squinted her eyes, attempting to see through the multiple layers of dense, gray steam floating near the base of the mountain. "What's down there?" she thought to herself, intrigued at the scene. "Where's all the mist coming from?"

She watched the steam and mist for several minutes, until, finally, a small area below the steam cleared momentarily. Hannah's eyes grew bigger and she gasped for air. Her heart pounded harder and faster in her chest then she had ever felt before. She quickly placed her hand over her mouth as she realized what she saw below. The steam and mist were caused by the water from the waterfall flowing freely into a raging river of hot lava at the base of the plateau. Sure there must be an erupting volcanic mountain close by, she followed the mist and flowing lava as far as she could see, hoping to find the source. But, she could not see all the way around the plateau. Bewildered, she stood up, frightened at what was below her, and slowly started to inch her way back away from the ledge.

"Hannah, get down before someone sees you!" insisted Alli.

Without responding to Alli, Hannah continued to inch her way back toward the mountain. Still holding her hand over her mouth, her eyes open wide, and fear clearly evident on her face.

"What's the matter, Hannah?" questioned Alli, as she watched her friend's unusual behavior. "Did you see something bad down there? Are we in trouble?"

Several seconds passed and Hannah still didn't reply.

Alli now frightened herself, called loudly, "Hannah! Please, tell me what you saw?"

Startled by Alli's comments, Hannah shook her head, trying to clear the foggy feeling she had, hoping everything she had seen had been a figment of her wild imagination.

"Hannah! Will you please answer me? What is wrong?" Alli demanded. "You're starting to scare me."

"You startled me, Alli!" Hannah replied calmly, as she dropped her hand from her mouth, trying to act normal. "I thought you were gonna stay back in the bushes and wait for me."

"I was, but you were taking so long and nothing bad was happening, so I changed my mind and decided to come over by you," Alli quietly replied. "Sorry I startled you. Now really, you have a scared look on your face. Tell me, what's the matter? What did you see? What happened to make you act so funny?"

"Nothing. Really, everything's fine. Nothing's wrong," replied Hannah, shaking her head back and forth, trying to convince Alli. "Everything is gonna be fine. The only problem we have is that we don't have a clue where we are, what we need to do and..."

"And what?" interrupted Alli, not believing anything Hannah had said.

Hannah paused, knowing how frightened Alli had been the night before. She smiled, not wanting her to be any more scared, and tried to be positive. "And nothing. I promise, everything is going to be fine."

"Come on, Hannah. Give me a break. You know you can't lie to me. I just saw your face and something is really wrong. Besides, I'm your best friend, remember? I can tell when there is a big problem. Now tell me, did you see something bad?" Alli demanded. She started to crawl on her hands and knees toward the edge of the cliff, determined to look over the ledge.

"Alli, there's nothing over the edge. We need to get moving and see what we can find. Come on, let's go," insisted Hannah, trying to steer her friend away from the edge.

Alli turned her head and looked at her friend. "You know you're a terrible liar, right?"

She continued crawling until she reached the edge. She laid on her stomach and peered over the ledge, scanning every inch of more than one hundred fifty feet of jagged rocks lining the mountain to the bottom. She wanted to see what had frightened Hannah.

"Alli, really, I think you should stay away from the edge. I don't want you to get hurt. Now come on," Hannah insisted.

"If you won't tell me what you saw, then I will have to find what scared you myself!" Alli's eyes slowly drifted down the mountain. She, too, was mesmerized by the beautiful waterfall flowing gracefully into the steam below. She turned her head, quickly looking back at Hannah, and asked, "The waterfall is beautiful. What are you so afraid of?"

"Keep looking," Hannah thought to herself. She shrugged her shoulders as she leaned against the mountain wall, trying as hard as she could to smile, and replied, "See, I told you everything was fine. Now get over here, and let's figure out what we're going to do next."

With Hannah's smug reply Alli was still not convinced. She turned back to the waterfall and glanced one last time, sure she was missing something. Still unable to find what it was, she climbed onto her hands and knees and slowly started to back away from the cliff's edge. Suddenly, through the billowing white steam below, she caught a glimpse of something bright red. Unsure what she had seen, she paused to get a better look. As she stared through the mist at the thick steam below, she again saw a brief flash of red. Afraid she might be seeing things, she reached up and quickly rubbed her eyes. She maneuvered back down on her stomach and leaned her head over the side.

"Come on, Alli. Let's get moving," urged Hannah, sure she would find the lava below, any moment.

"You are so hiding something from me, Hannah. And you only want to go because I'm getting close to finding it," Alli replied smugly. "So you can wait a minute until I see what's down here."

Hannah, afraid of how her friend would react to a canyon filled with lava, watched Alli closely, hoping the clouds, steam and mist would remain thick and not reveal the burning red embers below.

As Alli watched the steam float just above the ground for several moments, it cleared abruptly, revealing a raging river of hot lava below. Every muscle in her body froze in fear. Confused by what she saw, she tried to run, move, do anything, but her body would not budge. She could not look away from the red-hot lava below. Alli tried hard to make her lips move and nervously whispered, "Hannah, please tell me my eye's are playing tricks on me?"

"What are they seeing?" Hannah asked evasively, not sure Alli had seen the hot lava below.

"Hannah! Tell me, did I just see lava down there?" Alli demanded heatedly. She flipped over to her back and scowled at her friend. "Is that lava? Lava like would come out of an erupting volcano?"

"Well," replied Hannah, pausing briefly as she took a deep breath, "I don't know for sure. But, it looks like lava, and it's flowing like I think lava does or at least the way that I have seen lava flow on television. The only difference is that I have never seen water fall on hot lava, causing mass amounts of steam. But...yes, I think that is hot lava from a volcano down there."

"A river of hot lava is flowing a hundred or so feet below us? Just like we have watched on T.V.? You've got to be kidding me," shouted Alli though a crackling, terrified voice, as she tried to hold back the tears. "Can you see where it's coming from? Is an actual volcano erupting right now? Are we in serious danger? Where in the world are we?" she demanded.

"Hey, wait a minute. One question at a time. I'm not sure where the lava's coming from, and I have no idea if a volcano is or has been erupting. I can only assume that we are in serious danger, but we have been since we left on this adventure. And I'm positive I have no idea where in the world we are, Alli," Hannah whispered softly, hoping to ease her friend's fear. "I do know one thing, I haven't heard of any volcano not sending out a cloud of dust, ash and smoke when it erupts. I can't see any ashes floating in the sky right now. So I'm wondering if the lava we can see flows around the mountain continuously, but a volcano never erupts?"

"Maybe, you're right. We fell deep inside the earth, and the lava doesn't erupt down here," reasoned Alli, trying to control her fear.

"Maybe," replied Hannah, shrugging her shoulders. "I don't know. But, if we're in the middle of the earth, then how are we seeing the sun and sky?"

Alli thought for a moment before she replied, "Maybe the middle of earth has its own sun and sky like we do."

"Don't you think that scientists would have discovered that already?" asked Hannah.

"No, not necessarily. If the Lord didn't want them to know, then middle earth would never be discovered!" Alli said matter-of-factly.

"I guess you could be right, but I would think someone, somewhere, somehow would have found something by now," replied Hannah.

"Well, no one has. We're the first to find this place!" Alli replied smugly. "I sure wish I knew where we were, I really don't like the unknown. And what if the people that live here don't want us here?"

"Wherever we are, there is a mountain top in front of us that we have never seen before. The mountaintop has a beautiful flat plateau, which, by the way, is odd for the top of a mountain that is covered with bushes, trees, foliage, and colors that we can't describe. A waterfall more beautiful than I have ever seen before pours off the entire mountaintop, and falls into a river of hot lava at the base of the mountain. Lava only exists around an active volcano, which is nowhere in sight. And the mix of water and lava is causing more steam and mist than I have ever seen. So, all I know is we've got to find out where we are and if any people live here. If there are people here, and if they are from one of the ten tribes, we've got to talk someone from the tribe into going back with us to the twenty-first century, so that we can do as the Lord has asked us to. That is, if we can somehow climb several miles back up a slippery rock tunnel that brought us here. I'm not worried about who found this place first!" Hannah snapped.

The girls stared quietly at the lava for several minutes, trying to figure out what to do next. Hannah squealed excitedly as she noticed a suspension bridge running from the edge of the plateau to the mountain ledge, not far from where the girls were standing.

"What? What now?" demanded Alli, startled by Hannah's scream. "What do you see?"

Hannah ignored Alli's question as she stared at the bridge. Following the bridge from end to end, she noticed that it was very long—at least two or three hundred feet. The span was so wide that the bridge sagged noticeably closer to the lava in the middle, although it still seemed to be more than one hundred feet above the valley floor. The bridge was made out of rope and wood. The timbers were chiseled flat on top and rounded on the bottom. The rope was frayed and the timbers were split and cracking, they looked weathered and the bridge looked very old. As Hannah looked to see if they could cross the bridge, she noticed that every third or fourth plank was rotting or completely missing.

"Look, Alli, a bridge to the city," Hannah finally replied, as she pointed toward the bridge.

Alli turned to follow Hannah's pointing finger, quickly spotting the suspension bridge in the distance. "I can see it," Alli replied anxiously. "Do you think that's the only way over to the plateau?"

"That's the only way that I can see to get over there," Hannah replied excitedly.

"I take it by the sound of your voice that you want to try and cross it?" Alli asked hesitantly.

"Why not? We've got to get to the other side," Hannah replied through a huge grin. "Who knows, maybe we'll actually find the lost tribes."

"But...Hannah? Do...Should...Really?" stammered Alli. "The bridge doesn't look like it has been used in years—thousands of them. It can't be safe."

"We can't just sit here," Hannah replied. "We've got to do something. And we know for a fact that we have to find the lost tribes. It only makes sense that some of the tribes might be here! And we were told to locate them and bring them back home."

"That's exactly right!" squealed Alli. "They probably are here. The only problem that I see is that we are two girls, by ourselves, and we have no way to know whether the ten tribes are good, righteous people or not! What if we get over there and they're not? We could really get hurt, or worse, killed!"

"Why wouldn't they be good? Weren't they good when they disappeared?" asked Hannah. She continued to watch the steam and mist from the lava below floating up toward the bridge. "I can't imagine the Lord would save them only so they could be unrighteous."

"Why wouldn't they be good? Are you completely serious? Can you hear what you are saying?" Alli asked angrily, as she looked at Hannah in disbelief.

"Yeah, I'm serious, why wouldn't they be good?" Hannah asked.

"Hannah, have you ever read the Book of Mormon?" Alli snapped, as she carefully crawled back toward the bushes, hoping not to be seen by anyone from the plateau.

"Yes, Alli! For your information, I have read the Book of Mormon. What does that have to do with anything?" Hannah replied abruptly, scowling at her friend, annoyed by her question. "Have you read the Book of Mormon?"

"Actually, I have. And I know that time and time again, the stories in the Book of Mormon tell how the righteous turn their hearts away from the Lord and become wicked. I have also read that the wicked would kill anyone who would not deny Christ. Quite frankly, Hannah, the lost tribes were taken to the North Country hundreds of years ago, and plenty of time has passed for them to become wicked," Alli firmly responded. "And I really don't want to be captured or killed when I won't deny Christ."

Hannah took in a deep breath and held it for a few seconds in an effort to calm her nerves. Then she replied, "You have a point, Alli. I hadn't thought that they might also follow the pattern in the Book of Mormon. I guess you can't expect people to stay righteous forever. But still, I have no reason to believe that they would hurt us."

"Well, Hannah, they could, you know," Alli insisted angrily, as she quickly moved behind the bushes. "So, you tell me, what are the plans?"

"We've got to get over to the city and find out if people still live there. If they do, we need to see if we can find out which of the ten tribes they are from, then somehow we need to convince one of them to come back to the cave with us," replied Hannah. "This is not going to be easy."

"We haven't traveled back in time, have we?" Alli asked anxiously.

"I don't know. I don't think so," replied Hannah.

"I sure hope their calendar is close to the same year as ours," added Alli.

"So, do you think that we should try to cross the bridge over to the plateau, Alli?" Hannah asked, hopeful her friend would agree.

"Is there any other way to accomplish what we need to do to get home?" asked Alli, fully aware of what the answer had to be.

Hannah shrugged her shoulders as she smiled, then motioned to Alli to follow her.

"Wait!" exclaimed Alli. "What about Hunter and Hayden. Shouldn't we wait here for them, in case they come to look for us?"

"We could, but why?" questioned Hannah. "If we head over to the plateau now, we might be able to answer some of the questions we have, making finding the tribes easier and faster when the boys get here."

"How much longer before they get here, do you think?" asked Alli.

"I'm wondering if they will get here. We could just be on our own for this mission, you know?" replied Hannah. "I think if they were going to come and save us, they would have been here by now."

"Oh, don't say that! I sure hope they are coming!" exclaimed Alli, frightened at the thought of the girls completing this mission on their own. "I don't want to do this by ourselves."

"Come on. Let's get moving! I have not seen any movement or one single person over on the mountain the entire time that we've been here. I think we're safe to stand up and try to get across the bridge," insisted Hannah.

"I bet that's why the bridge is in such disrepair. Maybe whoever lived here at one time no longer does," said Alli.

"That's possible. There's no better way to know than to get over there and check it out," suggested Hannah. She stood up, moved from behind the bush, and started walking around the ledge toward the bridge.

Nervously looking around, Alli stood up and followed Hannah. As the two girls reached the suspension bridge, Hannah took hold of the ropes, checking to see if they were strong enough for the girls to get across. The ropes were old, frayed and worn, but felt strong and secure.

Hannah placed her foot on the first plank, testing it as well. The wood felt strong and secure, but there were only one or two planks about every three feet.

"Stay about five or six feet behind me so that we don't put too much weight on one plank. But don't get too far behind me either. That way, if either of us has a problem, we can help each other. Is that okay?" asked Hannah, as she bravely grasped the rope handrail and stepped onto the bridge.

"Are you sure you don't want me to go first?" Alli asked quietly, hoping Hannah hadn't heard her.

"Do you want to go first?" asked Hannah, looking over her shoulder at her scared friend.

"Not really!" replied Alli.

"Then follow me! Here we go. Remember, this is not going to be easy, but if we're really careful, we should be able to get across without any problem," said Hannah, trying to be positive.

"I know," replied Alli softly. "You know what I wish?" she asked, as she took hold of the rope and stepped onto the first plank.

"What do you wish, Alli?" asked Hannah, hoping to keep Alli's mind off of the lava below.

"Well, I can't tell you how many times in the last few hours that I've wished Hayden and Hunter were here with us," she replied.

"Yeah, I know what you mean. I can't tell you how many times I've wished I'd let Hunter enter the dark cave ahead of me. Then he would be here in this predicament instead of us," chuckled Hannah. "With the boys help, this would be a lot easier and safer. Or at least I would feel better!"

"Even if we had the boys' help, I'm afraid this wouldn't be easy," replied Alli, as she continued to follow Hannah across the old bridge.

The girls had crossed nearly half the bridge when Alli noticed a giant bird in the sky. Frightened by its size, she screamed in terror. "Hannah, what in the world is that? I thought you said we weren't in Jurassic Park!"

Startled by Alli's unexpected scream, Hannah looked up to see what was wrong. No longer concentrating on which wooden slat to step on, she placed her weight on a board that was cracked and rotting. Before she knew what was happening, the board she had stepped on snapped in half and she started falling forward. Struggling to grab hold of something to stop her fall, she screamed before she realized she was able to quickly maneuver her leg to the next plank. As Hannah jumped forward trying to get her balance, the bridge suddenly started to sway back and forth, knocking Alli to her knees, leaving her teetering precariously on a rickety, rotting, broken plank. As the bridge swayed from the girls' movements, the ropes made horrifying sounds. Alli watched as several puffs of dust floated above the ropes as they stretched and moved with the swaying bridge. The bridge could break apart at any moment, sending them both hurling to their deaths, and the girls knew it.

"Come on!" screamed Hannah. "We're running out of time."

Panicked, Alli struggled to her feet and stumbled

recklessly to keep up with Hannah, tripping over her own feet. As Hannah reached the end of the bridge, she jumped about five feet from the last plank to reach solid ground. The bridge made a horrible crunching sound, followed by a loud crack. Hannah rolled to her back, sure the bridge had snapped and Alli was swinging to her death on the broken bridge. As she looked over the valley, she was amazed to see the bridge still there and her friend standing eight feet away from her on the last plank.

"Hannah, how am I going to get over there now?" screamed Alli, sure the bridge would break at any moment. "You broke the last plank when you jumped!"

Hannah leaped to her feet and rushed to the edge of the bridge. "You'll have to cross on the rope," replied Hannah as she quickly surveyed the situation.

"How am I going to do that?" shrieked Alli. "You've got to be kidding."

"Take hold of the top rope, steady yourself as best you can, then step onto the bottom rope and slide across."

"Are you crazy?" squealed Alli. "I'll kill myself. I'm not that coordinated!"

"Come on. You can do it," urged Hannah.

"That's easy for you to say," muttered Alli, as she took a hold of the top rope and cautiously stepped onto the lower one.

Alli slowly moved inch by inch toward the safety of the mountain plateau, hoping the bridge would be strong enough to hold her weight as she shuffled. Several anxious minutes passed as she struggled to keep her balance.

"Alli, you're gonna have to go a little faster, the bridge

is swaying again, and I think the ropes could break any minute," Hannah said nervously as she listened to the rope creak under the pressure.

"This isn't easy, you know," shrieked Alli, as she scowled at Hannah. All of a sudden, she lost her balance as the rope on top went one way and the rope on the bottom went another.

Alli let out a blood-curdling scream. Hannah watched helplessly as Alli struggled to maintain her balance and fear spread across her face.

"You only have a few more feet. Come on, Alli, keep going. You can make it," urged Hannah, trying to encourage her friend. "Pull yourself up. You can do it."

"No, I can't!" Alli replied angrily, shaking in sheer terror. "I told you we should wait for the boys!"

"Yes, Alli, yes you can. Pull yourself up and finish the last four feet. You can do it. You're almost here," begged Hannah.

Hannah watched as her friend used all her strength to pull her feet back underneath her and straighten up her body. Relieved to see Alli start shuffling across the rope toward her, Hannah released a cautious sigh of relief.

Finally, Alli was across the bridge. She jumped the last foot to the safety of the land. Stumbling as she landed, Alli fell forward, automatically putting her hands out in front of her to stop her fall. She twisted her arm as she landed on the dirt and started to cry. Alli's heart raced in relief and fear. Nearly five full minutes passed before her heart began to beat at a normal pace. Hannah watched, unsure how to consol her friend.

"Don't cry, Alli. You made it!" Hannah exclaimed as she placed her hand on Alli's shoulder.

Alli grimaced in pain from Hannah's hand and looked up at her friend as a tear rolled down her cheek. "I know I made it. But I could have been killed," Alli replied gruffly.

"But you weren't, so everything is alright," Hannah insisted in a calm voice.

"You know, Hannah, I wasn't sure I wanted to go on this journey. Now I know why I felt so much reservation. I'm probably going to end up dead in a land where no one will ever find me!" said Alli.

"Come on, Alli. Try to be positive. We're going to make it back to the Hill Cumorah, and everything is going to be just fine," said Hannah.

"Oh, it is, is it?" squealed Alli. Unexpectedly, she jumped to her feet, grabbed Hannah's hand and ran for the cover of the trees twenty feet into the distance.

"What is it? What's wrong?" demanded Hannah, as she quickly followed Alli to the trees.

"That bird, the one I told you about earlier. I think it's about to eat one of us for supper," she replied, pointing to the sky.

"Oh, my!" responded Hannah, looking up as she ran. "It's almost here. When I tell you, fall flat on the ground as fast as you can," said Hannah. "Ready...One... Two...Now!"

The girls quickly fell to the ground, covering their heads with their hands. As the bird swooped in for the grab, it had misjudged their height and missed catching either girl. They only had a few more seconds to scurry into the safety of the trees ahead.

CHAPTER SIX

WITH THE HELP of the plant, the boys quickly found a small hole in the cave wall. Hunter peered inside hoping to see the girls. With no sign of them anywhere, he crawled inside, followed closely by Hayden and unexpectedly started falling into the mysterious and frightening darkness.

Sliding for what felt like an hour, Hunter cringed every time he crossed another rough spot in the rock tunnel. Unable to rub his legs or see how bad his pants were torn, he hoped the ride through the dark tunnel would end soon. Moving quickly across the slick rock of the tunnel, Hunter could see nothing, the tunnel looked as though it went on forever.

"I thought for sure I would see a light at the end of the tunnel by now," he thought anxiously to himself.

Grimacing from the pain in his side and legs, he was surprised as he finally shot out the end of the tunnel. Hayden, following closely behind, screamed frantically as he shot abruptly out right behind him. They both landed in the gooey pile of mud fifteen feet below.

Both boys landed with a thud. Hunter quickly pulled his head out of the mud, wiped his blond hair away from his face and tried to clear the mud and goo out of his eyes. Blinking several times to help clear the mud, he was finally able to view his surroundings. Several anxious seconds passed as he searched for Hayden, and was relieved when he located him just a few feet away, near the edge of the gooey mud pile.

Once Hunter was sure Hayden was okay, he quickly turned to scan the area, desperately searching for any sign of the missing girls. Unsure whether their lives were in danger, his heart sank when he could find no sign of them anywhere. He thought the girls might be hiding. He quickly jumped to his feet and slid down the muddy hill. He grabbed Hayden's shirt collar as he passed and nervously pulled him behind a large stone.

"What? What is it, Hunter?" Hayden asked, hastily looking around. "Do you see something?"

"No, but I don't see the girls anywhere. And if they're hiding, it's for a reason. Now, be quiet, while I try to see for sure what is out there," Hunter whispered. He held his finger to his mouth, signaling for Hayden to be silent.

Hunter quickly dropped onto his stomach and slowly inched his head out from behind the bushes. Cautiously, he scanned the area and was surprised to find a mountain plateau with a beautiful deep-blue waterfall circling it as far around the edge as he could see. He watched in disbelief as the water poured mightily over the mountain's edge, almost as if it was falling off the side of the earth. Unable to see over the ledge to where the water was falling, he cautiously crawled toward the edge.

Suddenly, he had a horrible thought. "What if the girls fell off the edge?" He shook the thought from his mind and continued crawling. He peered over the side, frantically searching for any sign of the two girls. He followed the falling water more than a hundred yards down until it reached billowing clouds of steam below. The steam filled the entire valley. Curious as to what was causing the steam, Hunter watched, just like his sister had earlier, searching through the mist to see what was hidden below. As the mist cleared, momentarily allowing Hunter to see to the bottom of the valley, he could not believe what he saw.

"What is it, Hunter? Is everything okay?" Hayden called worriedly. "The girls aren't hurt, are they?"

Hunter turned and looked over his shoulder toward Hayden and quietly replied. "Everything's alright. No worries, Hayden!"

"Then what are those faces you're making? I'm not dumb, ya know!" Hayden replied.

Hunter scratched a glob of dry mud from the top of his head, looked up at Hayden and replied, "I'm a little surprised to see flowing hot lava from a volcano here, that's all."

"Lava? Come on, be serious, Hunter. What's the matter, really?" insisted Hayden. He mumbled under his breath, "Lava. You know, I am old enough to handle things!"

"I am very serious. There is lava flowing at the bottom of this mountain!" Hunter exclaimed.

"Can you see the girls? Is that what's wrong?" Hayden called nervously. "They didn't fall into the lava, did they?"

"I doubt it," Hunter replied calmly. "Hannah's, way to stubborn to fall into lava and I can't see anything that would make me believe they might haven fallen over the ledge."

"And she's too smart to fall into lava, right?" asked Hayden. "Can you imagine how mad it would make her if she fell into the lava!"

Hunter nodded his head, smirked a little and replied, "Not to mention, dead!"

As the two boys laughed to relieve the tension, Hunter turned to continue searching across the valley, hoping he could somehow locate the girls. He looked back at the plateau where the waterfall started and noticed a tall stone. He also saw the thick, lush foliage of the trees and shrubs that covered the mountaintop.

"Hayden, come here, quick!" demanded Hunter, motioning with his hand for his brother to crawl next to him. "You've got to see this!"

Hayden, not sure he wanted to leave the safety of the bushes, called, "Hunter, I don't want to go out there. What do you want?"

"I want to throw you into the lava below, now get out here so I can!" Hunter replied sarcastically, frantically motioning for his brother to join him. "Come and see this. You'll be fine."

"No way, I don't believe you. I'm not coming out there now!" replied Hayden.

"Hayden, I'm serious. Get out here. You've got to see this!" Hunter insisted again.

Hayden reluctantly crawled out from behind the rock and maneuvered his way on his hands and knees next to Hunter.

"What's so important, Hunter?" questioned Hayden.

Hunter quietly looked at his brother, grabbed hold of his shirt and pulled him toward the edge, pretending he was really going to throw him over.

"Hey, what are you doing?" screamed Hayden.

"I'm throwing you over. I tried to warn you," Hunter replied, with a serious look on his face.

"Wait! What? Come on, you're scaring me. Stop!" Hayden cried.

"I'm only kidding, Hayden," Hunter chuckled, as he released the tight grip he had on his brother's shirt.

"Look," he said, as he pointed across the ravine toward the mountain plateau.

"Alright, what am I looking at, Hunter? Why is it so important for me to come out here in the open?" questioned Hayden, as he gazed out across the valley.

"Look at the wall hidden in the trees, about thirty yards from the edge of the plateau," Hunter instructed.

"Yeah, so?" quizzed Hayden.

"That could be where the girls are. It could be a city hiding one of the Lost Ten Tribes," Hunter replied excitedly. "This may be where we find the people we need to take back to the Hill Cumorah."

"If the girls shot out the end of the tunnel like we did, why in the world would they go over to that city by themselves? Besides, how do you suppose they could have gotten there?" questioned Hayden, looking around. "Do you see a way to get across the lava?"

Hunter shrugged his shoulders and replied, "You said yourself, Hannah's smart. She must have found a way. Besides I don't see her having the patience to sit here and wait for us"

"I can't see anything we can use to get us from where we are now over to that wall," said Hayden, scanning the area.

"Well, I bet if we follow the ledge that we're on around the side of the mountain, we'd find something that could get us across to the plateau," said Hunter as he jumped to his feet and started maneuvering around the ledge.

"Wait for me, Hunter!" yelled Hayden, afraid to be left alone. "Are you sure it's safe to walk in the open? Someone could see us."

Hunter stopped and shook his head. Without a word he turned and started walking again. Hayden hurried to his brother's side. The two started walking along the ledge as it wrapped around the mountain. They traveled nearly thirty yards before Hayden excitedly announced, "Look, a bridge! Hunter, I bet you're right. I bet the girls found this bridge. They've already crossed it and they're working on finding a way to get through the wall and hopefully into the city."

"Yep, I bet you're right," replied Hunter. "If the girls are on the plateau somewhere, the bridge is exactly how they got there."

"Do you really think the girls are over there?" asked Hayden as he gazed at the rickety old bridge. "I'm not so sure Hannah could get Alli to cross that bridge."

"Knowing Hannah, she's over there," replied Hunter. "But, can I tell you how bad I wish those girls would have waited for us?"

"Hannah, wait around for anyone?" chuckled Hayden. "Hannah and patience don't go together in the same sentence. I only hope we can find her before someone else does."

Hunter quietly laughed and shook his head as he thought about his sister, then replied, "You know, Hannah could have already found a way into the city, discovered a member from the lost tribes that was willing to return to New York with her and she has already returned without us. That is, if she found another way out of this land."

"What do you mean?" asked Hayden.

"There is absolutely no way that we'll be able to climb back up the slippery rock tunnel we fell through. I'm not sure how we're going to get back to the Hill Cumorah," said Hunter.

Hayden stood quietly for several minutes before he finally responded. "Hunter, if the Lord really wants us to come to this land and help bring back the lost tribes, wouldn't he also provide us a way for us to get back?"

Hunter could sense the nervous tone in Hayden's voice. He patted his brother on the shoulder and said, "I'm absolutely sure He would. I'm sure there is nothing to worry about."

"So, should we try to cross the bridge, hope the girls

already have, and are patiently waiting for us to find them?" asked Hayden grinning.

"Yep, I think we should. I haven't seen any other place they could have gone, and I haven't seen anyone move over on the mountain. The area may be totally deserted," replied Hunter.

"Deserted would be good," said Hayden.

"Unless it's only deserted because the people of the city have already captured the girls and they are currently preoccupied getting them ready to be sacrificed or something," Hunter added.

"Are you serious? Sacrificed?" questioned Hayden.

"Well, people did do sacrifices in olden times," said Hunter. "It is possible."

"Then we better hurry, just in case Hannah and Alli have been captured," said Hayden. "I don't want to tell dad that the girls were captured and used as a sacrifice!"

"I can only imagine how Alli's handling all of this," Hunter said chuckling. "She's got to be scared to death."

"Let's get moving. I don't want either of those girls to get hurt," insisted Hayden.

The two boys continued around the mountainside, running their hands along the dirt wall as they followed the ledge toward where they hoped the bridge began. They walked slowly for several moments. The ledge they were walking on seemed to be getting narrower and narrower with every step they took. They had walked for more than ten minutes, covering nearly one-half mile, when Hayden spotted the beginning of the bridge and excitedly started to run.

Surprised by the noise of Hayden's shoes on the rocks behind him, Hunter turned around just in time to trip Hayden's as he tried to pass on the narrowing rock ledge. Hayden screamed in terror as he tried to maneuver his feet under him before he plunged to his death in the boiling hot lava below.

"Oh, uuhh, uuhh, oohhh, helppp meee!" screamed Hayden.

He started to slide forward, unable to get his feet underneath him to stop the fall. He frantically grabbed at the dirt as he fell, hoping to find something to stop him from going over the ledge.

Hunter moved as fast as he could, hastily trying to catch Hayden before it was too late. He felt like his feet were stuck in concrete as he tried to move. He watched as his brother continued falling forward, suddenly slipping off the narrow twelve-inch, ledge.

"Hayden! Hayden!" screamed Hunter.

He fell to his knees, quickly looking over the edge, hoping Hayden had found something to hold on to.

Almost afraid to see what had happened, Hunter looked over. His heart almost stopped when he saw that Hayden was nowhere in sight.

"No! No! This can't be happening. Hayden! Hayden! Where are you?" screamed Hunter, as tears started to swell up in his eyes. "How am I ever going to tell Dad that I lost Alli, Hannah and Hayden? Who am I kidding? How am I ever going to get back by myself?"

Praying in his heart for a miracle, Hunter scooted as close as he dared to the edge. Then he screamed,

"Hayden, are you there? Hayden? Haayyddeennn!"

Several anxious seconds passed with no sign or sounds from Hayden.

"Oh, come on, bud. You can't be gone," cried Hunter, still trying to find his brother. "Hayden!"

Hunter dropped his head into his hands and started to cry. Suddenly, he heard a sound. His heart raced, and he quickly wiped the tears from his eyes. Again he tried to see his brother over the edge of the cliff.

"Hayden, is that you?" Hunter called nervously.

Several tense seconds ticked away, then finally he heard, "Hunter, please help me! I can't hold on much longer."

"Oh, yes! You're alive!" shouted Hunter, excited and relieved to hear his brother.

"But not for long if you don't help me!" Hayden screamed frantically. "Come on, Hunter. You've got to save me before I end up in that lava down there. Can you reach my hand to pull me up?"

Looking over the edge again, he saw Hayden's fingers start to lose their grip on the small tree protruding from the side of the mountain. Hunter reached to grab his brother, only to find that Hayden was just beyond his reach. No matter how Hunter moved, trying to get close enough to grab Hayden's hand, he was just inches from reaching his brother.

"Hunter! Help!" screamed Hayden. "I can't hold on much longer. I'm serious."

Hayden struggled to hold onto the branches. As his hand began to slip, he quickly released the tree with his left hand and tried to grab closer to the base of the small tree. His body swayed back and forth slightly as he pulled with all his might. He had barely grabbed hold of the base of the tree when the branch he had been holding in his right hand broke free of the tree, causing him to swing back and forth again. He screamed in fright, sure he was about to fall to the glowing red lava below.

Suddenly, Hunter had an idea. He pulled off his leather letterman's jacket, took a tight hold of one sleeve and threw the other sleeve down toward Hayden.

"Take hold of the jacket, and I will pull you up!" yelled Hunter. "Hurry!"

"Can the jacket hold my weight?" asked Hayden, nervous to release his grip on the tree.

"I sure hope so," Hunter replied tentatively.

As Hayden grasped the jacket, he looked up to Hunter and nervously asked, "If I let go of the tree, can you hold on to me and pull me up?"

"You bet I can," Hunter confidently replied. "I'm not gonna lose you again."

Hayden closed his eyes for only a moment before he nervously let go of the tree and grabbed hold of the jacket with his right hand.

Hunter, surprised by Hayden's weight, took an unexpected step forward, only inches from the edge. Hayden squealed nervously as his entire body dropped six inches toward the lava below.

"Don't drop me!" shrieked Hayden. "Pull me up! Pull me up! You promised you'd pull me up!"

Hunter took a deep breath and started to pull Hayden

up onto the ledge. Several moments passed as Hunter continued struggling to save his brother. The veins in Hunter's arms popped up all over his forearms, and his arms shook violently from the strain. Finally, Hunter mustered the strength to pull Hayden high enough that he could get his leg up on the ledge.

Afraid he might fall over the edge, Hayden refused to let go of Hunter's jacket until his entire body was completely on the mountain ledge and he was as close to the wall as he could be.

"Are you alright?" asked Hunter, as he shook his arms and hands and rubbed his shoulders, trying to relieve the muscle aches.

"No! I'm not alright," Hayden replied angrily. "You tried to kill me."

"I did not," retorted Hunter, angry at Hayden's comments. "If you weren't such a klutz, you wouldn't have tripped. I didn't make you trip."

"If you'd kept control of your big feet, I wouldn't have tripped on them!" snapped Hayden, as he looked over at Hunter, smiling at the silly comments.

The boys sat quietly for several minutes trying to catch their breath before Hunter asked, "Are you ready to keep going, buddy?"

"I can hardly wait," replied Hayden, smiling. "I wonder what's gonna happen when we try to cross that rickety old bridge. You know it's probably hundreds of years old."

"I bet it's thousands of years old," said Hunter, as he stared at the bridge a few feet in front of him. "Maybe we should wait here until the girls return."

"Yeah, that'll work," said Hayden sarcastically. "Come on. Let's get going," he insisted. He took hold of Hunter's arm and carefully maneuvered the final five yards to the beginning of the bridge.

Hunter stared at the bridge, carefully studying everything about the creaky, weathered, structure. He finally said, "The wooden planks are splintering and several of them are broken or completely gone. The planks that are still tied into the bridge look like they could be strong enough to hold our weight. The ropes are fraying all over the bridge, and several areas of the ropes look like they have frayed all the way through. But, I think if we're careful as we move from plank to plank, we should be able to make it across the bridge."

"Should we both try to cross at the same time, or should we cross the bridge one at a time?" asked Hayden, as he nervously stared at the bridge.

"I'm not sure how strong the ropes are, so we might want to try crossing one at a time. Why don't you start first, and then I will follow about ten feet or so behind you?" suggested Hunter

"No, I'm not going first. I'm not going to be the guinea pig. You go first!" demanded Hayden.

"Hayden, I weigh more than you do! I think the bridge will handle your weight better than mine," insisted Hunter. "The planks will be stronger if you start first. After I put my weight on them, they could become weaker."

"Come on, Hunter. I'm not dumb. You're afraid to go first," teased Hayden, smiling nervously. "What happens if a plank breaks or gives way? If I go first, I will be the one who falls into the lava below."

"Exactly. Now you go first, so I can see which planks are weak," replied Hunter, through a big cheesy grin.

"Oh, you're really funny!" replied Hayden.

Hayden turned toward the bridge and stared, obviously afraid to start across the old bridge.

"Would you feel better if I went across first?" asked Hunter, sensing Hayden's fear. "I will if you want me to."

"Would you mind, Hunter?" Hayden asked nervously as he looked over his shoulder at his brother. "I'm just not up for falling toward the lava again."

"No problem, buddy," said Hunter, as he reassuringly placed his arm on Hayden's shoulder and tentatively took hold of the three-inch-thick rope handrail on the bridge. He took a deep breath, and then pulled himself onto the first weathered wooden plank. "See, I told you everything would be fine."

The plank squeaked under Hunter's weight, but remained strong. Not wanting to stay very long on any one plank, he swallowed hard, located where to take his next step and quickly moved his foot to the next plank. Again, the weathered wood supported Hunter's weight until he was able to move to the next plank. Hunter breathed a cautious sigh of relief as the old bridge actually remained in tact and he continued the same sequence of events step after step.

Hayden waited for Hunter to get about fifteen feet ahead of him before he began to follow. He carefully started to move across, using the exact same planks and steps as Hunter had.

"Are you making it across okay, Hayden," called Hunter over his shoulder. "You know, with me going first, I won't see if a board breaks, or if you start to fall."

"I know, and I'm alright, I think," Hayden replied, moving cautiously, obviously scared.

"Well, whatever you do, try not to look down," suggested Hunter. "It's a long way to the bottom."

"Oh, man, you've got to be kidding," cried Hayden, quickly closing his eyes.

Hunter turned quickly on his plank, afraid Hayden was falling. "What's up, Hayden?" asked Hunter. "Are you alright?"

"You know, when someone tells you not to do something, that's the first thing you do," replied Hayden.

"Yeah, I do. Did you look down?" asked Hunter, smirking and shaking his head at his brother.

"I sure did," he replied nervously.

"Are you okay? Do I need to come back and help you across?" asked Hunter, pausing momentarily for his brother to respond.

"No, I'm gonna be fine. Don't worry about me. I can do this," he replied.

Cautiously, the boys continued crossing the bridge, carefully choosing each step they made. With only about twenty-five yards to go, Hayden asked, "Can you see anything yet, Hunter?"

Hunter stopped momentarily, staring at the bottom of the bridge, and looked up toward the wall.

"I can see less now than I could before, Hayden. I think if the people who live in this area wanted us captured or dead, we would already be caught or dead," said Hunter.

"With as quiet and lifeless as the area looks, I think we have more chance of being killed on this bridge when it breaks," replied Hayden.

"You know, I'd say you're right," laughed Hunter. "And by the way, this plank that I'm standing on right now is very loose, so when you get here be careful."

"How loose?" questioned Hunter.

"Just try to step on a different plank when you get here," suggested Hunter. "I think that would be better."

Hayden nodded and continued walking about three or four planks behind Hunter.

"This plank, right?" called Hayden, as he reached the area.

"Yeah, I think so," he replied. "Try to stretch to the next plank if you can."

Hunter watched as Hayden held the rope tightly and stretched out his leg, trying to reach the plank about three feet away. As his foot landed solidly on the board, Hunter breathed a sign of relief. Sure he had stepped securely on the board, Hayden quickly transferred all of his weight forward and started looking for the next plank. Suddenly, the board shifted slightly to the right, knocking Hayden off balance.

"Hey, careful, Hayden," called Hunter, watching his brother struggle to recover his balance. "Are you okay?"

Hayden struggled to gain his balance for several nerve-racking moments. Finally, somewhat steadying himself, he took his eyes off the board, looked up toward Hunter and answered. "I'm...alright, I think. No worries. I can do this!"

"Good! Now hurry up. We've got to go find those girls," replied Hunter.

Hayden nodded in agreement, looked down at the crumbling boards of the bridge, and gripped the ropes on either side of the bridge a little tighter. He nervously lifted his leg off the slat and reached forward for the next plank. The board he was standing on unexpectedly shattered into hundreds of tiny little pieces, falling rapidly toward the lava below.

As his legs dropped out from underneath him, Hayden was glad he had taken such a firm hold on the side ropes. Just then the side rope in his right hand started fraying.

Hunter watched as each thread of the rope snapped and started to pull apart, shredding piece after piece, as the weight from the bridge was more than it could hold.

"Hayden, grab the rope on the left side of the bridge, quick!" screamed Hunter. "The rope on the right isn't going to hold."

"Get me off of here, Hunter," cried Hayden, as he quickly followed Hunter's instructions, released his right hand and grabbed hold of the rope on the left.

Sure the bridge would give way at any moment, Hunter looked for any way he could help his brother.

Afraid to move and unable to see anything that could help, he held onto the last rope holding the bridge together. He prayed to Heavenly Father for help to get himself and his brother to the mountain plateau safely. Listening to the creaks and squeaks of the rope, Hunter knew the boys had very little time to get someplace safe.

"Hunter, if I die, would you please tell Mom that I love her," whispered Hayden, sure at any moment he would fall to his death.

"Hayden, please don't talk that way!" begged Hunter. "We're going to be alright, I promise. We'll find a way to get to the mountain."

CHAPTER SEVEN

HANNAH AND ALLI watched in horror as Hayden hung precariously from the ancient bridge. They knew that at any moment the ropes holding the old bridge together could shred, sending both boys to their deaths in the hot lava below. Afraid to run into the open, sure the giant bird was watching their every move, Hannah felt paralyzed, unable to make any part of her body work correctly. She felt helpless as she watched the nightmare her brothers faced.

Afraid to move a muscle, Hunter watched as his brother hung unsteadily from the rope that was still holding the bridge together. Nervous that the rope could give way at any moment, Hunter scanned the area for a way to save himself and his brother. As the bridge teetered back and forth, the wood started to creak and moan loudly.

"Hunter, I can't stand the sounds," cried Hayden. "They're eerie. I don't want to die!"

Hunter took a cautious breath before he said, "Hayden, do you think you can climb up on the ropes at all?"

"Did you hear me, Hunter? I said I can't stand the noise!" he replied.

"I heard you!" snapped Hunter. "There's nothing I can do about the spooky sounds out here right now! I need you to block them out and focus. Can you get your feet on the rope you're holding with your hands, reach up to the hand rope above your head, then using both ropes slide your feet across the bottom rope while you steady yourself with the top rope? Or do I need to think of another way to save you?"

"I can try," replied Hayden, startled by the tense tone of Hunter's voice.

He swung his leg back and forth trying to build enough momentum to hook it over the rope above him.

The ropes and boards moaned in pain under the newly added pressure.

"Wait! Wait! What are you doing?" squeaked Hunter. "You're gonna snap the ropes."

Hayden quickly stopped swinging his leg, holding it motionless underneath him. "I can't just pull myself up. I don't have that kind of arm strength!" he yelled. "What do you want me to do?"

"We'll have to find another way. The ropes will never hold with you swinging back and forth!" replied Hunter.

"I would already have hooked my leg over the rope if you hadn't stopped me," Hayden complained.

"If I hadn't stopped you, you'd already be dead!"

shouted Hunter. "Wait a minute, I'll figure out something else."

"Well, I'm gonna try my way first. I can't hold on forever waiting for you to think of something. My hands are already starting to slip," said Hayden.

Hayden began to swing his legs back and forth, trying to get them high enough to catch the rope with his foot. He tried not to cause the bridge to sway back and forth too much, but he knew without momentum he could not get his leg high enough to reach the rope.

After several failed attempts, Hayden wanted to quit. He took a deep breath and looked up to where Hunter was waiting. Suddenly, he saw a giant bird flying directly toward them

"Hunter, what in the world is that thing flying at us?" Hayden asked nervously, as he tried one last time to reach his foot over the rope.

Hunter did not have to turn around, but he heard the bird squawk loudly. "That sounds like a condor to me," he nervously replied, finally looking over his shoulder.

"Are you sure? It doesn't look like any condor I've ever seen before. Can you see it?" asked Hayden.

Hunter was shocked by the unusual size of the bird. Starring at its large wingspan, his mouth hung open for several moments. Then he looked back at Hayden, who had finally maneuvered himself up the ropes.

"You made it!" Hunter declared excitedly.

"What am I suppose to do now?" asked Hayden.

"Well," started Hunter, as the giant condor suddenly squawked loudly. "This is nuts! I almost feel like we're in one of those old dinosaur movies!" Hunter exclaimed nervously, as he watched the large bird circling overhead. "At any moment, we could be attacked or eaten!"

"Dinosaurs? Eaten? Are you serious?" asked Hayden, anxiously as he struggled to keep his balance.

"Oh, come on, Hayden. I don't really think that bird is a dinosaur," Hunter replied reassuringly.

"Well, you're the bird expert. What kind of bird is that? I'd like to know at least the name of the animal that eats me," insisted Hayden, trying to slide his feet across the frail ropes.

"A large, no wait, a very large bird of some kind," replied Hunter, as he cautiously watched the bird flying above them.

"So, tell me, why this bird is circling our heads?" asked Hayden, moving slowly. "Are you sure it's not getting ready to eat us? I thought birds circled their prey before they ate it."

"You're right," replied Hunter. "We better hurry. There's a good possibility the bird thinks we're lunch. Do you need any help moving on the ropes?"

"No, not really. I think I can make it. All I really need is for you to stop shaking them, and I'll do just fine," teased Hayden.

"Sorry, I'm trying to be careful," replied Hunter, as he carefully moved toward the mountain's edge.

Several tense minutes passed before Hunter finally reached the edge. He carefully climbed off the ropes and nervously watched Hayden. Hayden continued to move his feet side-to-side, sliding with small baby steps toward his brother. Hunter knelt down next to the pole where the rope was connected and tried to help steady the rope. He noticed the bottom rope starting to fray apart. He looked to see where Hayden was and saw that he was still at least twenty feet away.

"Not to put any added pressure on you, Hayden, but I really think you ought to try moving a little faster if possible," suggested Hunter, as he took hold of the fraying rope trying to relieve some of the weight.

Hayden, hearing the worry in Hunter's voice, looked up to see his brother holding onto the ropes and asked, "Why, Hunter? Is something wrong?"

"Not yet, bud. But there could be very soon," replied Hunter.

"Come on, be serious. Is there a problem?" demanded Hayden, trying to move faster.

"Seriously, there's not a problem yet. But if you don't hurry, there could be a big problem," replied Hunter. "You better get to the edge as quickly as you can."

Hayden wasted no more time asking questions, and moved as quickly as he dared. He moved faster than he was comfortable with, but he was sure he did not want to find out how hot the lava was beneath his feet.

Hunter kept a close eye on the twenty or so strands of rope tightly twisted together, updating Hayden every time another strand began to fray.

"Hayden, you better hurry. I'm not sure this rope is going to hold your weight much longer," Hunter urged nervously.

"Quiet!" replied Hayden. "I'm trying to concentrate. I don't want to slip and fall."

"Well, whatever you're doing, hurry up!" Hunter replied.

Hayden continued at steady pace, moving closer and closer to safety. He paused slightly every time the rope bounced as another strand snapped.

Suddenly, the last strand broke, falling quickly toward the lava below. Hunter gasped in terror and leaned over the edge of the mountain, praying somehow Hayden would be holding onto the edge of the mountain. As Hunter gazed in horror at the lava, he could not find any sign of his brother.

"So, are you going to find another way to help me?" asked Hayden, as he dangled precariously from the bottom rope.

"Man, Hayden, you scared me to death!" declared Hunter.

"I scared you? Give me a break," replied Hayden. "I'm the one about to fall to my death! Now, how do you suggest I get over to you?"

"You're gonna have to maneuver, hand over hand, across the rope toward me. I can't see any other way," replied Hunter.

"Hand over hand? I'm not sure..." Hayden paused.

"You've got to!" insisted Hunter, reaching toward his brother. "You're too far away for me to reach you."

Hayden took a deep breath, not sure he would be able to carry his weight. He looked down toward the lava, swallowed hard and carefully started to move one hand at a time across the rope. His hands ached as he gripped the rope tightly. His shoulders burned as they supported the weight of his body, and his arms throbbed from holding them over his head. Unable to hold on much longer, Hayden focused on the rope and reaching the mountains edge as fast as he could.

Seeing Hayden's desperation, Hunter scanned the area, searching for anything that he could use to help his brother, but he could find nothing.

Unable to think of anything else, he yanked the belt from his pants and quickly threw it over the rope toward Hayden.

Hayden flashed a cheesy but nervous grin at his brother as the belt landed inches from his hand.

"Grab the belt if you can," Hunter called excitedly. "Hang in there. You've almost made it!"

Hayden reached his hand toward the belt, stretching as far as he dared. He was ready to take hold and have Hunter pull him to safety. Suddenly the rope snapped, and Hayden was falling toward the lava below.

"Aaaaaaaaaaaaahhhhhhhhhhhhhh!" Hayden screamed uncontrollably. "Aaaaaaaaaaaahhhhhhhhhhhhhhhhhhh!"

Hunter, sure this time his brother was falling to his death, dropped to his knees, leaned forward, and looked over the edge. Suddenly, the belt he held in his hand jolted with the weight of his brother. Unprepared for the weight, Hunter lurched forward, almost falling head first off the mountain ledge. Quickly securing a solid hold on the belt, Hunter tried to pull his brother to safety.

"Don't let me fall, Hunter!" shrieked Hayden from below. "I'm gonna be really, really, really mad at you if you let me die!"

"I've got you. Hold on! I'll have you up here in just a second," Hunter replied, as he grimaced and struggled to lift his brother to safety. Hunter pulled with all his might, fighting to maneuver his legs underneath his body for added strength. Several anxious seconds passed before Hunter was finally able to pull his brother to safety.

Hunter smiled as he watched Hayden crawl up the ledge onto solid ground, flop on his back and take a deep breath, relieved to finally be safe.

"So, exactly how are we gonna get back to the Hill Cumorah now?" asked Hayden as he rolled on his side and glanced over the edge of the mountain to the lava below.

Hunter, relieved to see his brother safely across the bridge, grinned and replied, "We might be livin' here forever, now that you knocked the bridge down. And by the way, I don't think my arms can handle you falling over a ledge one more time today, okay. They need a break."

"I'll try, but you know me. I'm just drawn to excitement. Oh, and living with the bird, that'll be fantastic! You, me and the giant bird. That sounds like tons of fun. I can hardly wait," replied Hayden.

"You forgot about Hannah and Alli," added Hunter chuckling. "They'll be here with us, too."

"That's right. I forgot they're here, too. But, they will only be here if they actually crossed the bridge ahead of us," replied Hayden.

The boys sat quietly for several minutes trying to catch their breath. Hayden scanned the area while he tried to calm the rapid beating of his heart, and noticed a figure waving in the shadows of the trees.

"Hunter, look over in the trees!" squealed Hayden excitedly, as he pointed to the figure. "I think someone is waving at me."

"Waving? Where?" demanded Hunter, scanning the area where Hayden was pointing.

"Who is it?" asked Hayden. "Could that be the girls?"

"If it is the girls, why didn't they come and help us?" questioned Hunter as he continued to watch the figure jump around, wildly waving its arms.

The figure pointed into the sky, then ducked for cover just as a loud squawk sounded above the boys' heads. Frightened by the dreadful noise, Hayden screamed. Hunter looked up toward the sky and spotted the bird.

"Relax, Hayden, it's only that bird again," Hunter said calmly.

"How am I supposed to relax? Have you seen the size of that beast? Can you hear the noise that thing is making?" questioned Hayden.

"I can see it, but I don't think the bird is after us," Hunter said reassuringly.

"Oh, really? Then what's the bird doing right now?" exclaimed Hayden, frantically pointing toward the sky.

"Well, it looks to me like we're about to be attacked!" squealed Hunter.

The bird swooped down toward the boys, stretching its large clawed feet straight toward Hunter's chest. Surprised by the animal's attack, Hunter rolled from his back to his stomach, watching every move the bird made.

As the bird moved closer, opening the claws on its feet, Hunter instinctively twisted his body, barely staying out of the bird's grasp.

Missing its prey, the bird flapped its wings and climbed back into the sky, squawking multiple times angrily. Several hundred feet in the air, the bird started circling above the boys' heads. Hunter, sure the boys were in grave danger, jumped to his feet. He grabbed Hayden's arm and yelled, "Quick! Follow me. We're gonna be dinner if we don't find a place to hide fast!"

"Where are we going?" screamed Hayden, following closely behind Hunter.

"Run to the trees!" Hunter yelled.

"The bird is attacking again!" screamed Hayden, trying to keep an eye on the bird as he ran. "We'll never make it to the trees."

"We'll make it! Just keep running," insisted Hunter.

As Hunter reached the cover of the trees, he turned and watched as the giant bird flew closer and closer to Hayden.

"Hurry, Hayden! It's right behind you!" screamed Hunter. "Move it!"

Hayden, afraid to turn and see how close the bird was, ran as fast as he could toward Hunter and the cover of the trees.

"It's close, Hayden! Zigzag around, or it's going to get you!" shouted Hunter from behind the base of a large Manzanita Tree.

The bird opened the claws on both of its feet, spread its wings out as far as he could and then screeched a loud, victorious squawk.

As the bird stretched to capture its prey, Hayden suddenly changed direction, causing the giant bird to grasp a large green bush instead. The bird angrily flipped the bush to the ground, squawked again and watched as Hayden ran swiftly into the cover of the trees.

Hunter moved quickly toward his brother, grateful he was able to successfully maneuver into the safe cover of the trees.

"You made it!" Hunter exclaimed. "Nice job! For a minute, I thought you were a goner"

"Thanks," panted Hayden. He fell to the ground and dropped his head between his knees, trying to catch his breath. "Now, what are we going to do about the figure we saw?"

"I forgot about that," replied Hunter, quickly scanning the area for the figure.

"Maybe the people here are nice and were worried for no reason," whispered Hayden. He stood up and moved closer to his brother. "I could really use a break."

"I wouldn't count on it!" said Hunter. "But, I do think the shadow was trying to warn us about the bird."

The two boys nervously scanned the area for any sign of people. Unable to see anything, including the waving shadow they had seen earlier, they wandered into the lush green forest, searching for any sign of the girls. As they looked around the area, they were sure they were being watched, although they could not see anyone.

The trees and foliage in the forest were amazing. The leaves were a beautiful green and were the size of textbooks. Moss covered vines and leaves hung from the branches of the trees all the way to the ground. Bright red, orange, yellow and even blue flowers covered the trees and shrubs everywhere they looked.

"Something doesn't feel right, Hunter," said Hayden, cautiously scanning the area. "Everything is beautiful here. But something doesn't feel quite right."

"Like what?" asked Hunter, continuing deeper into the forest.

"I don't know for sure, but I think we should find a safe place to hide until we figure out what our next move should be," suggested Hayden, following closely behind his brother.

"I guess we can, if you think that's what we need to do," replied Hunter, looking at Hayden oddly. "But, do you want to tell me why first?"

"Oh, I don't know. I was thinking we've almost fallen into hot lava, had a bridge crumble beneath our feet, been attacked by a huge bird, had a dark, mysterious shadow waving at us, and that's just so far this morning," replied Hayden. He took a deep breath and then continued. "And, we've seen absolutely no sign of the girls! According to the letter Joseph Smith left, we're supposed to help the lost tribes return, and we haven't found any of them yet. Mom and dad are going to be worried sick about us, I'm sure the police are already involved. And, in case the people that live here aren't friendly, I thought we could use a safe place to make plans."

"Alright, I understand. You don't have to recap the entire morning," teased Hunter. "Let's find a safe place to hide."

The boys located a large tree with exceptionally big leaves that covered hundreds of long-hanging branches. Sliding the leaves to the side, Hunter motioned for Hayden to move underneath the cover of the leaves, then quickly followed, sliding the branches back into place. With the thick foliage all around them, Hayden finally felt somewhat secure. He snuggled safely into the dense undergrowth and breathed a cautious sigh of relief.

"I wonder how many scary things have to happen today, Hunter," whispered Hayden. He closed his eyes, leaned his head against the base of the tree and pondered the day's events.

"I hate it when you talk like that," snapped Hunter. "Try to think of something positive, will you?"

"I can think of one positive thing," he replied.

"What's that?" asked Hunter.

"The leaves on this tree are prettier than any other I've ever seen," Hayden replied, smirking.

"How would you know that?" snickered Hunter, grateful for the relief in tension. "You're eyes are closed."

Hayden opened his eyes and looked at the leaves. "I didn't have to open my eyes. I could see them in my dreams. They're identical to leaves I would expect to find in paradise!" Hayden replied, as he gazed in awe at the greenery completely surrounding him.

Hunter smiled at Hayden, laid back into the bed of greenery and looked up toward the deep-blue sky.

"Did you see that, Hunter?" whispered Hayden pointing nervously.

"Did I see what?" asked Hunter.

"I thought I saw someone moving out there," replied Hayden.

"Did you see who it was?" asked Hunter, as he quickly sat up and looked out to where Hayden was pointing.

"No, not really. All I saw was a shadow," he quietly replied.

"How does the shadow know that we're hiding?" asked Hunter.

"I don't think the shadow knows where we are. I think it's searching for us," whispered Hayden.

Hunter carefully moved a few tree branches aside. He soon located the mysterious shadow about fifteen yards in the distance.

"Have you heard the shadow say anything?" whispered Hunter.

"No, not a word," replied Hayden. "Why?"

"I'm not sure, but I think there's only one scary shadow searching for us," Hunter answered quietly. "If it gets too close to us, I think we might be able to capture it."

"What if the shadow has a gun or something? We could get hurt."

"Hayden, that's a risk we're gonna have to take—unless you want to be captured!" Hunter snapped angrily. "And I don't think the people here have guns. I think they fought with bows and arrows and things like that!"

"Oh, great! Arrows are painful!" Hayden whispered hysterically.

"How would you know?" demanded Hunter. "And by the way, guns are painful, too."

"Quiet, it's close!" whispered Hayden, holding his finger to his lips.

The boys watched as the shadow moved closer and closer toward them. Hayden's heart raced, as he carefully planned how they would capture the shadow.

"I think I can take the shadow by myself," whispered Hayden. "That way if it's not alone, and another one comes after me, you'll be able to surprise them and save me."

Hunter grabbed Hayden's shirtsleeve, shook his head and insisted Hayden wait. But, Hayden ignored Hunter, threw aside the leaves and jumped out of the protection of the trees. He charged the shadow, hoping to grab and tackle the mysterious figure and take it captive.

Hunter watched for a moment, stunned by his brother's actions. He closed his eyes momentarily and shook his head in frustration. He took a deep breath and remained helplessly hidden behind the leaves of the tree, watching the crazy actions of his foolish brother.

Confused by Hayden's actions, the shadow moved swiftly to the side and watched as Hayden's face crashed straight into the ground.

"I can't believe this," Hunter muttered under his breath. "What is he doing? How am I going to be able to save him now?"

Hunter watched as the shadow moved toward Hayden. It grabbed Hayden's arm, rolling him from his stomach to his back. Then it wiped the dirt and mud from Hayden's face and asked, "Hayden, Hayden, are you okay?"

Hunter rubbed his eyes and shook his head, sure he was not hearing correctly. "How did the shadow know his name?" he thought to himself. As he continued watching, he again heard the shadow say, "Hayden, are you alright?" Then it tapped Hayden softly on the cheek. "Come on, buddy, wake up. You need to tell me where Hunter is hiding so we can all get out of here!"

Hunter sprang to his feet, rustling the leaves in the tree. The shadow shot a glance at the tree, frightened by the noises.

"Who's there?" it demanded.

"It's me, Hannah!" Hunter yelled excitedly. "We found you!"

CHAPTER EIGHT

HANNAH, EXCITED to see her brother, rushed to Hunter and threw her arms around his neck.

"I didn't think I would ever see you again," she whispered in his ear. "And just so you know, I found you."

Hunter smiled as he looked at his sister, relieved she had made it across the bridge and was safe. "Well, you almost didn't find us. A few more seconds on that bridge, and we wouldn't be here right now," he replied.

"I know. We watched you two. Talk about exciting!" exclaimed Hannah.

"Exciting? Don't you mean terrifying?" Hunter questioned.

"We weren't sure you were really gonna make it across," replied Hannah. "We wanted to come help, but we were afraid to of being attacked by the bird."

"By the way, I'm really mad at you," added Hunter.

"Why?" Hannah asked innocently.

"Hello, Hannah. I asked you to wait for me, remember?"

replied Hunter as he puckered his lips and squinted his eyes at her.

"I'm sorry, Hunter. I didn't mean to slide down the opening," Hannah said smiling.

"I'm sure you didn't, but I sure wish you would have waited for me. Hayden and I have been worried sick about you two. Terrible things could have happened to you without us there to protect you," said Hunter.

"Well, if it's any consolation, the adventure has been really exciting because I didn't listen to you," she teased. "And I've wished several times that I would have listened to you."

"Thanks," he replied smiling. "But from here on out, I was hoping for the non-stressful, easy, non-eventful adventure, if that's alright," said Hunter, as he squeezed Hannah's shoulder tightly. "I don't think my heart can take much more of this today."

"Okay, I'll try," she replied mischievously.

"Hey, where's Alli?" asked Hunter, as he quickly scanned the area for her. "Is everything alright?"

"She's hidden in the bushes at the edge of trees," Hannah replied, pointing to where the boys first entered the forest.

"Is everything okay? Is she hurt?" Hunter asked nervously, looking to where Hannah was pointing.

"She's okay," Hannah reassured him. "She doesn't want to be here anymore. She wishes she were back at home. But, physically, she's okay. I'm not sure about Hayden, though," she said. "He knocked himself out when he fell."

"I'll get him," replied Hunter. He walked to his brother, shook Hayden's shoulder several times and quietly called his name.

"What was he trying to do, anyway?" questioned Hannah. "Why did he try to attack me?"

"We couldn't see your face in the shadows and we were afraid that you were after us. So, Hayden was going to capture you, and find out what you wanted," Hunter replied.

"Hayden, come on pal, time to wake up," added Hannah, smiling as she shook her head. "You caught the shadow, and now we need to get moving," she teased.

Several moments passed in silence as Hunter continued trying to wake his younger brother. Finally, Hayden lifted his hand to his mouth and moaned.

"Don't touch my face. I think I might have broken everything on it! As bad as I feel, I hope I caught the shadow!" moaned Hayden.

"You sure did," giggled Hunter.

"What is so funny?" demanded Hayden. "Where is the shadow?"

"The shadow was me, Hayden," replied Hannah, smiling softly.

"Hannah? Is that you?" asked Hayden, straining his eyes as he looked at her.

"Yep, you caught me!" she replied.

"Funny, Hannah. Really funny," he replied, a little aggravated. "So, are you two girls okay?"

"Yes, we're fine," replied Hannah.

"What about Alli? Where is she?" questioned Hayden.

He sat up slowly, looked around the area and grimaced in pain.

"She's waiting for us," replied Hannah. "But, I think maybe we should try to find a way back to mom and dad at the Hill Cumorah, and I think you need a doctor."

"We've come this far and we've got to be really close to finding people from the lost tribes. I'm not going back now!" exclaimed Hayden.

"Are you strong enough to get up, let alone keep moving?" asked Hannah.

"Sure, I am! Where to from here?" Hayden asked, trying to smile as he moved to his feet.

"First, we've got to get Alli," replied Hannah. "Then, I think we should head for the wall and possibly the city inside."

"Are you sure there is a city?" quizzed Hunter.

"Yes. Alli and I saw the lights last night," replied Hannah.

"Lights? What kind of lights? I can't imagine they have electricity here," questioned Hunter.

"I don't know what kind of lights they were. But, when the lightning flashed, Alli and I could see everything on the mountain—including lights from what we thought was a city," replied Hannah.

"Where did you see the lights?" asked Hunter excitedly.

"Somewhere over here on the mountaintop. I'm not sure exactly where, but there seemed to be a lot of them around," replied Hannah.

"If there is a city, I bet it's hidden by the forest of trees.

All we have to do is move inland to find it," Hayden suggested eagerly.

Once Hayden was stable enough to walk, Hannah led the way to Alli's secret hideout. Excited to see the boys, she jumped from behind the foliage. She quickly threw her arms around their shoulders and yelled, "I'm so glad you're both here! I was so scared."

"Well, no reason to be scared now!" insisted Hayden, smiling through the cuts and scrapes on his face.

"We better get moving. I don't know how safe we are out here in the open," said Hannah, as she looked nervously around.

"You haven't seen anyone, have you?" asked Hunter, suddenly leery of his surroundings.

"No, but someone could be watching us right now, and we wouldn't know it," insisted Alli.

"Let's go, then," agreed Hayden. "Everyone, follow me!"

Hayden turned away from the mountain's edge and the hot lava. He started walking inland, hoping to find the mysterious city.

"Where do you think we are, Hunter? Any idea?" whispered Hannah, staring tentatively into the dense forest of tall trees.

"Boy! That's the question of the day! I have no idea where we are, Hannah," replied Hunter. He smiled and shrugged his shoulders. "But, I'm sure we're gonna figure it out really soon."

"You mean after we've been captured?" Alli questioned fearfully.

"I hope not!" exclaimed Hunter.

"Then, don't you think we better get moving?" Alli insisted. "The longer we stay in one area, the better our chances are for being captured."

"I agree," said Hayden. "Let's go find the lost tribes."

They cautiously maneuvered their way through the dense leaves, beautiful foliage, and vibrant green forest toward what they hoped was the city. They struggled to move through the vines hanging from the trees and the roots scattered endlessly underneath their feet. The group moved slowly, hoping not to get hurt, as they inched deeper and deeper into the growing darkness.

"I can see some light up ahead," Hayden announced excitedly. "Could that be the city?"

"Let's go find out," said Hannah, as she ran toward the lights.

Small strands of light broke through the leaves, allowing a beautiful, bright light to dance across the wall.

"Oh, man," whispered Hayden. "You don't think...we haven't really found...this isn't one, is it?" he stammered.

"I guess we better go and see, hadn't we?" said Alli.

They hurried through the thick foliage of the forest to a beautiful wall that was nearly thirty feet tall. They hoped the wall surrounded a long—lost city. The sun shone through the trees onto the wall in small rays, splashing a random design of leaves and flowers across the wall.

"How are we going to climb over this wall?" asked Hayden. He leaned his head back as far as he could, attempting to see the top.

"I know I can't climb over this wall!" screeched Hannah. "I'm not even going to try. You know I'm afraid of heights."

"There has to be a door, gate, or some other way in, besides climbing over the top," Hunter said, reassuringly. "Not even I want to attempt climbing over this huge beast."

"We could follow the wall until we find a gate," suggested Alli.

"I like that idea," said Hannah.

Hunter smiled at the expressions on the girls' face, then quickly turned and led the search for an opening to the mysterious, hidden city inside.

CHAPTER NINE

THE KIDS CIRCLED the wall, searching for a way to get inside. After an hour, Hayden finally gave up and sat down on the ground.

"I can't go on one more minute! I haven't had anything to eat in...I don't know how long, and I'm starving," Hayden exclaimed. "Besides that, we must be walking in circles. If you look, you can see the trampled weeds and grass where we've already walked."

"I'm starving, too, Hunter. I need some food," added Hannah. "And if we've already circled the wall, we need to make a plan before we go on."

"I agree. We need to eat and decide what we're doing next," replied Hunter. "But, I haven't seen any food anywhere."

"Haven't you guys eaten?" asked Alli, with a surprised look on her face.

"No, have you?" asked Hannah suspiciously.

"You betcha, I did. I ate while you were looking for the boys," replied Alli.

"What did you eat? Did you bring food with you?" asked Hunter, holding his hand out toward her, waiting for Alli to share her food. "We're all famished, and you're hiding food?"

"I didn't bring anything from the Hill Cumorah with me, Hunter!" exclaimed Alli. "I'm not hiding anything!"

"Then where did you get food?" questioned Hayden. "I'm starving!"

"I gathered fruit and berries here on the mountain," replied Alli. "And everything I found tasted really good."

"From where?" demanded Hannah. "Where did you find the food? And why didn't you say anything to me?"

"The food is everywhere. I didn't say anything because I thought you saw me. I figured if you were hungry, you would gather some of the fruit and eat," answered Alli. She pointed to something hanging from the tree branch. "Hanging from that branch is one of the fruits I like the best."

"What are they?" asked Hayden. "Do they taste good? Will I like them?"

Alli shrugged her shoulders, walked over to a tree and grabbed a large, round, yellow fruit. "I don't know if you'll like this one, but it was my favorite," she said, as she smiled and held the fruit out for Hayden.

"Ouch!" whined Hayden as he took the food from her hand. "What are all these bumps?"

"Oh, come on, you big baby. It's not like they hurt," teased Alli.

"They're a little prickly," Hayden replied, as he gingerly held the fruit. "So, how exactly do I eat this?"

"Break it open like you would a melon and eat the inside," replied Alli. She took the yellow fruit from Hayden's hand and hit it on the edge of a rock. "Here you go. Try it now."

Hayden skeptically took the fruit from Alli's hand, looked at the inside of the fruit, nervously looked up at Alli and asked, "Are you sure it tastes good?"

"I guess if you're really hungry, you'll try a bite, Hayden," teased Hunter. He slapped his brother on the shoulder and took the other half of the fruit from Alli's hand.

Hayden slowly lifted the fruit toward his mouth. He sniffed the inside and finally took a bite.

"Hey, this tastes like the filling in lemon meringue pie," he announced excitedly. "I like it!"

"I told you it tasted good," exclaimed Alli, smiling proudly.

Hannah ran to another tree and quickly pulled a bright red, plum-sized fruit off the lowest branch. Hunter finished his first piece and found a tree with an orange colored fruit similar to an apricot. Alli found one she had not tried yet. It was hidden behind a beautiful purple flower. The outside of the fruit was a dark olive color, with a fuzzy, leathery skin. Hunter found a safe place to hide, and then they all sat down to enjoy eating the fruit and discuss the events of the day.

"That tasted sssooo good!" exclaimed Hayden, as he licked the juice off his fingers. "I knew I was hungry, but

I didn't know I was twelve pieces of fruit hungry."

"Should we gather any fruit to take with us?" asked Hannah, as she swallowed her last bite of food.

"We don't have any way to bring it with us," answered Hunter. "But, I think with all of the trees around the area, we should be okay if we get hungry again."

Hannah nodded in agreement, kneeling up on her knees, barely able to see over the top of the shrubs they were hiding in and asked, "So, where do we go from here?"

"I think we need to get to work. Somehow we must have missed the entrance the first time we circled the wall, so this time we need to watch even more closely for any sign of even the smallest opening," suggested Hunter. "Do you want me to lead the way?"

Hannah shrugged her shoulders and nodded her head in agreement. Acting like an undercover spy, Hunter slowly poked his head over the top of the bushes. His eyes barely high enough to see, he scanned the area looking for any sign of people.

"There's still no sign of anyone in the area," he reported, slowly lowering his head. "I think we're safe to start searching again. Follow me, and let's go find a way inside," he said excitedly. Then he stood up and cautiously walked toward the wall.

Excited to begin their adventure again, the girls stood and followed him. Suddenly, a loud squawk bellowed through the trees, startling the girls. Alli, terrified by the noise, ducked back down in the bushes, quickly searching the sky through the trees. She was positive the squawk was from the large bird they had seen earlier, and at any moment, he would swoop down to get her.

Unexpectedly, another loud squawk rattled through the trees. The noise was followed by several large tree branches crashing to the ground, barely missing Hannah's head. Startled, she jumped backward, gasping for breath. Hayden yelled at the top of his lungs. Hunter spun around rapidly, holding his hands up in front of his chest with clenched fists, ready to defend the group, sure they were under attack. As he looked around, quickly searching for their attackers, he could not find anything.

"What's going on around here?" Hunter demanded angrily. "I thought we were under attack. You guys scared me to death!"

"Sorry, Hunter. I thought that big bird was trying to attack us," replied Hannah, nervously looking up toward the sky. "We've already been attacked once."

Hunter shook his head. He took a deep breath, released it loudly, rolled his eyes and turned back toward the wall.

"Do me a favor, will you, Hayden?" Hunter asked angrily.

"What's that?" asked Hayden heatedly.

"Try not to squeal like a girl, will you?" he said sarcastically. "I hate being surprised with girly screams, especially when they're not from a girl."

"I didn't squeal like a girl!" Hayden protested, struggling to keep up with Hunter's rapid pace.

"Yes, you did!" teased Hunter.

"I've heard you squeal like a girl," Hayden insisted, unable to think of anything else to say.

"Slow down, you two," interrupted Alli, hurrying through the vines and bushes. "You're going too fast. We can't keep up with you."

"Move faster then. I want to find a way through the wall before it gets dark," replied Hunter, moving even faster. "I can't believe we haven't found a gate, door, or some way for us to enter."

"I might squeal like a girl, but you're the one who's afraid of the dark," said Hayden, not listening to anything Hunter said.

Hunter ignored Hayden's comments, and moved faster through the thick grass, making it harder and harder for the girls to keep up with him.

"Hold it, you two!" screamed Alli. "We can't keep up with you!"

Hunter turned around just in time to see Hannah trip over a large, brown tree root protruding up from the base of a canopy tree. Unable to reach her before she hit the ground, Hunter watched in horror as Hannah's arms flailed in the air. Unable to find anything to stop her fall, she crashed head first into the wall surrounding the city.

"Uuuuhhhh!" she squeaked in pain, as she slid down the wall to the ground. When her body finally came to a stop, Hannah was crumpled in a pile on the ground.

"Hannah! Hannah, are you alright?" called Hunter, moving quickly toward her. "Come on, talk to me. Are you alright?"

Several tense seconds passed in silence, with no response from Hannah. Hunter moved her head away from the wall, carefully straightened her body out, and quickly felt her neck, searching for a pulse.

"Hunter, is she breathing?" questioned Alli nervously.

"She's breathing, relax, Alli," replied Hunter calmly. "I'm sure she's okay."

"Is she gonna be all right, Hunter?" screeched Alli tearfully. "Did she knock herself out?"

"I think so," Hunter replied, kneeling at her side.

Hannah moaned as Hunter slid his hand under her head, carefully raising it just high enough to slide his sweatshirt underneath.

"Hannah, Hannah," called Alli softly, as she picked up her lifeless hand, patting it several times.

"Do you think she has a concussion?" questioned Hayden, watching Hannah's eyelids move around rapidly.

"She might," replied Hunter. "But, I sure hope she doesn't."

"Come on, Hannah. Try to wake up," insisted Alli, now patting her cheeks softly.

"Don't hurt her, Alli," said Hunter, worried about his sister.

"We've got to wake her up," said Alli firmly. "Hannah, wake up!"

"Hayden, Alli is right, come around here and help us wake her up," suggested Hunter.

He picked up Hannah's other hand and followed Alli's example, patting it softly as he called her name. Several anxious minutes passed before Hannah softly moaned, batted her eyes several times, pulled her hand away from Hunter and tried to lift her head.

"Mom, do I have to wake up?" she angrily replied.

"Can't I sleep a few more minutes?" The sudden throbbing in her head made her nauseous. Quickly lying back on the ground, she whimpered, "Please mom, my head is killing me, I think I need to rest for awhile. Everything is spinning."

"Hannah, I'm not Mom," replied Hunter quietly. "Can you remember where you are?"

Hannah blinked her eyes, looked at Alli, Hayden and then Hunter and replied, "I can't quite focus. Remind me where we are, and why we're all here."

"We're looking for the lost tribes. Can you remember?" asked Alli, tenderly patting her friend's hand.

"My head is pounding," Hannah replied, as she slowly tried to sit up. "I'm not really feeling very good."

"You fell and hit your head. Can you remember?" asked Hayden.

Several moments passed as Hannah thought about the question. She rubbed her aching and spinning head and finally replied, "I remember everything, I know exactly what we are doing, I just forgot for a minute. You don't need to worry about me, I'm tough!"

Hunter smiled, looked over at Alli and said, "She must be feeling alright, with that sassy attitude."

Hannah returned the smile, still holding onto her aching head.

"But, you need to be careful, Hannah. Don't try to do anything too fast. Sit and rest for a minute," Hunter insisted. "I think you might have a concussion."

"My head is killing me, Hunter!" Hannah whined, as a tear trickled down her cheek. Hunter placed his arm around Hannah's shoulder and helped her slowly back down to the soft blanket of leaves on the ground.

The huge bird again squawked eerily, sending a nervous tingle up Hayden's spine. Sure the bird was a giant condor, and afraid it might attack at any moment, Hunter looked up to Hayden and said, "Keep watch as I try to get Hannah to her feet. I don't want to get attacked."

Hayden nodded and frantically searched the sky for the bird.

"We better get moving, Hannah," he insisted as he took hold of her hand. "Can you walk or do you want to stay here and rest while we find an opening?"

Hannah rolled her head to the side, opened her eyes, looked at Hayden and replied, "Hayden, if you leave me here because you're afraid of that bird, I'm gonna tell Dad what you did."

Hayden knew she was serious by the sharp tone in her voice. Chuckling, he replied, "I'm only teasing, Hannah. I'd never leave you here alone."

"That's what I thought!" she snapped, again attempting to lift her head and sit up.

Overcome by the intense pain, Hannah quickly laid her head back down on the leaves. She rolled over to her stomach, hoping to have better luck getting to her feet in that position. Hunter tried to help her, but she pushed his hand away and insisted on standing up by herself. She pulled her knees under her body, put her hands on the ground in front of her shoulders and pushed with all her might to lift her head. Grimacing from the intense pain as she moved, several moments passed before she had successfully maneuvered her body up onto her knees.

"Will you let me help you yet, Hannah?" asked Alli, watching her friend struggle to stand. "I'm worried about you."

"No, I can get up," she replied. She held her pounding head with both hands, not sure she was quite ready to stand. After several moments, she opened her eyes to see everyone watching her. She quickly took a deep breath, slowly placed her arms in front of her on the ground, and used the strength in her legs to push her body to stand. As she struggled to get to her feet, she reached out to the huge wall in front of her for support. She placed her hands on the stone for leverage and tried to push herself to her feet.

Unable to watch Hannah struggle any longer, Alli moved to her side, took hold of her friend's arm and helped support her weight. "Don't say a word. I don't care if you want my help or not, I'm not going to sit there and watch you struggle. That's not what best friends do!"

Hannah smiled softly, grateful for the help and struggled to steady her legs.

Blinking her eyes several times, trying to focus her vision, she exclaimed, "Hey, look at that!" pointing to the bottom of the wall.

"Look at what, Hannah? What is it?" asked Hunter, as he turned his head to see where his sister was pointing.

"Hieroglyphs and writings over here on the wall," she replied, excited to have found something they had not seen the first time around the wall. "Lots of them."

"What writing?" asked Hunter. "What are you talking about? Where do you see writing?"

"The pictures are carved into the wall," explained. Hannah, as she dropped back down to her knees and ran her fingers across the soft, white stone wall. "Right here. Can't you see them?"

Hunter shook his head. "Are you sure you're alright, Hannah? You did hit your head pretty hard. I'm afraid you really might have a concussion."

"They're right here," she insisted, still pointing at the wall. "Both pictures and symbols, hieroglyphics I'm sure of it!"

"Hannah, I can't see anything either. The wall is blank," added Hayden, scanning the wall closely, searching for the objects she could see.

"Alli, can you see them?" Hannah asked anxiously, looking worriedly at her friend. "You can't, you?"

"I'm sorry, I can't see anything either, Hannah," she answered, shaking her head and shrugging her shoulders. "There isn't any writing on the wall, Hannah."

"Are you serious? There is a ton of writing here. It covers a two-foot by two-foot area. I'm not making this up. I can describe what each symbol looks like, I swear, I can see it!"

"You know, you're eyes are really dilated. I don't know how you could even focus enough to see writing on the wall," said Hunter, trying to comfort his sister.

"Quit messing around, guys. You're not funny," snapped Hannah, annoyed at their jokes. "My head is hurting too bad for you to be playing a joke on me!"

"I'm not joking. I'm serious, Hannah, I can't see any writing on the wall," insisted Hunter. He rubbed his hand across the stone wall. "I can't even feel any indentations. Hannah, I don't think anything is there."

"Me neither, Hannah," added Alli, shrugging her shoulders. "I can't see anything on the wall."

"What about you, Hayden? Can you see the writing or pictures?" demanded Hannah nervously. "Please tell me someone believes me."

"I'm sorry, sis. I can't see anything either. Are you sure you can see something?" Hayden asked, as he placed his hand on her shoulder, trying to comfort her. "You could just be imagining there are hieroglyphs."

"There really are hieroglyphs carved into the stone!" Hannah insisted, suddenly grabbing her head with both hands, trying to control the pain.

"What do they look like?" asked Alli, wanting to believe her friend. "Maybe the Lord is only allowing you to see them."

"Yeah, maybe Alli is right, and you're the only one who can see them," agreed Hunter, hoping she had found something. "Maybe the writings can help us find what we're looking for."

Hannah looked dejectedly at her brother. She slowly turned back to the wall and carefully looked at the mysterious writing and symbols meticulously carved into the stone. Searching for any recognizable word or picture, she stared silently at the cream-colored wall.

Hunter, Alli and Hayden watched her stare for several minutes before Hunter impatiently asked, "Hannah, we've got to get moving. It's getting late, and I was hoping to find a passage into the city before dark. Can you decipher any of the writings that you see?"

Hannah turned to Hunter. Embarrassed by the tear streaming down her cheek, she quickly wiped it away. She looked down at the ground, trying to regain her composure. Then, she replied, "I really can see them, but I don't know what they mean."

Heartbroken at her tears, Hunter softly replied, "Well, let's try to figure them out, okay?"

"Can you explain to me what each symbol looks like?" interrupted Hayden. "Maybe I can help to decipher them. I can't read Egyptian, but I have done a lot of reading on Egypt and ancient hieroglyphics. I might be able to figure out some of the pictures."

Hannah smiled and replied, "Let me see if I can describe them to you, Hayden."

Hannah studied the writings carved into the wall. She rubbed her fingers over each one and tried to describe them to her brother.

"Before I start describing the pictures, do you know how hieroglyphics are read? Don't I need to read the characters a certain direction? I thought hieroglyphs were read top to bottom or something like that?" asked Hannah.

"Actually, hieroglyphs can be read in any direction, depending on which direction the images are facing. For example, if the profile of a bird is drawn with the beak facing to the right then you read starting from the right. Does that make sense?" asked Hayden.

"Yes, I understand," replied Hannah, pausing momentarily. "Then the first line shows a half-buried stone and a bird," said Hannah, looking up at Hayden. "Does that make any sense?"

"What kind of bird?" asked Hayden.

Hannah looked back at the wall, hesitated for a moment and then replied, "I think it's either a condor or a vulture."

"Does the half-buried stone look more like an upside bowl?" questioned Hayden.

Hannah looked at the wall and excitedly replied, "Yes! Does that mean anything?"

"Yes, the bowl represents the letters T and H in the English alphabet. And if the bird is a vulture, then it represents the letter E. So, I think what your describing is the word, *the*," explained Hayden. "What's next?"

Excited to have translated the first line so easily, Hannah quickly started describing the next. "Okay, first there is a clay pot with a light inside, then the shape of an eye, then a vulture again, followed by a mouth."

Hayden quietly thought for several moments before he replied, "I think that is the word, *great*."

"This next line looks difficult," said Hannah. "The line starts with a small bowl and a handle. Then it looks like the green flag waved when a car race is started. The half-buried stone or upside down bowl is next, and then there are two more of those green flags. Can you figure that out?"

Hayden closed his eyes and pictured what Hannah had described. Several moments passed before Hayden asked, "Does the green flag look anything like a leaf?"

"No, not really?" Hannah hesitantly replied. "At least it doesn't look like a leaf to me."

"Can you draw in the dirt exactly what it looks like?" questioned Hayden. "I think I might have a better idea what the picture is, if you show me."

Hannah quickly moved several leaves and vines lying on the ground and drew the picture for Hayden.

"That looks like a palm frond to me," exclaimed Alli, looking at the picture over Hayden's shoulder.

"Or a butcher's knife," added Hunter.

"Actually, I think Alli is on the right track," said Hayden. "I think it's a picture of a reed leaf. And if the picture is a reed, then the pictures represent the word city," replied Hayden. "Hurry go on to the next one."

"The next line of pictures start with a basket that has a handle again, an arm, and several squiggly lines," Hannah described quickly, excited Hayden loved history and had studied all about the Egyptian culture.

"Are there several squiggly lines on top of each other?" asked Hayden.

"No, it's more like what you would draw to show water. One line zigzags across the page," she replied.

"The basket is the letter C, the arm represents A and I think the squiggly line represents the letter N."

"So that word is *can*," interrupted Alli. "So far the sentence reads, *"The great city can.* Is that right?"

"I think so," replied Hayden.

"Keep going, Hannah," insisted Hunter.

"Okay, there are only a few pictures left in this box. The first line of drawings starts with the picture of a foot and the vulture again," said Hannah.

"What letter is a foot, Hayden?" questioned Hunter.

"The foot is the English letter B," he replied, matter-of-factly.

"I know that word then!" shouted Alli, excited to help. "*Be.*"

"I think you're right, Alli," agreed Hayden.

"The last set of pictures in this sentence starts with a vulture, squiggly lines, half-covered stone, a vulture again, an eye, another vulture, and it ends with the side view of a hand," Hannah explained.

"I know what letter the vulture represents," chuckled Alli.

"And I can tell you the squiggly lines," chimed in Hunter.

"And I know what the eye and the half-covered stone are. But what is the hand?" questioned Hannah.

"I believe the hand represents a *D*," replied Hayden.

"So, the last word reads, *entered*?" asked Alli.

"Yep," Hayden answered.

"So, the entire sentence reads, *the great city can be entered*," said Hannah.

"I think so," replied Hayden. "Are there many more sentences?"

"Five," replied Hannah.

"That's going to take forever," complained Alli.

"Not if we hurry. Be positive! We can do it," said Hunter. "Come on, start describing those symbols, Hannah."

Hannah nodded and started to read the symbols

engraved on the wall. After several minutes of describing symbols she declared, "This is the last word."

"What is it?" shrieked Alli.

"The word starts with a hand, followed by a baby chick, and finishes with the eye," said Hannah.

"That word is door," replied Hayden.

"So, read all the lines for us, Hannah?" asked Hunter.

"Alright," she said, as she took a deep breath and started to read.

> "THE GREAT CITY CAN BE ENTERED,
> WITH TRUE FAITH WITHIN THE LORD.
> FIND THE DATE THAT MORONI REVEALED IT,
> AND THE YEAR IT WAS RESTORED.
> CHOOSE THE MIGHTY PROTECTOR,
> THEN ENTER THROUGH THE HIDDEN DOOR.'"

"I guess we can enter, but only if we have faith. I think we have faith because we're here," Hayden reasoned.

"And we need to know the date that Moroni revealed *it*, but I'm not sure what *it* is," added Alli.

"The sentence has to be talking about the Book of Mormon," replied Hunter. "One of the very first things that you learn in Seminary is the date that Moroni visited Joseph and told him where the Golden Plates were hidden."

"Can you remember the exact date?" asked Hayden.

Hunter paused and slowly shook his head and sighed. "I know it was the year 1823, I just can't remember the exact date."

"I can," Alli, interjected. "The angel appeared to Joseph on my mom's birthday."

"So when is your mom's birthday," begged Hannah.

Alli smiled and said, "September twenty-second."

"Are you sure?" questioned Hunter.

"Positive," replied Alli.

"Okay, what else do we need to know?" asked Hayden.

"We've got to know the year *it* was restored," said Hannah. "Do you think the sentence is referring to the Book of Mormon or the Priesthood?"

"The sentence doesn't talk about the Priesthood anywhere, so my guess is the Book of Mormon," replied Hunter.

"Yeah, I think you're right," agreed Hayden.

"But was the Book of Mormon *restored*?" questioned Alli.

"Restored here to the earth," replied Hayden.

"What do you mean?" asked Hannah.

"Well, think about it. The Lord took the Book of Mormon away when He had Moroni bury the plates, right?" Hayden replied.

"Yeah," Hannah hesitantly answered.

"So, He restored the Book of Mormon to the people when He had Joseph translate the plates," explained Hayden.

Hannah looked up at Hunter and asked, "Do you think that's right?"

"Well, we're talking about the Book of Mormon. So, yeah, I think he's right," said Hunter.

"What year was the Book of Mormon given back to the people?" asked Alli.

"Come on. You've got to know that," teased Hayden.

Alli shook her head sadly and replied, "No, I don't know for sure. Do you?"

Hayden smiled and replied, "Of course I don't!"

Alli started laughing and said, "I hate it when I fall for your jokes."

"Does anyone know when the Book of Mormon was first published?" asked Hunter.

"I do," said Hannah. "1830, wasn't it?"

"Yeah. I think you're right," agreed Hunter. "I'm sure I read that at the very beginning of the Book of Mormon."

"What does the clue say to do next?" asked Hayden.

"Choose the mighty protector. What in the world is this sentence talking about?" asked Alli.

"I'm not sure," replied Hayden, shrugging his shoulders.

"Well," started Hunter, rubbing his chin as he thought, "What about the Lord? He is a mighty protector."

"I think the clue would have said, choose the Lord," replied Hannah. "The Lord is too obvious."

"Then what do you think the clue is referring to?" questioned Hayden.

"What is a mighty protector?" quizzed Hannah. "Could the sentence be referring to the condor that keeps attacking us?"

"Yeah, the condor could be a mighty protector," interrupted Alli, nodding her head quickly. "A protector for whoever lives behind this wall."

Hannah smiled at her friend's animated facial expressions and said, "But the condor, could be a mighty protector, right?"

"Yeah, Hannah. I think you're on to something here," replied Hunter. "Can you see any markings on the wall, engraved with the picture of an animal, like the condor?"

"Something other than the birds and animals, used in the clue?" she questioned.

"Yes, I think the mighty protector must lead us into the city," Hunter replied excitedly. "Because in the next line it tells us to enter through the hidden door."

"So, what are we looking for?" asked Alli. "I'm confused.

"Read the clue again, Hayden. Will you please?" asked Hunter.

Hayden looked at his scribbles in the dirt and read,

THE GREAT CITY CAN BE ENTERED,
WITH TRUE FAITH WITHIN THE LORD,
FIND THE DATE THAT MORONI REVEALED IT,
AND THE YEAR IT WAS RESTORED,
CHOOSE THE MIGHTY PROTECTOR,
THEN ENTER THROUGH THE HIDDEN DOOR."

"Okay, then. We need to start with faith that we can find the entrance," started Hunter.

"We already have that," interrupted Hayden.

"Yep," answered Hunter. "We do! Next, we need the date Moroni revealed it, which I think we decided was September 22, 1823, right?"

"Yes, that's the date we picked," replied Hannah. "Now what?"

Hunter took a deep breath and started, "We need the year it was restored, and I think we decided that was the year 1830."

"Next, we need to choose the mighty protector and then we can enter," announced Hannah.

"So, where do we go? What do we know?" asked Hayden impatiently. "I'm ready to find the entrance! Where is the mighty protector?"

"I don't know," replied Hunter. "I think we've got to find some more hieroglyphs."

"What are more hieroglyphs going to tell us?" Alli asked, confused at what Hunter meant.

"I think, there are hieroglyphs engraved somewhere on the wall that will lead us to the way inside," answered Hunter. "And the entrance is marked by the mighty protector."

"Is that why we need to know specific dates?" asked Alli. "So, when we find the protector we will have what we need to enter?"

"Could be?" replied Hunter. "But, I'm not positive."

"We can't see anything on the wall," exclaimed Hayden. "How are we going to find a picture when we can't even see anything on the wall?"

"We can't, but Hannah can," replied Alli, excitedly. "Hannah, you're gonna have to find them for us!"

"I'm already looking," Hannah shouted from several feet away as she rubbed her hand across the wall searching for more engravings.

"Hannah, wait!" called Hayden. "Come back here."

"Hayden, I need to hurry!" exclaimed Hannah, as she moved farther into the distance.

"No, Hannah wait," called Hayden again. "I think the hieroglyphs are back here."

"What makes you think that, Hayden?" quizzed Hunter suspiciously. "Do you know something?"

"Hieroglyphics are drawn together, they are not spread over large areas," Hayden replied. "In most cases, hieroglyphs start in one area and then every inch of the stone is used from one side to the other."

"What," exclaimed Hannah, startling the two boys. Hannah giggled at their nervous reactions and asked, "Okay, guys. What do you need?"

"I think the hieroglyphs have got to be right here in this area," replied Hayden, pointing to the wall. "Wherever the hieroglyphs are that you described earlier, is most likely where all of the drawings will be."

"I didn't see anything else before, but I will look again," she replied, as she moved toward the engravings on the wall.

Hannah scoured the area for several moments, looking for anything that might lead to a secret entrance. Frustrated she could not find anything, she looked over at the boys and said, "Hayden, all I can see are the pictures I described earlier, outlined by a box. Next to that are several lines and squiggles, but no hieroglyphic letters. Above that box, there are several more squiggles and lines and there are an additional four boxes that look the same way."

"Hannah what exactly do those squiggles and lines look like?" questioned Hayden, sure they had a meaning. "Can you describe them or draw them in the dirt for me?"

"I think they are just engraved on the wall for decoration, Hayden. But I can describe them for you if you want," Hannah replied.

Hayden nodded, so Hannah began.

"Okay, in the box to the right of the hieroglyphics, there are eight squiggly lines, they are all identical and they sort of look like a large letter *e* without the bottom line curled. Then, there are three figures that look like tunnels and one straight line," Hannah described. "Do those mean anything to you, Hayden?"

"Well, yes. I think you're describing numbers," he replied excitedly. "Hieroglyphic numerals."

"The squiggly line stands for one hundred, the tunnel represents the number ten and the straight line is the symbol for one," Hayden replied. "I think!"

"Then what number would the symbols that Hannah just described represent?" asked Alli.

"Eight hundred-twenty-one," chimed in Hunter. "What do the other boxes have, Hannah?"

"Let's see, there is one that looks kinda funny. It has a heart shape on a stick that is wrapped in a burlap bag at the bottom, followed by eight of those squiggly lines, two tunnels and three straight lines," Hannah replied, looking quickly to the next box.

"Wait a second," insisted Hunter. "Hayden, what was the first symbol Hannah described?"

"I think it's the symbol that represents one-thousand," he replied. "So, that number would be, one thousand eight hundred twenty three."

"That's one of the numbers we need!" exclaimed Alli. "Are there any more?"

Hannah quickly described the last three boxes of symbols, identifying all of the numbers they needed along with several that they did not need.

"Is that everything, Hannah?" asked Hayden.

"The only other symbols carved into the stone wall are characters representing the one, tens, hundreds, thousands, and ten-thousands," she replied.

"Just one of each number?" asked Hayden, making sure they were not missing anything.

"Yep, carved across the top line of boxes," she replied. "So, now what do we do, Hayden?" asked Hannah nervously excited.

"Somehow we use the numbers to open a secret door or something," Hayden replied. "Does it look like you could push the numbers or boxes?"

"No, not really, but I could try," Hannah replied, as she quickly moved to the engravings on the wall and pushed the stone. "Which stones do you want me to try?"

"Start with the box that represents 1830 and then try pushing the box that represents 1823," answered Hunter.

Hannah nodded, looked at the stone wall, chose the numbers she needed and pushed both at the same time. Several anxious moments passed before she stood up and looked bewildered at Hunter.

"Did it work?" asked Alli, frustrated she could not see

what was happening.

"Yeah, what's up, Hannah?" asked Hunter. "Did a secret doorway open?"

"Both of the stones moved slightly, but it feels like something is holding them back from being pushed all the way in," Hannah replied, as she turned and pushed with all her strength.

"But, the stones did move a little?" asked Hayden.

"They seemed to, a little," Hannah replied.

"What about the mighty protector?" asked Alli. "We haven't found the protector yet."

"Or, what about faith we can find the opening?" quizzed Hayden. "Do we have the faith we need?"

"I've got plenty of faith," replied Hannah. "But, I cannot find the protector, I can't see..." she paused.

"What? What, did you find, Hannah?" questioned Hunter, sure Hannah had found something.

Hannah stared at the wall for nearly a minute before she finally took a breath. Leaning her head slightly to the right and squinting, she continued to stare.

"Hannah, wake up!" demanded Hunter.

"Yeah, tell us what you found!" exclaimed Alli.

Hannah turned and looked at Hunter, still contemplating what she thought she could see.

"Hunter, could you sketch the lion that was etched into the glass of Grandpa's lamp?" she asked, with a distant look in her eyes.

"I could try to," he replied, as he kneeled down on the ground and looked up at her. "Can you tell me why?"

Hannah blinked several times, trying to clear the fog

from her head, before she replied, "The hieroglyphs engraved on the wall have a shape the way they are written. When you imagine all of the words and numbers together, you can almost see the shape of a lion. I thought maybe the Lion could be the great protector."

"Hey, wait a minute. In the original paper Grandpa showed us, there was a letter from Heber C. Kimball. In that letter, didn't he tell us to have faith and courage like the lion?" asked Hayden.

"Yes, you told me about the letter, did it say that," replied Alli. "Didn't you tell me the letter also said the lion would be a protection?"

"Yeah! The letter did say something like that too," replied Hunter.

"Okay, okay, back to finding a way through the wall, if Hannah can see the shape of the mighty protector, and we have found the numbers we need, then why aren't we able to see a secret door or something?" quizzed Hayden.

"Hannah what numbers did you push?" asked Hunter.

"I pushed the boxes that represent the number 1830 and 1823," she replied.

"What about the numbers for September twenty-second?" questioned Alli.

"I can't see anything that represents a month and a day," replied Hannah.

"What about the numbers nine or twenty-two?" asked Hunter. "Are there boxes with those numbers engraved inside?"

"There are boxes with both of those numbers," exclaimed Hannah.

"Then that has to be it!" replied Alli. "Try to push those two stones as well."

Hannah quickly pushed the stones representing the number nine and twenty-two. Then she again tried to push the stones with the number 1823 and 1830. All four stones moved nearly five inches inside the huge stone wall.

"They are all pushed in what do I do now?" questioned Hannah.

"What does the clue say we need to do next?" asked Hunter.

"The clue reads,

'CHOOSE THE MIGHTY PROTECTOR,
THEN ENTER THROUGH THE HIDDEN DOOR'."

read Hayden.

"How do we choose the mighty protector?" asked Alli.

"I think we have already," replied Hayden. "We chose the mighty protector when we translated these hieroglyphs."

"So, what do we do now?" questioned Alli. "What have we missed?"

"We must just have to enter somewhere," replied Hannah.

"But where?" questioned Hunter. "Can you see any openings, anything that looks like it could be an entrance?"

Hannah looked at the hieroglyphs and visualized the outline of the lion. She found could see the lion was standing on his hind legs with his front paws up, ready to attack, just like on the lamp. She could see that the four stones she had pushed into the wall outlined the lion's body, forming four corners. She stood wondering what to do for several moments, praying for guidance from the Lord, when she suddenly had a thought.

"I wonder what would happen if I pushed on the lion," she said.

She placed both of her hands on the stone wall and pushed with all her might.

"What are you doing, Hannah?" asked Alli.

"Trying to open the secret door," she replied.

"Can I help?" asked Alli as she started pushing the stone.

"The corners of where I think the door might be, are marked by the four stones I pushed into the wall. So, I'm hoping they are also the four corners of the secret door," she explained, still pushing.

"Hey, I think the stone just moved," exclaimed Alli. "Guys come help us."

Hunter and Hayden moved quickly to the wall and helped the girls push. Several long and frustrating minutes passed before a small opening to the mysterious city was revealed.

"I think that's far enough to squeeze through," said Hannah as she stopped pushing the wall and brushed the sand and dirt from her hands.

"Should we go inside?" Alli asked tentatively.

"We're not going to find the lost tribes if we don't," replied Hunter, as he carefully peeked through the crack in the wall.

"Who thought finding our way inside the city would

be so simple?" asked Hayden, as he peered over Hunter's shoulders, trying to catch a glimpse inside.

"Simple for whom? My head is still really hurting," complained Hannah. She rubbed the egg-sized lump on her forehead. "If I hadn't just about killed myself we would never have found those engravings."

"I guess you're right. Finding our way in wasn't as simple for you," agreed Hayden. He moved away from the opening in the stone and quickly stepped to the side. Smiling a cheesy grin, Hayden said, "After you girls."

"This is no time to be gentlemen, Hayden," Alli protested. "You go first in case someone is waiting to capture us just inside the wall.

Hayden grinned at Alli and replied, "Oh, you're right, girls. I mean, everybody follow Hunter!"

Hunter smiled at Hayden, shook his head and agreed. "That's right! Everybody follow me, and stay close!"

CHAPTER TEN

AS EACH OF THEM carefully slipped through the small opening in the wall, they were greeted by an exquisite pool of dazzling blue water that shimmered like diamonds in the late afternoon sun. Amazed at the vibrant colors and scenery, they stood motionless for several minutes, taking in the view. As a bird softly trilled in the distance, Hayden was sure this must be what heaven was like.

The wind blew softly, causing the leaves to sway back and forth slowly. The water fell over the hillside with grace and beauty. The scene was truly mesmerizing. Peace and calm filled every open space around them. All of a sudden, a loud boom sounded, startling the four visitors back into the present.

"What was that?" exclaimed Alli, holding her hand up to her chest.

"Was that a cannon?" asked Hannah, still holding her pounding head.

"No, I don't think that was a cannon," replied Hunter, grinning.

"Then what?" demanded Alli. "The sound and vibrations felt awfully close."

"The sound was more like a volcanic release of air," replied Hayden confidently. "Especially with the low level vibrations it caused."

"A volcanic release of air? What are you talking about?" teased Hannah. "I might have a concussion, but come on, Hayden. You sound like a release of volcanic air!"

"Seriously, Hannah. I think a build up of pressure underneath the lava, that we crossed earlier, finally released an air pocket, causing a loud boom," insisted Hayden. "I've read about them before."

"Sounds like something you made up to me, but okay," replied Alli, smiling at Hayden's explanation.

"I sure wish I knew where we were," muttered Hannah. "I really don't like not knowing."

"Me neither," agreed Alli.

"I wish I knew so I could come back again. This place is amazing," added Hunter. "Don't you think Mom would love it here?"

"Yes, she'd love everything—except the huge, attacking condor," replied Hannah, looking up toward the sky. "I don't think she'd like it very much."

"Your mom would like the water. I've never seen anything like this," whispered Alli. "The water in the waterfall pouring over the ledge sparkles until it falls into the pool of water below, then it shines with the prettiest colors I've ever seen."

"I think so, too. I've never seen anything so beautiful. Not only the colors, but the trees, plants, sky, water—it's all amazing!" agreed Hayden softly. "I wonder why everything is so pretty?"

"Maybe because of the weather, who knows," replied Hunter, as he shrugged his shoulders and smiled. "But everything sure is pretty!"

"We need to make a plan, night's gonna be here soon and I'm not sure we want to be out in the open when it hits," said Hannah.

"Hunter, how are we ever going to convince someone that lives here that the Lord wants us to bring them back?" Alli asked.

"You know, I'm not really sure. But, we have enough faith that the Lord will provide a way for us, don't we?" he softly replied. "Otherwise, why did we even try to follow Joseph Smith's letter in the first place, right?"

"You're right. I'm just scared," Alli replied.

Suddenly, a fist sized rock tore through the leaves of the trees making a loud thump as it hit the tree right next to Hunter's shoulder. The rock rattled its way down the tree trunk to the ground, quickly followed by a twig loudly snapping in the distance. Someone was coming. Hunter nervously scanned their surroundings, searching for a safe place to hide. He was afraid that at any moment, they would be captured. Spotting a dense grove of small trees and bushes ten feet in the distance, he motioned for everyone to stay quiet as he hurried toward it. He checked to see if the trees would provide adequate shelter. Finding the area large enough for them to hide, he turned and frantically waved his arms, motioning for Hannah, Alli and Hayden to quickly follow.

Slipping between the trees and bushes, Hunter smashed down the small foliage, forming a hideout inside. "Climb in quickly," he whispered anxiously, holding back several branches.

Once inside, the four watched nervously to see who was coming.

"Hunter, what about the opening? We didn't close the opening in the wall," declared Hayden, in a low nervous tone.

Hunter gasped in terror and replied, "We've got to close it, or someone will know we're here," he replied fearfully.

"I'll go. I'm smaller and I'll have a better chance of not being seen," insisted Hannah, starting to pull back several branches of the tree.

"Not a chance," whispered Hayden, grabbing her arm and pulling her back. "You're not going anywhere."

Without a word, Hayden swiftly slipped out of the cover of the shrubs and into the dangerous open area. Luckily, towering trees surrounding the area delivered hundreds of twisting branches everywhere, providing an umbrella of hanging vines and leaves for Hayden to hide behind. Hayden moved like a jaguar, ready to attack his prey. He was quiet and agile. He moved quickly, like the wind, to the opening in the wall. With only pale streaks of light from the sky penetrating the umbrella of leaves, his silhouette was hard to see.

"I think he's almost there," Hunter nervously reported to the girls.

".What's taking him so long?" questioned Alli, anxious for Hayden to return.

Without a word, Hunter shrugged his shoulders and strained to watch, praying for his brother's safe return. "He's moving pretty quickly, Alli. I'm sure he won't be much longer."

"Hunter, did the stone door make a lot of noise when it opened?" asked Hannah, afraid the sounds might give away Hayden's position.

"I don't remember. Did it?" he asked, looking nervously at Hannah.

"I can't remember either. I didn't pay attention," she cried softly. "I really don't want Hayden to be caught."

The sound of rocks grinding together suddenly filled the air. Several moments passed as the three waited in horror for the noise to end.

"I guess that answers that question," Alli said sarcastically. "At least there's no sign of whoever is coming."

The last remnants of pale light faded from the sky, and the cover of darkness finally came. Several nervous minutes followed as Hunter, Hannah and Alli waited for Hayden to safely return to their hideout.

"I can hear voices, Hunter!" exclaimed Hannah. "They must be close."

"Can you tell where the voices are coming from?" asked Hunter, as he surveyed the area.

"No, I can only hear them," she replied. "What if the people caught Hayden, and that's why he's not back yet?"

"Hayden's smart, I'm sure he's safely hidden," Hunter said reassuringly.

"There they are!" exclaimed Alli, pointing toward the pool of water. "Two men—they look like guards."

"Do they have Hayden?" asked Hunter, searching in the darkness.

"I don't think so," Alli replied hesitantly. "I wish I could tell what they're saying. That way I would know if they've caught Hayden or not."

"Me, too," agreed Hannah. "I don't even recognize the language they're speaking."

"Hey, wait a minute," exclaimed Hunter. "I can understand every word they're saying, and I know I've never heard this language before. Can you understand them?"

"No, everything sounds foreign to me," replied Hannah.

"I can't understand a word, either," whispered Alli. "Although I think I heard someone speak this language before, on the Discovery Channel."

"So, Hunter, if you understand them, what are they saying?" asked Hannah. "Tell me, have they found Hayden?"

"Quiet so I can hear them," Hunter barked. "If you want me to find out what they know, be quiet for a minute."

Several tense minutes passed while Hunter listened to the men speak. "I can't hear everything they are saying, but what I can hear is something about their king or leader Tantua, not Hayden."

"What about the king?" questioned Hayden, startling the group as he climbed inside the hideout.

"I almost screamed, Hayden. You scared me!" snarled

Hannah, pushing his shoulder.

"You made it!" said Hunter, relieved to see his brother. "Nice job!"

"Yes, I did," Hayden, boasted through a huge grin. "Sorry I took so long. I could hear the men, so I crept back here slowly and carefully so I wouldn't make any noise."

"We're glad you made it!" exclaimed Alli. "I was sure the noise made by the wall closing gave you away."

"So, tell me, what are the men out there talking about?" asked Hayden, pulling the leaves aside far enough to see the men. "Anything that might tell us where we are?"

"You don't understand them either?" questioned Hunter. "I was hoping one of you would be able to understand what was being said."

"Nope, sorry. I take it you're the only one who can understand what they're saying," said Hayden, with a grin.

"Yep, it looks that way," replied Hunter. He turned back toward the men and tried to concentrate on their conversation.

"So far, Hannah can see ancient writing that no one else can, I'm able to translate the writing that no one else is able to figure out, and Hunter is able to understand the language the people here are speaking and no one else can," recounted Hayden. "Sounds to me like the Lord is helping us to get done what He has asked."

"Ssshhh," insisted Hunter, as he held his finger to his lips. "They're moving this way," he whispered.

Hannah pulled the huge leaves from the Elephant Ear

plant across her body, hoping the added camouflage would prevent the men from spotting her bright pink shirt through the leaves. The sound of the men's voices and the unrecognizable words they were saying came closer and closer, then suddenly stopped directly in front of the hideout.

"Hold your breath," Hannah thought to herself, sure the men knew the kids were hiding there.

Hunter motioned for everyone to remain still and quiet. Hannah agreed, although she thought running for her life might be a better option.

The men talked and pointed to the crushed greenery on the ground. They walked back and forth to the wall several times, looking for anything suspicious. More than five minutes passed before the men were satisfied that nothing was wrong, and finally continued on their way.

"What was that all about, Hunter?" asked Hannah. "Did they see something?"

"They know something has been here, but they don't know what," he replied, whispering.

"Do they know we're here?" Hayden asked fearfully, sure the men were going for reinforcements and would be back momentarily.

"They don't know that we're here—only that something has been here recently," Hunter whispered. "Now ssshhhh, I need to hear what they are saying."

Alli waited impatiently several moments before she asked. "Have they said who they are?"

"Why would they tell each other who they are, Alli?" asked Hayden.

"I don't know. I was just hoping..." replied Alli.

"Will you two please be quiet!" demanded Hannah. "They're going to hear us."

Hunter placed his finger to his lips, signaling for them to be quiet and whispered. "The tall man's name, on the right, is Heth. And the other man's name is Midian. Both men are soldiers in Tantua's army. They are supposed to report any inconsistencies to a man named Bashan; I guess he is the captain, but I can't tell if they are going to for sure. The three of you won't be quiet long enough for me to hear their conversation!" Hunter snapped. He turned and tried to focus on the men.

Hannah and Alli listened quietly to every word the men said, hoping they would be able to understand something in their language. Unable to comprehend even one word, Hannah was grateful that Hunter could translate the soldiers' conversation for them.

"Do you think someone from the village has been out here spying on us?" asked Heth, in a deep baritone voice.

"I don't know. I guess Tantua could have sent someone to watch us. But why?" asked Midian.

"Well, if you don't think someone was spying on us, is there any chance someone could have entered the city? There has to be a reason that Tantua has us patrol the walls of the village everyday," reasoned Heth.

"No one has entered our city in more than a thousand years. What could possibly make you think that someone, after all these years, has entered?" questioned Midian.

"I just thought that there might be a reason why we have walked around the village every day for the last three months!" said Heth.

"Not that I'm aware of. I think this is another unnecessary job Tantua requires us to do," replied Midian. "If he gives orders and looks busy, then I think he feels better about his appointment to be prophet."

"How does patrolling the village wall for the protection of all the citizens help Tantua?" questioned Heth.

"When his soldiers are away from the city, Tantua is able to do secret things back at the temple," replied Midian.

"Come on, Midian. You can't be serious?" questioned Heth.

"Well, I am. You know that I think Tantua is up to something. How do I know what he's thinking? None of the other prophets had the soldiers patrol the walls," replied Midian.

"Do you think it is because of the prophecy that was written on the tablets thousands of years ago?" asked Heth.

"Are you talking about the prophecy that reads, 'Four will come to return the tribes, over the great highway, home to our brothers in a new land'?" questioned Midian.

"Yes. Doesn't the prophecy also say that the four will come shortly after Tantua becomes a prophet?" asked Heth.

"Yes, but do you really believe the writing of the old prophets?" asked Midian.

"I do, and maybe Tantua does, too. So, to protect himself, he sends his soldiers to protect the city," suggested Heth.

"I don't know, maybe. But I still think he's up to something that's not good," replied Midian.

"We've been out here a long time. Longer than usual. I don't want anyone to come looking for us. We better get back to the village and find out what's going on. Besides, it's almost time," said Heth.

"Should we tell Tantua about the smashed foliage?" asked Midian.

"Maybe. Let's see if anything is happening first," replied Heth. "Besides, we don't know what smashed the bushes and grasses, I don't want to frighten anyone in the city, for nothing. Okay?"

Midian, cleared his throat, looked at Heth, nodded his head and they quickly walked into the mist and disappeared.

CHAPTER ELEVEN

HAYDEN WATCHED until he could no longer see even their shadows through the trees. He remained quiet, straining to hear every word of their conversation until he was sure not another word could be heard. When he was sure the soldiers could not hear him, he turned to Hunter and impatiently asked, "Where to from here, Hunter? Do you think they're heading to the center of the city we just snuck into? Did they say which of the ten tribes they belonged to? Do you think we should follow the soldiers or search on our own?"

"I...I...I don't know," stammered Hunter, overwhelmed by all the questions. "I'm not sure what to do. You heard those men, they're planning something. I don't want to get caught up in any secret combinations against the leaders here. That could spell real trouble."

"No, I couldn't understand what they were saying. What plans? What secret combinations? I think we should follow them, Hunter," insisted Hayden. "We'll at least know exactly where the center of the city is. Maybe, by following them, we can get there safely."

"He's got a point," agreed Hannah. "I think we should follow them. Even if they are planning secret combinations, we might be able to warn their leader."

"Oh, you're not going, Hannah," snapped Hunter. "Hayden and I will follow the soldiers. We'll come back for you and Alli when I'm sure everything is safe."

"You're not leaving us here! No way, Hunter!" Alli protested. "What if we're caught by the soldiers, or attacked by that huge bird!"

"I agree," added Hannah angrily. "You're not leaving us here alone. I want to go with you. Please."

"Sssshhhhh, girls," snarled Hayden. "We won't have to worry about following the soldiers, we're gonna end up their prisoners if you're not quiet."

"Sorry, Hayden," replied Hannah. "But there's no way you two are gonna leave us here alone."

"Okay, let's all follow them," Hunter agreed hesitantly. "We have to be careful and not get to close. I don't want to get caught."

"Me, neither," added Alli. "I don't think we'd be able to complete our mission for the Lord if we get caught. Hannah and I will be very quiet. I promise."

"We better hurry. If we wait much longer, we might not be able to catch up with the soldiers," said Hannah as she pointed into the distance.

Hunter pulled the thick blanket of vines and leaves to the side and quietly led the way out of their hideout.

"One last thing before we go," said Hunter, stopping

abruptly. "If, for any reason, we get separated, we are to meet back here in this hideout. Okay?"

Everyone nodded. The kids, anxious and excited to follow the soldiers, quickly slipped into the open forest of trees and mist. Hunter was grateful for the cover of night. He used the darkness to rapidly catch up with the soldiers. He was able to stay hidden and keep everyone at a safe distance. The kids were lucky that the soldiers were preoccupied with the current problems and events of the city, because they did not hear Hayden trip over a large vine and crash loudly to the ground, grunting in pain as he landed.

"I thought the girls would be the noise problem, not you," teased Hunter, as he reached out his hand and helped Hayden to stand. "Are you alright?"

"Yeah, I think so," Hayden slowly replied.

"Good. Now, be quiet will ya?" teased Hunter.

Hayden rolled his eyes, shook his head and whispered back, "You're really funny, Hunter."

"Will you two quit messing around? The soldiers are getting away," squawked Alli, pointing into the distance. "We better start moving a little faster."

Alli took the lead, being careful to stay hidden behind trees and bushes. They followed the soldiers for nearly thirty minutes before the first rays of light, from the city, shone in the distance

"Can you guys see that?" Alli asked excitedly, pointing toward the light.

"I can," replied Hannah, eager to see the ancient city.

"We've got to be really careful, guys," whispered

Hunter. "We're really close to the city now, that is, if we're not already in the middle of it, and there's bound to be more soldiers and guards posted here."

"Should we find a place to hide for the night and continue searching the city in the morning, when we can see better?" quizzed Alli, not wanting to be captured.

"I think we should follow them a little longer—at least until we can see more than just the shadows of a city," answered Hayden. "We'll have better cover during the night than we will in the morning."

"I agree. Let's follow the soldiers as close as we can to the city," said Hunter. He turned and continued carefully walking through the dense trees and vines.

"We might be hidden better at night, but we can't see better," whispered Hannah, as she stumbled through the forest.

They traveled in silence, struggling through the thickest brush they had encountered. They had moved in a single-file line for thirty or forty yards through the thick bushes when the group reached an unusual clearing in the trees. The clearing was barely big enough to accommodate a large forty by forty foot pool with an exquisite waterfall cascading down from the side of a small thirty-foot hillside. The transparent blue water fell from the hillside filling the large, pool which was encirlced by a sandy beach, before it continued on, meandering down a small stream in and out of nearby bushes before it disappeared out of sight, deep into the forest. Both large and small rocks lined the hillside on either side of the pool, precariously reaching the top of the waterfall.

As Hunter scanned the rocks, following them from the pool to the top of the waterfall, he noticed another waterfall on the opposite side of the hill. Suddenly, a small movement caught the corner of his eye. Twisting his head rapidly to the side, he was shocked to see a group of teenage kids. The group sounded like they were playing, laughing and splashing in a pool, similar to the pool Hunter was standing by. Hunter motioned for Hayden, Hannah and Alli to follow him as he quickly moved through the area. Excited to find people, Hunter rushed into the forest toward the noise and searched for the kids he heard. Quickly finding the loud group, he scanned the area and was thrilled to find them all about his age. Hunter quickly motioned for Hannah, Hayden and Alli to hide. Frantically, each one scrunched into the protective leaves of the nearby Elephant Ear plant.

"Can you see them?" asked Hunter, pointing to the group at the top of the waterfall.

"Do you think they're from one of the lost tribes?" asked Alli.

"Where else would they be from?" teased Hannah. "I wonder how they would react if we casually walked out and talked to them."

"They would probably freak out!" chuckled Hayden. "Um, excuse me. We're from another world, and the Lord told us we should take you back there. So grab your stuff, we need to get going," he whispered jokingly.

"I know what my reaction would be," Alli snickered.

"Oh yeah? What would you do?" asked Hayden, smiling as he waited for Alli's reply.

"Scream!" interjected Hannah. "Alli, would start screaming and never stop."

"Oh, I would stop screaming," replied Alli. "But, not until the soldiers came to rescue me!" Alli announced proudly.

Hunter silently watched for several minutes as Hayden, Hannah and Alli, giggled about how much fun it could be to frighten the teenagers and how frightening it would be to have soldiers chasing them through the unknown land.

Unexpectedly, a loud horn blew three times. Then footsteps grew louder and louder in the area. Rapidly, the kids playing in the waterfall, scurried out of the water and watched as several of the city's soldiers suddenly appeared.

"Get back to the city!" a tall, bald man shouted. "You know the rules. You should have been back an hour ago," said a soldier.

"Yes, Moniah," one of the boys nervously replied.

"Don't break the rules again! If we hadn't found you, who knows what could have happened. It's almost time," Moniah announced.

Hannah looked at Hunter confused by what the soldier was talking about and whispered. "Time for what Hunter?"

"That is the second time that a soldier has said something like that," replied Hunter. "But, I don't have a clue what he means."

"Look at the kids. They're all moving pretty fast," said Alli, as she watched them disappear into the jungle foliage.

"Whatever it's time for, must be really important."

"I hope it's not something dangerous," added Hannah.

"Where did the soldiers go?" asked Hayden, searching the area for their whereabouts.

"We better find them. We must be getting close to the city, and I don't want to lose them now," insisted Hunter.

"Look!" exclaimed Hannah quietly. "There's the soldier who yelled at the kids."

"I can't see any sign of the two soldiers we followed earlier. Should we follow this soldier instead?" questioned Hayden.

"I don't see why not, I'm sure we'll get to the same place," reasoned Hunter. He stood from his hiding spot and motioned for everyone to follow him.

Hunter had barely passed the waterfall and pool when he stopped abruptly, causing Hayden to slam directly into his back.

"Careful, Hayden," whispered Hunter. He stood quietly in awe at the scene before his eyes.

Hunter quickly motioned for everyone to crouch down in the tall grasses. Then he cautiously leaned out, just beyond the tree line, attempting to locate the soldier they had been following. In the center of the clearing was a large, round stone wall, which Hunter estimated was approximately ten feet in diameter. The stone wall was at least thirty feet tall and had beautifully decorated carvings covering two large doors on the right side of the wall. In the center of each door was a large, round handle seemingly made of gold.

Unable to see the soldier, Hunter cautiously stepped from behind the shelter of the trees into the clearing. He was surprised to step onto perfectly manicured grass. The lush green grass sloped downhill slightly, toward the only change in the natural beauty of the area—the large stone circle.

"Can you see where the soldier went?" Hannah called impatiently, startling Hunter.

Angrily, he turned around, and glared at Hannah. "You scared me, Hannah. I will let you know as soon as I see something," he snapped. "Now, be quiet for a minute, will ya?"

Hunter nervously scanned the area for the soldier who seemed to vanish into thin air.

"Hunter?" Hannah called again catching Hunter off guard.

"What?" he called anxiously. "What do you want?"

"Is there any sign of the kids?" she asked, smiling.

"Are you purposely trying to torment me?" he asked, purposely ignoring her question. "Now, will you please stay quiet and remain hidden in the trees until I call for you?"

"No one can see us, Hunter. The darkness of night gives us added cover. Can we come and help you search?" she called ready to help.

"Hannah, please," he angrily replied. "Will you give me a break for just a minute?"

Hannah moved back into the cover of the trees, and just in time. The large bird, that seemed to be following them since the bridge, squawked loudly, right over Hunter's head.

Panicked, he instinctively dropped to the ground. He rolled to the right, just as the bird swooped down to catch him, causing the bird to again miss him by inches.

"Hunter!" Hannah called again, afraid the bird's claw might have grabbed him.

"Not now, Hannah. I'm kinda busy," he replied, still trying to wiggle out of the bird's grasp.

"Hunter!" she screamed desperately.

"What, Hannah? What?" he demanded, finally looking at her.

"The soldier," she cried, pointing behind him.

Hunter, still struggling to stay out of the bird's sharp claws, spun around quickly to find soldiers racing straight toward him and the giant bird. Afraid the soldiers had seen him, Hunter scooted back into the covering of the trees, quickly hid and motioned for Hannah, Hayden and Alli to move closer to him.

"What have you done, Hunter?" asked Hannah. "If the soldier saw you, everyone in the city is going to be out here in the forest searching for us now."

"Hurry, we've got to find somewhere else to hide," he insisted. He started crawling on his hands and knees through the thick brush.

"No!" Hayden called quietly. "Look!"

Hunter turned, looked into the clearing and watched as the soldiers raced to the bird's side.

"The bird must be their pet or something," whispered Alli, as she watched the soldiers attend to its every need.

"That bird has seen us three or four times today," said Hannah worriedly.

"It's not like the bird can talk," teased Hunter.

"No, but it could direct the soldiers straight to us," replied Hannah.

"Can you hear what the soldiers are saying, Hunter?" asked Hayden.

"They're talking about a storm. They think the bird is all upset about a storm that is approaching," he replied. "I guess they didn't see me!" he exclaimed relieved.

"Do you think this storm is what the soldiers have been talking about today?" Hannah asked worriedly.

"Could be," replied Hunter.

"Well, if the natives are this scared about a storm, shouldn't we be scared also?" asked Alli as a concerned look rapidly spread across her face.

"No, not necessarily," Hunter replied. "We've probably lived through the same kinds of storms back home."

They quietly watched as the soldiers worked to calm the agitated bird. Then they watched it fly away and the soldiers hurried back inside the protection of the wall.

"What is that wall? Do you think that's the city?" asked Hannah.

"I can't imagine that wall is big enough for everyone in the city," shouted Alli. "I'm not sure the area inside is even big enough for the few soldiers and the kids we saw at the waterfall!"

"Are the lights on the wall the lights you saw through the storm last night, Hannah," asked Hunter.

"They could be, I don't know for sure," she replied. "All I could see were lights."

"Hayden, about how big is that wall?" asked Hannah.

"The wall the soldiers are hiding inside?" he asked.

Hannah nodded.

"I would guess about ten to twelve feet in diameter," announced Hayden, pointing toward the wall in the center of the clearing.

"I agree," said Hunter. "That's exactly what I guessed the size of the wall was, too."

"Why are there two walls?" asked Alli. "The big one we already entered and now this smaller one?"

"Maybe the small wall is where the people from the city hide when there is going to be a bad storm," replied Hayden. "Something like a bomb shelter back home."

"Do you really think all the people from the city can fit inside that small area?" asked Hannah, as she stared at the wall.

"No way," exclaimed Hayden. "Unless, the people in this city have almost all perished and the few people we saw are all that is left."

"No, way. That can't be it," shouted Hannah. "There has to be more people than that here."

"Then, how are all the people from the city living inside that small area?" he asked, perplexed.

"Tightly?" replied Hunter, with a grin.

"Wow, you are so funny!" Hayden said mockingly.

Hunter smiled at his brother and shrugged his shoulders. Then he replied, "Honestly, I have no idea how they can all fit inside there. We're going to have to go check out the wall and see what's going on inside."

As the last soldier entered into the stone wall and closed the door, Hunter stood up and stepped carefully into the clearing, anxiously watching the sky closely for the possible return of the large scary bird.

"Do you think we're safe to go check out the wall?" Alli asked nervously. "The soldiers barely went back inside."

"I can't see anyone or anything," Hunter replied. "Hopefully, we'll be alright. Come on, let's go see if we can figure out how to get inside that wall without being caught by more soldiers or attacked by the bird."

They all raced excitedly toward the stone door, everyone except Alli. Suspecting that they could be walking into a trap, she moved warily across the clearing toward the stone door.

CHAPTER TWELVE

AS THE KIDS REACHED the door, they were amazed at its beauty. The stone was an exquisite white with small gold flecks scattered throughout. Ornate carvings covered the edges surrounding the door, with protruding stars at each of the corners. A large round handle, which looked to be made of gold, was in the center of both doors.

"What do you think the soldier meant when he said, 'Prophets of old foretold about four coming with a message from the Lord to help return them to Zion'?" asked Hannah, as she continued to survey the area.

"I'm not sure," replied Hunter, trying to ignore the question.

"Do you really think the prophets of old knew that we would be the four?" she asked inquisitively.

"Sure they did," answered Hayden. "The Lord revealed that to these people, the same way our prophet reveals what the Lord wants us to know."

"I hope they believe we're the good guys," interjected Alli, finally reaching the wall.

"I'll bet they have to believe on faith, the same way we do," replied Hayden.

"And I'll bet that some believe and some don't," added Hunter. "Just like people back home."

"Are we ever gonna go inside?" questioned Hannah.

"Hunter, did you see how the soldiers opened the door?" asked Hayden.

"Yeah, I think they pulled the large ring on the front," he replied, shrugging his shoulders.

"Seriously?" asked Hayden.

"I think so. Why?" asked Hunter.

"The ring looks like it's made of gold," Hayden replied.

"Is that a problem?" questioned Alli.

"No, not necessarily," Hayden replied, examining the handle. "I just wondered if the gold is strong enough to pull the heavy stone."

"I guess the only way to find out is to try," reasoned Hunter.

He took hold of the ring and pulled with all his might. The huge stone door did not budge at all. Frustrated, he rubbed his hands together and pulled again. Nothing happened.

"I guess I'm gonna need some help," Hunter snarled angrily.

Hayden and Hannah took hold of the door along side Hunter. Alli counted, "One, two, three, pull!"

Again, they pulled the ring, but to their dismay, the door would not budge.

"When the soldier pulled on the door, it slid open and closed easily," exclaimed Hunter. "I don't think he was any bigger than I am. Why was it so easy for him?"

"It looks like the soldier was a lot stronger than you are, Hunter," teased Hannah.

"He couldn't have been stronger than all of us together," replied Hayden.

"Okay, so now what?" asked Hannah.

"There has to be a latch or button to push," insisted Hunter. "Something that triggers the door to easily slide open. Help me look."

Quickly running their hands over the wall, they searched for any sort of latch. But they could find no switches, nor buttons, nor anything that indicated how to open the door.

"There's nothing here, Hunter," complained Hannah, as the wind suddenly tore through the area, rattling the trees and bushes.

"Feels like the storm they were talking about earlier is getting close," said Alli. "We better hurry so we don't get caught out here in the open."

"Then we better hurry and find that switch. It's got to be here somewhere," insisted Hunter. "We didn't come this far to turn around now!"

"What about the symbols?" asked Hayden, pointing to the designs surrounding the door. "Do they mean anything?"

Hannah studied the designs carefully, looking for any recognizable writing. As she ran her fingers over the protruding symbols, she looked at Hayden and replied, "I can't see anything that looks like the hieroglyphs I was able to see before."

"In all the designs and decorations, there's no Egyptian writing?" quizzed Hunter.

"Not really," she replied.

"What do you mean, 'Not really'?" asked Alli. "Is there any writing that you can see that we can't?"

"Well, I'm not sure what you can see," Hannah replied. "Can you see the condor at the base of the door?"

"Yes," replied Alli. "And the stone flowers, leaves and stars."

"What about the tiny pictures inside the stars? Can you see those?" Hannah questioned smugly.

"Nope, I can't see those," Alli replied excitedly.

"Hayden, translate these for me, will you please?" Hannah asked, hoping this was the key to getting through the doors.

"Anytime you're ready," he replied.

"Okay, on this star," she started, pointing to the bottom left side, "there's a small baby chick, a leaf, and a half-buried stone."

Hayden thought for a moment, then replied, "I think that means, *with*."

"The star at the top left corner has a snake, or it could be a worm, an arm and the same half-buried stone," Hannah continued smiling at her descriptions.

Picturing the images in his mind, several seconds passed before Hayden replied. "Using the snake instead of a worm, I believe the word is *faith*."

Hannah, moved to the right side of the door. Then she

said, "The star on the top right corner has a picture of a tall leaf, then squiggly lines, possibly depicting water."

"That's easy," Hunter smugly replied. "That means in."

"The last star, down on the bottom right, has pictures of a clay pot, a baby chick and a hand," Hannah finished, looking up to Hayden.

"Those pictures mean, *God*. So, put together, the words read, 'With faith in God'." Hayden looked at Hannah and asked, "Is there anything else?"

"Only one thing. Under each star, there is a picture of a growling lion standing on its two hind legs. The engraving is really small, so it's hard to see, but I think it's kinda like the picture on Grandpa's lamp. Does that have any meaning?"

"Just the lion alone?" asked Hayden.

"Yep," she replied, straining to see the picture clearly.

"No, the lion is not a symbol used in the Egyptian language," he replied, confused as to why the lion was engraved by the stars.

"If the lion doesn't have a meaning, what does the phrase, 'With faith in God' mean?" questioned Alli.

"Probably that we need to have faith to get inside," replied Hunter.

Hunter took hold of the handle and pulled again with all his might, but the stone door still did not budge. "Well, that didn't work. Do you have any other ideas on how to get inside?" questioned Hunter, annoyed that he was unable to move the door.

"With faith in God," Alli mumbled under her breath. "That has to mean something," she thought, as she ran her fingers over the star. All of a sudden, she had a thought. "Hey, didn't the original letter inside the lamp say something about needing to have courage like the lion or something like that?"

"You're right. I think it did," Hannah replied excitedly.

"So, do you think the lion is engraved in the stone just for us?" asked Hayden, cautiously optimistic.

"They have to be," replied Hannah. "They were placed there so that we could find the opening."

"Okay, I still don't know how to get inside," complained Hunter angrily. "What do we need to do?" he asked, as he wiped a raindrop from his face.

"We better figure this out quickly," insisted Hayden. "The rain is starting to join the howling wind. We don't have long until the storm hits."

Hayden hurriedly inspected each star on the door. Then he said, "Hannah, stand by the bottom right star. Alli, you stand by the bottom left star, Hunter you stand by the top right star, and I will stand by the top one on the left."

"Now what?" asked Hayden.

"You tell me, " snapped Hunter.

"Okay, when I tell you to, try to push the star into the door. Okay," replied Hayden.

"What do you mean, push the star?" asked Hunter.

"Push the star like it was the button to open the microwave back home," replied Hayden. "Do you know what I mean?"

"Yeah, I get it," replied Hunter.

"Any other questions?" asked Hayden. "Everybody else understand?"

Everyone understood. They nodded quickly moved to their assigned positions and waited for Hayden.

"What now, Hayden?" asked Hannah.

"I guess we should and see if my idea works," replied Hayden. "When I say, everyone push your star."

Alli placed her hand on the star and waited for Hayden's signal.

"One, two, three, push," called Hayden excitedly.

Everyone pushed their assigned star trying with all their might to get them to budge.

"Nothing's happening," announced Alli. "My star won't move at all."

"Neither is mine," Hannah disappointedly reported.

"Same here," added Hunter. "Did you have any luck, Hayden," he asked.

"No, mine didn't move either," he replied sadly.

"Well, that was a good thought!" said Alli, trying to cheer Hayden up.

"Do you have any other ideas, Hayden?" asked Hunter.

"Not really," he replied, racking his brain for what to do next.

"We don't have a lot of time," said Hannah as soft rumbles started to echo through the area.

"Then help us come up with another idea," snapped Hunter.

Hannah, annoyed by Hunter's response, scrunched up her nose and made a face at her brother, took a deep breath and leaned back against the wall to think. Suddenly, she heard a click and felt something move behind her back.

"Hey, something happened over here," she said nervously.

"What?" asked Alli.

"I think something moved on the door," she replied, searching the area.

"What moved," questioned Alli.

"The star moved," screeched Hayden, excitedly pointing at the star. "Look!"

"It did move!" exclaimed Hunter.

"What do we do now?" asked Alli, sure they were on the right track.

"Maybe, we have to push the stars one at a time rather than all at once," replied Hayden, rubbing his chin as he spoke.

"So, let's try pushing them one at a time," said Hannah.

"Okay, I'll go first," Hayden anxiously replied, as he placed his hand on the star and pushed. Excited that the star pushed in easily, he quickly turned to Hunter and urged, "Push yours quick."

Hunter pushed and seconds later the star slid into place on the door.

"Alli, it's your turn," Hayden said.

Excitedly she pushed the star and waited for something to happen. Nearly thirty seconds passed as they waited anxiously for something to happen.

Suddenly, a loud click sounded, rattling the doors.

"Did they open?" questioned Hannah. "Was that the lock I heard click open?"

"There's only one way to find out," replied Hunter.

He again grabbed the gold handle on the front door and pulled with all his might. But still, the stone door did not budge an inch. As he looked to see where the loud click had come from, he noticed that every star had suddenly popped out into its normal position.

"Man, that didn't work either. Now what are we going to do?" moaned Hayden.

"Any other ideas?" Hunter asked sarcastically.

"I have one," replied Alli, as she raised her hand, like she was waiting for the teacher to call on her.

"We're not in school anymore, Alli. You don't have to raise your hand. Tell us what your idea is," chuckled Hunter.

Alli smirked as she tilted her head to the side and asked, "What if we all push the stars in one at a time. And then hold them in until we hear the click."

"We could try, we've got nothing to lose," Hunter replied, as he slicked his hair back off his face. "Everybody, get next to your star. When I say to, push in your stars," Hunter instructed. He looked down at his watch, took a deep breath and said, "Ready? One, two, three... now!"

Everyone pushed and held their star into place. Again nearly thirty seconds passed when suddenly, the door made a loud click, followed by a quiet moan. Then unexpectedly, the door lunged forward an inch or so.

"I bet it will open now," said Hayden, excited to finally be entering the city.

Hunter took hold of the handle and closed his eyes momentarily. He took a deep breath, and then he pulled with all his might. Without warning, the door flew open, knocking Hunter to the ground. In an instant, their whereabouts were revealed to everyone on the other side of the wall.

CHAPTER THIRTEEN

"HIDE, QUICK!" yelled Hunter, rolling behind the door, afraid the soldiers would be arresting them any second.

"Hide from what?" asked Alli, as she carefully peered inside the wall. "I can't see anyone inside here."

"What do you mean you can't see anyone? Where are all the soldiers?" questioned Hayden, as he stepped inside the wall. "More than two or three dozen came in here. I saw them with my own eyes!"

"And the kids?" added Hannah. "We saw all those kids come in here, too."

"Something's not right, Hunter," warned Alli. "Where did everyone go?"

"We'll have to figure it out," Hunter replied calmly. "We know that they entered through the door. What we don't know is what happened after they came in. So, what clues can we find?" he asked, smiling. "Come on, everybody. Look for something that will give us a clue."

They carefully entered through the stone door and

cautiously inspected the area. All of a sudden, a swift burst of wind forced Hunter backwards against the stone door, loudly slamming it shut, startling the kids. Frightened by the loud noise, Hannah spun around quickly to see where the noise came from.

"Everything's alright, Hannah," Hunter said reassuringly. "I fell against the door, and it slammed shut."

"Oh, great," cried Alli. "Are we trapped in here forever?"

Hunter firmly pulled the gold handle attached to the inside of the door, closing the door tightly. Then he replied, "We found out how to get in here. I'm sure we can find a way to get out of here, if we need to!"

Alli took a deep breath and nodded her head as she exhaled. Leaning back against the wall, she searched the small area for any indications of where the soldiers had gone, and any clues that might lead the kids to find them.

The wall was built in a circle, approximately twenty feet from side to side. There were three steps down from the door to a landing. Directly in the center between the walls was a pool that filled almost the entire open area, leaving only three feet from the pool's edge to the wall. Several trees were scattered throughout the walkway surrounding the interior.

Alli slowly walked toward the pool and noticed small shrubs, flowers, and lily pads scattered across the top of the water.

As she looked down at the water, she strained to see her reflection in the dark water. Finally finding it, she stared past her reflection and was surprised to see that the pool was only about two feet deep.

"Hey guys, come here. Look at this," she called.

"Look at what?" asked Hannah, as she peered down at the water. She was startled by her vivid reflection in the dark water. "Wow!" she exclaimed. "My reflection looks so real in the dark."

"Is that why you called us over?" questioned Hayden, annoyed as he looked in the water. "You know, there could be traps set in here for trespassers."

"No!" Alli replied gruffly. "I didn't call you over to look at yourselves. Look through the water."

"What am I looking for?" asked Hunter, staring into the dark, blue water.

"Can you see that the pool is only about two feet deep? Isn't that odd?" insisted Alli. "I thought it might be a clue."

"This entire area is odd," added Hayden, looking around the opening. "Look at all the stepping stones and rocks in the pool. Who would've put rocks in a pool?"

"Who would build a large pool and make it only two feet deep?" asked Hannah. She swirled the water with her hand, disrupting the images reflecting back at her.

"I wonder if the pool is a clue," said Hunter.

"A clue to what?" asked Hayden, with a confused look on his face.

"Well, think about it—a pool is built in the middle of nowhere, surrounded by a huge stone wall with a bunch of stones and rocks scattered randomly through the water," replied Hunter. "The pool has to have something to do with where the soldiers disappeared to."

"Yeah, but what?" asked Alli.

"That's what we've got to figure out," replied Hayden. He jumped onto the edge of the pool to get a better look at the rocks. "Hunter, quick! Check this out!"

Hunter jumped onto the edge of the pool next to Hayden and looked across the pool to where Hayden's finger was pointing.

"What is it?" asked Hunter, baffled as to where Hayden was pointing. "I can't see anything."

"Look at the figure the stones and rocks make in the pool," replied Hayden. "They looked almost uniform— like they mean something."

"Like they mean what?" questioned Hannah. She and Alli, climbed onto the pool's edge and looked out across the water.

"Can you see the design the stones and rocks form?" asked Hayden, pointing toward the pool.

Hunter squinted his eyes and twisted his head to the right, searching to find the figure Hayden could see in the water. "Now I can see what you're pointing to in the water. You're right. The stones do look like they've been placed."

Suddenly, a loud boom sounded, sending vibrations through the area. The sound was followed by a sudden burst of light, which seemed to release static into the air.

As the static from the light flashed inches above her head, Hannah's hair stood on end. She squealed in terror, afraid of being hit by the lightning that seemed to flash across the ground.

"This is the storm that the soldier was talking about, isn't it?" asked Alli. She held out her hands to keep her balance on the pool's edge.

"It must be," whispered Hannah, slightly crouching down. "This is just like the storm that we watched rage through the valley last night."

"You've seen a storm like this already?" questioned Hunter.

"Yeah, last night. I was so scared, I couldn't sleep all night. I was sure I was going to be hit by lightning," explained Hannah.

"The storm was different than any other I have ever seen before. Everything seemed to happen upside down," added Alli. "The weather was really weird."

"What do you mean 'upside down'?" asked Hayden, confused by her statement.

"Well, the lightning flashed across the ground. The clouds built from the ground and billowed up toward the sky. The rain came from every direction. I couldn't tell if it was above me or below me," replied Alli.

"Could a storm like this be dangerous?" asked Hannah.

"Far more dangerous than the storms we have back home," replied Hayden. "Especially if lightning is on the ground rather than in the sky and the clouds make it so you can't see."

"What can we do to be safe?" asked Alli, nervously looking around.

"We can find a safe place to hide," answered Hunter.

"Where would that be exactly?" questioned Hannah.

"Probably wherever the soldiers and people of the city are hiding, I bet it is safe there," Hunter replied, smirking at his sister.

"Then we better hurry and find out where the people of the city are hiding," insisted Hayden. "We shouldn't have too much trouble in this small area."

"Hey, look. I think I found a clue," Hannah excitedly called from the other side of the pool.

"What is it?" asked Hunter.

"There are broken branches and leaves all over the ground here. A path has formed that leads toward two small steps up to the pool," she excitedly replied. "Do you think those people disappeared in the water?"

"Where would they go? The water is only two feet deep," snapped Hayden "I don't think that many people could disappear in water that shallow. There has to be somewhere else."

"So then, where'd they go?" Hannah demanded.

"That's what we have to figure out," Hayden called, matter-of-factly. He walked toward Hannah and the steps into the pool.

"Do you think there's a secret tunnel in here?" Hannah asked excitedly.

"There has to be," replied Hunter. "That has to be the way the soldiers disappeared."

"Where are we going to find the secret entrance?" asked Hayden, looking around. "There's practically nothing in here."

"Let's start looking next to the tree where Hannah found all the leaves and broken branches on the ground," suggested Hunter. "Branches and leaves torn from the tree indicate that maybe the people broke them entering a secret tunnel over there."

Abruptly, an ear-piercing boom exploded over their heads, sending all of them frantically to the ground for cover. A bright flash of light, shooting in jagged lines across the valley, immediately followed the boom. As the lightning slammed into the tree next to Hannah, it caused an unexpected explosion and shattered fiery wood pieces all over the area.

"Hunter, my pant leg is on fire!" Hannah screamed in terror.

"Smother it, Hannah," called Hunter as he frantically crawled toward her.

"I can't! I can't!" she screamed, swinging her hands at the flames.

Hunter reached her just as she started screaming wildly and kicking her leg in the air. He grabbed her and pulled her rapidly toward the pool, plunging her leg into the water. Smoke from her pants rose slowly, sending an awful burnt smell through the air, as the water rapidly extinguished the bright yellow flames.

"Are you okay, Hannah?" asked Hunter, as he examined the charred edge of her jeans.

"I think so," she replied hesitantly, as she rubbed her leg. "It feels like the only thing burned was the hair off my leg."

Hunter grinned as he shook his head. "The storm is getting worse. I don't think it will be long until the rising clouds start sending rain," he said.

"We'll lose any sign of clues left behind by the soldiers if we don't hurry," added Alli.

"I think all our clues are burning up as we speak," said Hayden, pointing to the small fires scattered throughout the area. "I'm sure the secret entrance to the hidden tunnel was inside that tree that was just struck by the lightning."

"If the hidden entrance is in the tree, we should still be able to find it. We just need to figure out how to open it," said Hannah, as she walked gingerly toward the tree.

"I think the stones in the water have something to do with opening the secret tunnel," insisted Hayden. "If you look, they're not scattered randomly throughout the pool. The rocks are carefully placed throughout the pool!"

"How do they have anything to do with opening the tunnel?" questioned Alli. "Do they form a shape that gives a clue?"

"I don't recognize the shape," Hayden replied disappointedly.

"Okay, if they don't form a shape that reveals a clue, then how can the rocks possibly help us find the opening?" asked Hunter.

"Is there a sign that points a direction to something?" asked Hannah.

"I can't see a sign," replied Hayden. "The stones start at the edge of the pool, then swirl into a circle in the middle of the pool."

"If they're stepping stones, do we need to step on them to trigger the opening?" asked Alli, as she pushed on the stone closest to the pool's edge.

"Maybe," replied Hayden. Nervously he stepped onto the first stone.

"Hey, wait a minute. I want to step on the stones, too," insisted Hannah "Wait for me!"

Hannah followed Hayden as he started to cross each of the stones to the center of the pool.

"Come on, guys. Follow us," Hannah insisted, motioning for Alli and Hunter to come.

"Are you serious? We're in the middle of a thunder and lightning storm. The last place I want to be is anywhere near water," replied Alli, pointing to the sky. "Just standing here on the side of the pool is scary enough."

"Hunter, come check this out!" Hayden called excitedly. "There are several foot prints smashed in the moss on the stones."

"Really?" asked Hunter. "Maybe, the stones are the path to the secret entrance?"

"Come on, Alli. Let's go check this out," said Hunter. He held out his hand to help her onto the first stone.

"But...Hunter, what if the lightning strikes again?" she said hesitantly.

Abruptly, a fierce wind started to blow. Rain immediately followed. The rain got heavier with every passing second. Finally, the rain blew in every direction Hunter turned. Holding his hand up to shield his eyes, he squinted tightly, hoping to see through the large drops of water now soaking his clothes. He looked toward the ground, hoping to relieve the stinging from the rain, only to find that the rain was also coming up from the ground.

Unable to see Alli, as sheets of rain poured over their heads, he frantically called her name, still holding out his hand for her.

"I'm right here, Hunter," she calmly replied, as she reached out to him.

"Come on. Let's go see if Hayden has found the opening to the tunnel yet," he yelled.

Keeping a tight hold on the back of his shirt, Alli moved cautiously from one moss covered stone to the next.

"Hayden, where are you?" screamed Hunter, hoping Hayden could hear him over the noise of the rain, wind, thunder and lightning.

"We're at the last stone, Hunter!" called Hayden. "Hurry up!"

"We're trying," Hunter shrieked. His foot suddenly slipped on the moss, and he struggled to keep his balance.

"Don't fall, Hunter," begged Alli, not wanting to fall into the water.

"I'm not trying to," Hunter said, struggling to maintain his footing.

As the two cautiously continued, as fast as they dared toward Hannah and Hayden, another bolt of lightning whizzed over Alli's head.

As tears of fear flowed freely from her eyes, Alli whispered to Hunter, "Please don't let me die here."

"Don't worry. I promise everything's going to be all right, Alli. We're almost there," Hunter reassured her.

"How do you know that?" she cried. "I can't see anything, so I know that you can't either. If we get hit by lightning, we're both dead!"

"I promise, Alli. I have faith the Lord will lead us to where we need to go," he replied.

She reluctantly agreed, and continued following her friend. The storm continued to get stronger and stronger with every passing second.

"Hayden, did you find anything?" hollered Hunter. "Can you see a secret entrance?"

"I can't see anything yet. I need your help. Are you close?" screamed Hayden.

"I'm not sure. I can't see anything either," he replied nervously.

"I counted thirty stones. Keep coming," urged Hayden.

"Do you have Hannah with you? Is she okay?" yelled Hunter, suddenly worried about his sister's whereabouts.

"I've got her," Hayden called, as another burst of lightning rattled through the area.

"We're gonna get hit if we don't hurry!" yelled Hunter. "Those strikes are getting closer and closer."

Suddenly, another tree was struck by a bolt of lightning, sending scattered balls of fire flashing through the pouring rain. As one of the balls of fire skimmed Hunter's head, he grabbed Alli's arm and pulled her down as low as they could go on the stone.

Alli looked up at Hunter in horror. She screamed and started swinging wildly at Hunter's head.

"What are you doing, Alli?" Hunter yelled, as he grabbed for her hand.

"Your hair! There's a burning ember that landed in your hair," she replied, in a panic.

Hunter calmly let go of her hand, knelt on the edge of the stone and dunked his head into the pool. Seconds later, he lifted his head out of the water, quickly flipping his hair back. He rubbed his hand over his hair, pressing all the water out that he could. "Are the embers out?" he asked.

Alli nodded, as a tear trickled down her face.

Hunter gently took her hand, smiled and said, "I guess we better hurry and get out of here." He turned quickly and felt for the next stone.

"Look, you can see the stones," shrieked Alli excitedly. "And I can see Hayden and Hannah."

"You're right!" exclaimed Hunter, elated at the sight of them. "The burning tree is lighting the area. We better hurry before the rain puts out the fire and we can't see again."

Alli nodded, and the two quickly moved from stone to stone, hurrying as fast as they dared on the slippery moss toward Hayden and Hannah.

"I can see you!" shouted Hayden, excited at the sight of his brother. "You're almost here."

The words had barely escaped Hayden's lips when another deafening boom rang out across the valley.

Startled by the noise, Hunter struggled to keep his balance as he reached out with his foot for the next stone. He flailed his arms in the air and tried to get his feet set securely beneath his body. Alli reached out and, grabbed Hunter's shirt, trying to steady him. Several anxious moments passed as his lanky six-foot-two body struggled to regain his balance.

"Careful, Hunter. We're almost there," urged Alli. "Don't fall now."

Cautiously moving to the next stone, Hunter whispered, "Thanks Alli. I thought I was tumbling into the water for sure."

"Finally!" screeched Hannah, as she saw Hunter and Alli a few steps away. "You two took forever. We're gonna get struck by lightning if we don't hurry. How exactly, would we explain being killed by lightning to Mom and Dad?!"

"Relax, Hannah. We're here now," replied Hunter, unexpectedly calm. "Have you found anything yet?"

"Nothing, other than the stone we're all standing on, is the only stone without moss on it. Hannah said she could feel some engravings on the stone, but with all the rain, she hasn't been able to tell me if they are engravings for sure," replied Hayden.

"Sounds like that is where we need to start. Hannah, you've got to try and see for sure if what you could feel was engravings and if so, describe the writings to Hayden," encouraged Hunter. "They're probably the directions for opening the secret tunnel door."

"Hunter, it's impossible to see out here," she cried, as the wind whipped the rain unmercifully around her face.

"You've got to try, Hannah!" he demanded.

"Come on, Hannah. We'll all try to shield you from the rain while you look," added Alli.

Hannah agreed. She waited patiently a few moments

as Hunter and Hayden joined Alli in protecting her face from the rain, then started describing the hieroglyphs engraved on the stone.

"Okay, I can see two lines of symbols. The first has four engraved pictures. The first picture looks like a half-buried stone, the second looks like a hole, the third appears to be a baby chick, and the last picture resembles a huge vulture or bird," Hannah said.

Hayden closed his eyes and pictured the symbols that Hannah had described to him. Trying to determine what they meant, he tried to remember the symbols of the Egyptian alphabet. Several seconds passed before he finally motioned for her to continue with the second line.

"Are you ready?" questioned Hannah, unsure what he wanted her to do.

"Yeah, keep going!" demanded Hayden with his eyes still closed.

"Okay, the next picture is of a snake, an arm and that half-buried stone again," Hannah said. She looked up toward Hayden and watched as his eyelids bounced around from the movement of his eyes. She was sure he was picturing all of the images in his head.

"Translated, the symbols mean, *true faith*, I think," said Hayden. "That is, if I am remembering everything correctly."

"If that is right, how does, *true faith* open a secret tunnel?" questioned Hannah, frustrated that the message did not tell them exactly what to do.

"I don't know, but every message from the Lord so far,

has had something to do with *true faith*," replied Hayden.

"We had the faith to follow the stones," said Alli. "How else do we need to have *true faith*?"

"Maybe, the words mean, if you have true faith, that you'll find the entrance," suggested Hunter.

"What if the words have a hidden message?" questioned Hannah, still kneeling close to the drawings in the stone.

"What do you mean, Hannah?" asked Alli, sure Hannah had an idea.

"Well, if you can, watch the tree and tell me if anything happens," Hannah insisted.

"Like what?" asked Hunter. "With the rain, pouring down, it's really hard to see if anything is happening."

"Watch for a secret opening," she demanded gruffly.

Alli, intrigued at what information Hannah had found, let Hunter and Hayden watch the tree while she watched Hannah.

Hannah ran her fingers across the engravings and mumbled several letters under her breath before she looked up to Alli and said, "I think I've figured it out!"

"Well, quit talking about it then," insisted Hunter, annoyed she was taking so long.

"Okay," she snapped, with major attitude. "Heart, I think true faith starts with Heart. So, the word *faith* has an H in it," she said. She carefully pushed the symbol she thought represented an H, and was surprised that the stone seemed to slightly move. "Next is E. The word *true* has an E." She pushed the symbols that represented the letter E, and again the stone seemed to move slightly.

"Followed by A. The word *faith* has an A." She found the corresponding letter and pushed it, still surprised each time that the stone moved slightly. "Okay, now I need an R. The word *true* has the letter R," she said, looking up to Alli, sure she was talking loud enough for everyone to hear her. Looking back toward the stone she spotted the symbol she needed and pushed, smiling as the stone moved again. Excitedly, she announced, "And the last letter we need is a T. *Faith* has a T," she said, surprised to have spelled the word heart, using the letters from, *true faith.*

Looking up at her brothers, she nervously called, "Okay, I'm gonna push the last letter. Watch closely. Here we go!"

CHAPTER FOURTEEN

HANNAH LOCATED the symbol she thought repre-sented the letter T. She closed her eyes, hoping she was on the right track, and slowly pushed. The stone moved slightly, creaked, and then jolted abruptly upward. Not expecting the movement of the stone, Hunter lost his balance and began falling forward. Panicked, he started grabbing at anything he could to stop his fall. Hayden, standing directly behind Hunter, stumbled forward slightly as the stone moved, but was able to quickly regain his balance. Without thinking, Hayden was able to grab the back of Hunter's shirt, stopping him from falling into the shallow pool.

"What's going on?" called Alli. She held her arms out to her sides, trying to steady herself on the stone. "Why are we moving?"

"The stone doesn't open a door, it is the door," replied Hunter excitedly, as he balanced gingerly on the stone.

"What do you mean, 'it is the door'?" questioned Hannah, with a confused look on her face.

"Look, the tunnel isn't a tunnel we crawl into, like back in the Hill Cumorah. The tunnel is on the stepping stone, and it must be taking us to the lost tribes," he replied excitedly. "We were looking for a secret door, not a secret stone."

"This stepping stone is taking us toward the crazy lightning?" shrieked Hannah. "I don't want to go up there!"

"You're the one who found the secret stone, not me," replied Hunter, smiling.

Hannah looked up, nervously trying to see into the clouds above. Afraid the moving stone might be a trap, she searched frantically, but was unable to see anything through the thick, sticky, wet clouds.

"Can you see below us?" asked Hannah, closing her eyes, afraid to look down.

Alli peered cautiously over the edge, forgetting momentarily she was afraid of heights. As she looked, her body suddenly froze when she saw the distance between the stone they were standing on and the pool of water below. Pulling back from the edge, she replied, "Yeah, I can kinda see. Why?"

"How far up do you think we've gone so far?" asked Hannah.

Alli, not positive she could handle looking toward the ground again, closed her eyes and took a deep breath. She opened her eyes slowly and again peered over the edge to see how far they had risen above the ground. Her heart was racing as she looked and found the ground was covered with clouds. Shocked to be so high in the air, her body refused to move an inch, leaving her frozen and staring toward the ground.

Hunter noticed Alli and quickly moved to her aid. "Don't look down, Alli," he insisted, as he quickly pulled her away from the stone's edge.

Firmly grabbing hold of Hunter's arm, she looked up at him and nervously replied, "That was a long way down."

Hunter smiled and nodded in agreement.

"Where do you think we are we going, Hunter?" interrupted Hayden. "We could be in danger. Do you think this is a trap?"

"No one even knows we're coming," he replied, snickering. "How could this be a trap?"

"You know, Hunter, someone from the lost tribes could have set up several traps to keep people away, and this could be one of them," he answered.

Again, a loud boom roared across the valley, startling everyone. Alli grabbed her chest as her heart raced in fear, while Hannah dropped to her knees, sure the lightning would be close behind.

"We're sitting ducks up here," cried Hannah. "And I'm sure I'll be the one who gets hit! There's no way we're not going to be struck by lightning here in the middle of the clouds."

Hayden watched the ground slowly disappear through the clouds, as the stone they were standing on continued to rise more than one hundred yards off the ground. The storm worked its way through the area, filling the sky with mysterious, dark grey clouds.

Suddenly, lightning exploded across the sky. It struck the edge of the stone, unexpectedly sending shock waves of static electricity sparking through their feet.

Hannah was scared to death. With nowhere to run or hide, she sat down in the middle of the five-foot-wide stone and dropped her head into her hands. Tears quickly began to stream down her cheeks as she quietly cried.

"Come on, Hannah. We're going to be alright," said Hayden reassuringly. He sat down on the stone next to Hannah and placed his arm around her shoulders.

"I'm glad you're so positive," she replied sniffling. "I'm scared. This isn't fun or exciting, it's frightening."

"I'll take good care of you," Hayden replied as he wiped a tear from her cheek. "I promise."

"The stone is slowing down," exclaimed Hunter. "We must be close to where it stops."

"Oh, great," replied Hannah sarcastically.

Hunter, excited to see what was above them, looked at the girls and said, "Come on, girls. We might actually be able to do what the letter from Joseph Smith asks us to do and bring back members from the lost tribes. Look, the clouds are beginning to clear, and it looks like something's up here. Now, you know, there's no crying when we're searching for the lost tribes," he teased.

Hannah knew Hunter was trying to make her feel better. She forced a smile to cross her face. "You say that about everything, Hunter," she said.

"Exactly!" responded Hayden. "That's 'cause this is

exciting, not sad. Now, come on. Wipe off those tears, and let's get ready for whatever is above these clouds."

Several anxious moments passed in silence as the kids waited for the stone to come to a complete stop. Tension filled the air as the stone crawled at a snail's pace to its final destination.

"The rain has finally stopped," said Alli interrupting the tension. She was grateful her clothes might be able to dry soon. "Maybe the weather will be better up here."

"And the wind has stopped, along with the thunder and lightning," added Hayden. "No more noise or deadly lightning strikes."

As the kids anxiously scanned through the area several faint images were visible through the thick clouds. Fearful their lives might be in danger they all remained absolutely quiet until the images disappeared into the darkness. Suddenly, the rising stone came to an abrupt stop.

"Oh, great! How do we get off this thing?" asked Hannah. She glanced around, sure at any moment the stone would quickly start to descend, taking them back down to the raging storm below.

"So, now what do we do?" Alli questioned quietly.

"I think this is where we find true faith," replied Hunter.

"I'm not stepping into thin air, Hunter," exclaimed Hannah. "If that's what you mean by true faith, you're nuts!"

"Hannah, you're the one who found the clue, 'True faith starts in your heart'. Where's your faith?" asked Hunter, smiling.

"You step into thin air first. If you don't die, then I will follow you," insisted Hannah, as she returned the smile.

Hayden looked around, unable to see clearly through the clouds and fog. He took a deep breath and said, "I have true faith. I'll go first."

Hunter, not sure he really wanted anyone to step into thin air, replied, "Be careful, Hayden. Try not to get hurt."

Hayden lifted his leg into the air and cautiously started to step off the stone. "Wait!" Alli screamed. "Maybe it would be better if we felt for something to step onto before we leaped into thin air. I really don't want to see you fall to your death."

Hayden closed his eyes and retraced in his mind the steps they had taken so far in their quest to find the lost tribes. He was instantly comforted when a warm sensation sent tingles all over his body. Hayden was sure the Holy Ghost was urging him to have faith. He was positive the Lord had helped them find the stone that lifted them from the dangers of the storm below. He again took a deep breath, and blindly stepped off the stone platform.

Hayden's body fell several feet, causing the girls to scream in terror. Suddenly, he felt the strength of several branches beneath his feet, as he landed securely on the top of an umbrella tree.

"Are you alright, Hayden?" asked Alli, reaching out and taking hold of his shirt.

"I'm fine. Get over here, and let's see if we can find out what's going on around here," he insisted. He took hold of her hand and pulled her toward him.

"No, wait. I don't want to step off of the ledge," she squeaked.

"Hey, be quiet, you guys. I think I can hear voices," interrupted Hannah, as she held her hand to her ear, listening carefully.

"We could be in a lot of trouble if we get caught. We need to find a safe place to hide," suggested Hunter. "At least until we know for sure where we are and what we need to do."

"I don't want to get off the stone and step onto the branches of a tree, I don't know if they're strong enough to hold all of us," Alli said warily. "Why don't you guys go first, and Hannah and I will sit here and wait for you to return."

"Funny, Alli," replied Hayden.

The stone platform suddenly started to lower. Not wanting to be taken down to the ground below, Hunter followed Hayden and quickly stepped out onto the trees.

"Come on, you two. Get over here quick before you end up back in the middle of that storm," Hunter said adamantly. "We don't want you to get hurt."

Unsure what to do, Hayden, grabbed Hannah's arm, pulled with all his might, and yanked her off the stone and next to him on the tree.

"Alli, jump!" called Hannah. "You don't want to end up back down on the ground."

"I can't," she whispered, as she stood paralyzed with fear. "I'm afraid of heights."

"Try, Alli!" screamed Hannah.

"I can't," she softly cried.

"You have to try," Hannah insisted.

Unable to make even one muscle move, Alli watched

as Hunter, Hayden and Hannah started to disappear into the darkness.

Hunter panicked as he watched fear spread across Alli's face. He fell to his knees, reached over the edge of the tree and grabbed Alli's arms. Holding onto her for dear life, he watched as the stepping-stone disappeared into the dark clouds below her feet.

"Hunter, I don't want to stay. Please, let me go!" she screamed, as her feet dangled several yards above the stone. "The stone is still close enough I can fall onto it. Let me go back down to the ground. I'll feel safer there!"

"I can't now," he replied, motioning with his head for Hannah and Hayden to help him hold on to her. "Besides, you know I can't let you go anywhere alone. My Dad would be very angry with me."

"Alli, can you swing your leg up toward me so Hayden and I can grab hold and help Hunter pull you up a little easier?" asked Hannah, stretching her hand over the edge of the tree as far as she dared.

Alli struggled to raise her leg high enough that someone could grab hold. Petrified of heights, and of falling, she carefully swung her lower body back and forth several times, hoping one of them would catch hold of her leg and pull her to safety. After several unsuccessful attempts, Alli dropped her head and started to cry.

"Come on, Alli, keep trying," Hannah urged, afraid at any moment her friend would give up. "You can do it!"

"Hunter, pull me up. Save me," Alli insisted, shaking violently in fear. "I can't lift my leg high enough."

"I'm trying, Alli," said Hunter reassuringly, as he

watched his friend cry. "Hang on! I'll save you, I promise!"

Hunter struggled to keep hold of Alli's cold, clammy hands. He tightened his grip as her hands started to slip through his fingers. Hayden stretched toward her, as far as he could reach, and attempted to catch her belt when her body swung close. Hannah, feeling helpless, continued to reach for Alli's legs as she listened to her friend beg for help.

Alli grew more nervous with every passing second. She wiggled relentlessly as she tried to get her leg over the edge. As she squirmed around, Hunter fought to keep a secure grip on her hands.

"You've got to hold still for me Alli," insisted Hunter, squeezing his hands tighter.

Alli did not respond. She continued wiggling her body.

"Alli, I'm serious," screamed Hunter. "Quit moving. I'm losing my grip."

Hannah finally caught hold of Alli's ankles, and secured a solid grip on her legs. Suddenly Alli's fingers slipped through Hunter's grip and her body unexpectedly flipped upside down.

Screaming as she fell, Alli's body jolted to an abrupt stop. Hannah was able to hold the weight of her friend by gripping her ankle as tight as she could. But Alli's weight quickly pulled Hannah toward the tree's edge. Struggling to maintain her grip on Alli's ankle, Hannah screamed at the boys for help.

Hunter quickly jumped into action. He grabbed hold of Hannah's waist, stopping her from falling over the edge of the tree. Meanwhile, Hayden quickly grabbed Alli's ankles from Hannah, and waited for Hunter to help. When both boys had hold of Alli they quickly pulled her to safety. Overwhelmed by the events, Hannah sat down next to Alli and breathed an enormous sigh of relief.

"Well, that was sure a lot of fun," Alli remarked, as she sat up and crossed her legs.

"Don't be mad, Alli. You know I couldn't let you go back down to the storm below, especially alone," Hunter replied softly.

"You were frozen in fear, Alli," Hannah said gently, as she placed her hand on her friend's shoulder, hoping to consol her. "Hunter had to do something."

"No, I wasn't frozen in fear. I could have moved if I had wanted to," she snapped. "I didn't move because I wanted to leave."

"No, I don't think you could move at all," Hunter retorted, annoyed by Alli's ungrateful attitude. "Now, you're welcome for saving your life!"

He stood up and started to survey the area.

"Sorry, Hunter. Maybe, you're right. I was really afraid," said Alli quietly. "Thank you for saving me."

All of a sudden, Hunter dropped down to his knees and softly whispered, "I can see someone out there in the clouds."

"What?" asked Hayden, moving cautiously toward his brother. "Where? I don't see anything."

"I'm serious, I think I can see someone's shadow through the clouds," declared Hunter, pointing. He motioned for everyone to crouch down and stay quiet.

Hayden cautiously shifted onto his knees, lifted his head into the soft white clouds and scanned the area. "You're right. I can see shadows in the clouds, too. Maybe they're from the soldiers we saw earlier tonight."

"Do you think they heard Alli scream?" questioned Hannah. She worried that at any moment, the soldiers would break through the clouds and the kids would be caught.

Hunter guardedly searched for any sign that the soldiers had heard Alli's screams and replied, "The shadows aren't moving like they heard a girl scream. They're not moving around or hurrying this way at all."

"What is this place?" asked Alli, as she cautiously peered through the clouds at a beautiful city.

"Can everyone else see what I see?" Hannah asked wondering if her eyes were playing tricks on her.

"You mean the city built in the tops of the trees rising up out of the clouds?" Alli asked sarcastically. "Nope, I can't see a thing. If I could, everyone would think I was crazy."

"Okay, so you can see it, too. I was afraid I might be having a nervous break down or something. Then I thought maybe my eyes weren't working properly, especially after I hit my head," said Hannah, smiling.

"What is going on, Hunter?" quizzed Hayden. "Do you have any ideas? Where are we?"

"I can see a rope bridge a few feet ahead. I think the three of you should follow me to the bridge before we're all spotted. We need to find a safe place to hide," he insisted. He crawled across the top of the tree toward the small bridge, motioning for the rest of them to follow.

"Why build a city in the clouds and trees?" asked Hayden, as he scratched his head. "Why not build the city on the ground where things are more stable?"

"Hello, did you see what happens on the ground at night around here!" Hannah abruptly replied. "Besides, the top of this tree feels pretty stable to me."

"Yeah, I guess you're right. If storms like that happened back home, we couldn't live on the ground either. Houses wouldn't be very safe," agreed Hayden, through a cheesy grin as he carefully followed Hunter, Hannah and Alli onto the rope bridge.

Suddenly, without warning, a deafening boom rang across the valley. Alli nearly fell off the rope. Frightened she would fall to her death, she screamed with all her might.

Hunter grabbed her hand and whispered, "Ssssshhhhh, you're going to get us caught!"

"I'm sorry! The boom scared me," she tearfully replied. "I didn't mean to scream."

"Sssshhh, Alli. I'm serious! Be quiet!" insisted Hunter. "Hayden, look and see if there is anyone moving this way," demanded Hunter, as he continued to tightly squeeze Alli's hand.

The words had barely escaped his lips, when another unexpected boom pounded its way through the area. Amazingly, bright lightning flashed across the sky, lighting up the entire city.

"Wow!" exclaimed Hayden. "The city is beautiful. And it's easier to see when the lightning flashes through the sky."

"Is that lightning and thunder from the valley below, or is the storm moving up to the city in the clouds?" Hannah questioned nervously.

"I think the noise is echoing from the valley below," Hunter said calmly, trying to settle his sister's nerves. "And the lightning is coming from below us too. So, I think we're safe up here."

"But what if the soldiers can see us when the lightning strikes?" asked Alli, nervously looking around.

"Did you see anyone coming our way, Hayden?" asked Hunter.

"No. I couldn't really see anyone at all," Hayden replied, shrugging his shoulders.

"What if they're sneaking up and the soldiers are going to find us any second now?" Hannah cried softly.

"Then we'll shuffle across these ropes as fast as we can," replied Hunter, as he smiled.

"We really need to find someplace a little more secure than hanging on to these ropes," insisted Hayden. "Hannah could be right, and the soldiers could be sneaking up on us right now."

"And we need to cross this bridge before one of us gets hurt! Like me," added Alli.

"I agree," answered Hunter, again searching in the darkness for somewhere to hide.

"Where? Where are we going to hide in a city built on the tops of trees and in the clouds," asked Alli, frantically searching the immediate area. "It's not like there are bushes or trees to make a fort inside."

"Look at all of the bungalow houses and buildings

scattered around up here. Maybe there's one that no one lives in," suggested Hayden, pointing toward the city. "We should be able to find one of them that is safe for us to hide in, until we have a plan."

"I don't know if anyone has noticed, but we are standing on a fairly thin rope, and the rope isn't that easy to hang on to. How do you propose we move around easier so that we can even get to the houses?" Hannah asked sharply. "In fact, I can't even see anyway to get over to the houses."

"You know, the people that live here in the city must have a way that they move around that is easier than balancing on these ropes," replied Hunter. "We've just got to figure out what they do and how to do it."

"I agree. If we have to move around on these ropes, we won't find a safe place very quickly," added Hayden, as he inspected the flexibility of the rope. "And if we're spotted, then there won't be any quick getaways!"

"You're right," replied Hunter, chuckling. "I know we can't maneuver on these ropes very fast."

Not sure what to do, everyone remained quiet for several moments before Alli said, "Hey guys, I have an idea!"

"Let's hear it," replied Hunter, open to her suggestions. "We're in great need of ideas right now."

"If we can find someone in the area, why don't we watch to see what they do to move around?" she suggested.

"We are trying to get to safety, remember?" asked Hayden. "Not get caught."

"I know. But if watching for a minute helps us to get to safety faster, doesn't it make sense to try?" asked Alli.

"Yeah, I guess so," replied Hayden.

They all peered through the thick clouds, hoping to catch a glimpse of how the soldiers moved through the city.

Hannah was intrigued by the mysterious city, she stared through the darkness toward the lights, looking for a way to travel through the city. She found herself amazed at all the sights. The buildings were beautiful. Most of them were built out of wood and carved with incredible designs. The trees were giant and seemed to get bigger from the cloud line up, providing the same beautiful green leaves and vibrant flowers as they did back on the ground. The colors, although muted in the darkness, were deep and rich. Some of the colors were indescribable.

Polka dotting their way around the buildings, in the center of the city were small, round, adobe-like bunga-lows. Each bungalow hung higher than the buildings and swayed softly in the wind. Each had a unique carving engraved in the adobe mud above the door and a beauti-ful lantern dangling precariously in the trees or bushes to the right of the door. The lanterns were round, with several diamond designs around the base, revealing a soft yellow glow that flickered like a candle through the open-ings. She felt mesmerized by the lights' movements as she watched them twitch, flicker and glow. Each lantern had just enough light to fill the empty spaces between the bungalows. As she looked, she thought the floating fog and mist filled the city streets with mystery and intrigue.

"Hannah," called Hunter, as he watched her stare

into the distance. "Planet earth to Hannah."

Hannah blinked her eyes as she looked at her brother. She smiled slightly and replied, "Are we on planet earth?"

Hunter shook his head, smirked back at her and replied, "You know, I'm really not sure!"

"Did you see something that might help us, Hannah?" questioned Alli.

"No, not really. I was looking at the beautiful city. Have you noticed that nothing is out of place? There's no graffiti, no trash nor debris. Everything seems perfect," Hannah replied, still looking out at the city. "Almost too perfect."

"Yeah, I was thinking the same thing. Way too perfect. I don't know what it is for sure, but something really doesn't feel right," agreed Hayden.

"Hello! Have any of you paid attention to the fact that nothing has been right here?" asked Hunter, as he shook his head. "The thunder and lighting storms are on the ground, lava flows at the bottom of a waterfall, giant birds protect the city, and secret tunnels are above ground instead of below. Nothing is right here!"

"That's true. I hadn't thought about that," agreed Hayden, shrugging his shoulders.

"Maybe the people are really clean here," added Alli.

"And maybe life here is a lot different than ours," added Hannah.

"You mean they respect their environment?" questioned Alli, as she raised her eyebrows.

"No, I mean maybe the consequences are different here," replied Hannah.

"Like instead of jail, the penalty for littering or graffiti is death," suggested Hunter.

"That's a totally scary thought," whispered Alli. She crouched down on the rope, trying to stay hidden in the mist of the clouds. "You guys, I'm really afraid. Can we go home now?"

"Don't be afraid. We just need to find a safe place to hide. Then we can calm down and figure out what's going on here. And we can figure out our next move," suggested Hayden. "Besides, I don't think we can go home until we find the lost tribes. If you remember, the bridge we crossed to get here broke, leaving us no way back to the Hill Cumorah."

"I'd forgotten that! Thanks a lot for reminding me, Hayden," Alli said angrily. She tried as hard as she could not to cry. "Now I'm really scared."

"Come on, Alli. You know the Lord wouldn't send us here to do His work if he didn't provide a way for us to get home," Hannah said reassuringly. "Now, come on. Let's find a safe place to hide."

Hannah held Alli's hand, helping her to stand on the ropes. Then the two girls slowly moved through the clouds.

"Can anyone see how the soldiers are moving around the city?" asked Hunter, frustrated he could not find a path or trail.

"Yeah, I can see them. But I'm not sure I believe what I'm seeing," replied Hannah.

"I'm standing here with you, and I can't see. What can you see?" asked Alli.

"Well, it looks to me like the men are walking directly on top of the clouds," she replied. "Their feet sink about three or four inches into the clouds, and then the clouds seem to be solid."

"Come on, Hannah. Be serious," demanded Hunter, stunned by her comments. "We're not falling for any of your tricks."

"I'm serious. The mist from the clouds comes maybe three or four inches above their ankles, so I can't see exactly what they're walking on. But, I think there must be a walkway about six inches below the cloud line," Hannah insisted.

"Do you think stepping onto the clouds is another test of faith?" Alli questioned nervously. "'Cause if it is, I don't think that I can do this."

"Well, once we run out of rope to slide across, then we'll figure out what we have to do for sure," said Hunter. He was tired of waiting and ready to get moving.

"We better do whatever we're gonna do, quickly! The clouds are disappearing and so will our protection. We're gonna get caught for sure if we don't move now!" whispered Alli. She watched the silhouette of a soldier pass a few feet away,

"Hey, I noticed several dark, possibly empty, bungalows in the city," added Hannah. "Maybe we can find one to hide inside."

"We can't just assume because they're dark that they're empty," insisted Alli.

"Without knocking on every door, how are we gonna find out if they are empty?" asked Hayden.

Hannah thought as she stared out toward the city, then replied, "What about the lanterns hanging by the door of every house? If the lantern isn't lit, then maybe no one is home," she suggested. "We could try those houses first."

"That's not really logical thinking," replied Hunter as he searched through the mysterious city for the unlit lanterns. "Just because the lights aren't on, doesn't mean no one lives there."

"That's true, but if the lights are off, it at least gives us a place to start," replied Hannah.

"I agree, Hunter. There are several bungalows up ahead about fifty yards. Let's start with those," recommended Hayden.

"Hold on! Wait a minute! Before we go knocking on a whole bunch of doors, what if the wind has blown out the lanterns?" asked Alli, concerned that Hunter's plan would not work. "Then all we do is wake the people up that live inside!"

"Alli, we've got to do something. We can't sit here and wait all night," Hunter replied gruffly. "We're going to get caught out here if we don't move."

"Besides, we can peek in the windows of the bungalows before we knock or try to enter," suggested Hannah, trying to be positive.

"Okay," Alli agreed softly, as she shrugged her shoulders. "But, we'll have to be careful! I really, really, really don't want to get caught by the soldiers."

"Everyone, follow me. We've got to get moving. The clouds are starting to lift," Hunter whispered. "Be careful as you slide across the rope."

Struggling to keep their balance as they slid across the rope, they spent several minutes before they finally reached the end of the rope

CHAPTER FIFTEEN

"CAN YOU SEE a way to continue?" asked Alli.

Hunter scanned the cloud's lining where he hoped there was a floor.

"I can't, but we know that the soldiers were walking right in this area. So, I think we're gonna have to have faith like we did when we stepped off the stone earlier," he replied, looking into Alli nervous eyes.

"I don't want to die here!" Alli exclaimed tearfully. "I don't want to fall hundreds of feet to my death."

"Um, I think that's where the faith comes in to play," teased Hayden.

"Okay, then you step off the rope first. If you fall, then we'll know not to follow you," joked Alli, as she smirked at Hayden.

Hunter nodded his head at Alli and replied, "Fine, I'll show you it's safe. I'll go first—no worries!"

Hunter looked at the thick bank of clouds that started just beyond the end of the rope. Looking intently, he struggled to see anything underneath the clouds that could possibly support his weight. Unable to see through the thick clouds, his heart pounded in terror.

"Are you going to step off anytime soon?" teased Alli, as she watched Hunter struggle.

"I'm going. Give me a minute, will ya?" barked Hunter. "I'm trying to make sure no one is out here who might see us!"

He waited for only a moment, not daring to take a breath, his heart pounding uncontrollably, as he finally stepped out into the clouds. As his foot continued to fall deeper and deeper into the soft, moist wetness of the clouds, he panicked as the scream that was happening in his mind got stuck in his throat.

Finally, about six inches below the clouds, his foot reached something hard, and he was able to step out into the clouds.

"Hey, look at that. You must have had enough faith!" exclaimed Hannah, with a smile.

"Now all of you can see that I'm fine. Move it! Get over here! We've got to find a place to hide!" Hunter demanded.

Cautiously, Hayden, Hannah and Alli stepped off the rope into the clouds, following Hunter's example.

"See, I told you everything would be fine," said Hunter, grinning from ear to ear. "It's a good thing we all have enough faith to hold Alli on the clouds, otherwise she would have already fallen through," he teased.

"You're not funny, Hunter," cried Alli. She turned angrily and moved through the clouds. She was sure at any moment the bottom of the clouds would disappear and she would tumble hundreds of feet to her death.

She stumbled and fell toward the clouds. Unable to get her arms out fast enough to stop her fall, she slammed into the clouds and hit her head on something very hard.

"Are you okay, Alli?" whispered Hannah, as she hurried to her friend's side.

"Yeah, I'm alright," she replied softy, as she rubbed the top of her head.

"Come on, girls," whispered Hayden, frantically motioning for them to hurry. "Hunter's gonna check out a bungalow."

Hannah helped Alli to her feet. Alli rubbed her head as they hurried to catch up with Hayden. Trying to stay hidden in the clouds the best they could, they watched as Hunter grabbed hold of a windowsill and carefully pulled himself up high enough to look inside the bungalow.

"Can you see anything, Hunter?" whispered Hayden.

"Sssshhhh, Hayden," demanded Hunter. "You're gonna get me caught. Be quiet and stay hidden. I'll call you when it's safe."

Hunter looked back inside the bungalow, hoping not to see anyone inside. As he looked, he saw food on a table, clothes, blankets, and a heap of material on a chair. On the floor in the center of the bungalow was a bow, several arrows and a spear. Two bright-orange silk belts hung on the wall, and a bedroll was thrown right in the middle of the room.

"Doesn't something feel weird in the city tonight?" asked a tall, thin, dark-haired soldier, startling Hunter, as he stared inside the small, diamond-shaped window. Sure he would be seen at any moment, he hung motionless from the window, afraid to make the slightest movement.

Hunter watched as the two men walked to the door of the bungalow where he was perilously hanging. Afraid to take his eyes off the men, or even move a muscle, he remained motionless as the tall soldier turned toward him. The soldier took a beautiful, blue crystal necklace from around his neck. He carefully snapped the crystal in half and took a small white object from inside. Delicately holding the object in his left hand, he grasped the lantern hanging in the bushes, pulled open the thin, diamond-shape window and placed the small white object inside.

Hunter's hands and arms burned as he struggled to hold on to the windowsill. He knew he could not let go, or the men would surely hear the leaves from the bushes rattle when he fell.

After lighting the lantern, the two men continued talking on the front porch of the bungalow for a few minutes. Finally, the tall soldier opened the door, and the two men walked inside.

Hunter breathed a cautious sigh of relief. When the

door closed and the men were finally gone, Hunter quickly let go of the windowsill, falling into the shelter of the clouds and bushes below the window. He paused momentarily to rub his aching hands and shoulders before he stood up, when the soldier's voices inside the bungalow suddenly disappeared.

"Where'd they go?" Hunter thought to himself as he intently listened for their voices. Unable to hear the men, he stood up next to the window and concentrated on the sound he could hear inside.

"What's he doing?" asked Hannah.

"Yeah, why is he standing there?" questioned Alli. "If he's not careful he's going to get caught."

"I don't have any idea," replied Hayden.

Hannah, Alli and Hayden watched, as Hunter stood motionless for nearly a minute before he turned and scanned the area for danger, then hurried toward his friends. Hunter cautiously made his way back to where they were anxiously waiting.

"That was way too close!" exclaimed Hunter. "I was sure that guy was going to see me when he turned toward the lantern!"

"Me, too," replied Hayden. "I thought you were a gonner for sure."

"Are you okay?" asked Alli.

"Yeah, I'm fine. My hands hurt a little, but they're okay," he replied, holding them up for Alli to see.

"They hurt because they're bleeding," Alli said. She gently held Hunter's hands and looked at the cuts.

"Oh, they're okay," Hunter mumbled, as he pulled his

hands away and wiped the blood on his jeans.

Hey, we better get moving. We've got to find another place," insisted Hayden.

Suddenly, the door to the bungalow opened.

"What was the man doing with the lantern, Hunter?" asked Hannah. "We couldn't see from where we were standing?"

"I'm not sure exactly," Hunter whispered. He crouched down trying to hide. "He placed something inside. It looked like it was about the size of a battery, but he was holding the object tightly in his clenched hand. All I could see was that it glowed, a very bright, white."

"Could you hear anything the two men were saying?" questioned Hayden.

"I heard them talking about something that the men in town are planning. Then they walked inside the bungalow. I didn't want them to see me hanging there, so I just listened for a moment before I left," Hunter replied.

"What are the men planning?" quizzed Hayden. "Is that what you were listening to, after you dropped from the window?"

"I don't know what they're planning. But it had something to do with their prophet, Tantua," Hunter replied.

"What were they saying?" asked Alli.

"They were whispering, so I couldn't hear the entire conversation," Hunter replied.

"Of the conversation that you could hear, what were they saying?" asked Hannah.

"There are several men in the village that don't like the way he is leading the people," he answered.

"So what are they going to do?" asked Alli.

"I'm not sure, that's the part I couldn't hear," replied Hunter.

"Do we need to worry?" asked Hannah nervously. "Could our lives be in danger?"

"I don't know," Hunter whispered. "I hope not!"

"The stars are starting to shine brightly in the sky, guys. We can worry about what the men are planning after we find a safe place to hide," insisted Hannah, as she pointed upward.

"Come on, then. I can see another dark bungalow over there," whispered Hunter. He swiftly moved toward the bungalow, cautiously searching the area.

"Why are there so many dark bungalows?" asked Alli. "They're all over the city."

"Maybe people are just starting to go home for the night, and they haven't lit the lanterns yet," replied Hannah. "That makes finding a deserted bungalow a little more difficult."

"And maybe they're just empty," replied Hunter. "Quit being so negative, Hannah!"

They maneuvered quietly through the clouds and shadows, working their way to the bungalow. Suddenly, Hunter stopped dead in his tracks, causing Hayden to slam into Hunter's back.

"What gives, Hunter?" snapped Hayden, checking his nose to see if it was broken.

"Someone's watching us," Hunter whispered.

"What?" asked Hayden, sure he had not heard his brother correctly.

"Someone is watching us," Hunter repeated quietly.

"How do you know? Are you sure?" squeaked Alli, frightened by Hunter's statement.

"Yeah, he's staring right at us," insisted Hunter. "I can see him."

"Where?" asked Hannah, searching nervously around the area.

"Look up ahead, about twenty feet," he quietly replied. He lifted his hand slowly and pointed in the distance.

Hayden looked into the darkness and was startled as he stared into two glowing eyes. "Oh, Hunter, it's just a cat," he teased.

"I don't know, Hayden. Did you see how big its eyes are?" questioned Hannah. "I don't think house cats have eyes that big."

"Then what kind of a cat is it?" questioned Alli, afraid at any moment they could be attacked.

"I don't know!" snarled Hunter.

"Why don't we just pretend we don't see it and move on," suggested Hannah. "I'm sure it has been watching us for a while. If it is dangerous, it would have already attacked us, right?"

"You're right! Let's keep moving," said Hayden.

He continued toward the small bungalow. The girls cautiously followed Hayden's lead, moving swiftly toward the bungalow, pretending they had never seen the pair of eyes.

Hunter, afraid to take his eyes off the figure in the distance, moved slowly. He watched the intense green eyes glow through the clouds. Suddenly, the eyes moved. They were headed straight for Hunter.

Afraid the cat would pounce at any moment, Hunter froze. Not sure what else to do, he yelled, "Hayden, girls, wait! The cat is moving. I may need your help."

Hayden spun around just in time to see the graceful, sleek, lean body of the cat, dart straight toward Hunter. The yellow cat was beautiful, his fur looked long and soft and was covered with light brown spots all over its body. Its paws and face were a cream color. It had perfectly rounded ears and a two-foot-long tail.

"Run, Hunter!" called Hannah, frightened for her brother as the animal moved closer and closer toward him.

"No! Don't run. It will think you're food and run after you," called Hayden, scowling at Hannah.

"Then what do I do?" Hunter yelled, in a high squeaky voice.

"Hold still. Whatever you do, don't move—no matter what. Maybe the cat will pass right by you," he called, as he watched his brother shake in fear.

Hunter tried to remain still, as the animal neared his feet and started to sniff. Shaking in fear, he prayed for the strength not to move a muscle. Circling Hunter several times, the cat began rubbing its body and tail around Hunter's legs. Afraid of being eaten, Hunter shuddered at the thought, startling the cat.

"A cat?" he thought to himself. "A house cat wouldn't attack me!"

He glanced down at the animal wrapping its tail around his legs, trying to see what kind of ferocious animal was getting ready to attack. As he looked at the animal, he was not sure what kind of cat it was. He was sure it was not a lion or tiger—it wasn't big enough. He was sure it was not a jaguar or cheetah either—the animal was not small enough. "Either way," he thought to himself, "I don't want to be eaten by this animal."

Suddenly, the cat stopped, and sat on the edge of Hunter's shoe. It looked up toward Hunter's face with its intense green eyes. Then it simply began to clean itself with its long, pink tongue.

"Oh, great. It's cleaning up before it eats me," Hunter thought to himself. "Now if I try to run, it will know because it's sitting on my foot. It's probably a guard cat of some kind, and its job is to hold its prey until the soldiers come to take it."

Hayden watched as the cat sat down. Then he called, "Hunter, we've got to get moving."

"I know, but this ferocious cat is sitting on my foot," he replied.

"Maybe it's a domestic cat," called Hayden. "Why don't you try to move and see what it does?"

"Why don't you make choices like that with your own life," Hunter snapped. The cat momentarily stopped cleaning itself and looked at Hunter. Hunter watched the cat for several anxious seconds before it finally started licking at its fur again. "Besides this cat is about three or four times bigger than a domestic house cat," added Hunter.

"We've got to try something," insisted Hannah. "We can't stand here forever."

Hunter took a deep breath as he closed his eyes. He

prayed for the Lord to help him move safely away from the animal. He rubbed his hands together, and then quickly took a step away from the cat.

The cat looked up at Hunter and softly growled as if to ask, "Where are you going?"

Hunter felt compelled to answer. "I've got to find a safe place to hide. Everybody's counting on me!" he whispered to the animal.

"Are you talking to the cat?" called Hayden smiling.

"Yeah, do you have a problem with that?" Hunter asked sarcastically.

"Nope, just checking," Hayden answered, grinning from ear to ear.

As Hunter continued to move slowly, the cat jumped to its feet to follow. It looked over to Hayden and the girls and growled softly. It walked around Hunter's legs again, wrapping its tail tightly around one. And then, strangely, walked several feet into the distance.

"Where's it going?" Hannah asked softly.

"I don't know, but I'm gonna go in the opposite direction," replied Alli, with a sigh of relief.

Suddenly, the cat stopped, looked back at the kids, growled softly, and motioned with its head for them to follow.

"I think the cat wants us to follow it," said Hunter, as he watched the cat start to walk again.

"I'm not going to follow a cat that could eat me," replied Alli. "Be serious!"

"If the cat wanted to eat us, it would have done it already," replied Hayden.

"What if that cat is trying to help us?" questioned Hannah, as she slowly took a step toward Hunter.

"What if it's just taking us to the soldiers, or worse, more animals just like it!" Alli asked suspiciously.

Again the cat stopped, this time turning completely around and looked at the kids. Suddenly, it growled loudly, frightening the girls. It shook its head back and forth several times, dug at the ground with its paw, then turned and started walking.

"I'm gonna follow the cat," Hunter said matter-of-factly. "It could have attacked me earlier and it didn't. Maybe it's really trying to help us."

"How could an animal help us?" Alli asked skeptically?"

"I agree. I'm not sure about this, Hunter," added Hayden.

"You're not sure about this. What about me?" growled Alli. "I'm afraid of big cats."

Hunter did not want the cat to turn again and not see them following it, so he quickly motioned for everyone to follow. They walked at least the length of a football field, right through the center of all the city buildings. Hunter was grateful the clouds and fog were still thick enough to keep them hidden as they crept through the city, following the animal. Finally, at the opposite end of the city from where they started, the cat stopped and again growled. It led them up some steps to a dark, weathered and run down house.

"Where is the cat taking us?" whispered Alli. "This could totally be a trap!"

"I think to this bungalow," Hunter replied, pointing. "And we can only hope it's not a trap."

The cat jumped onto the stairs and pushed his way through the heavy door.

"The cat's out of sight. Should we run?" asked Alli.

"Alli, come on. Could you try to be positive for a moment?" questioned Hayden. "I think Hunter's right, the cat is trying to help us."

"It did help us through the city safely," said Hannah.

"And it hasn't attacked us," added Hunter.

"No, it's inviting us in now so it can eat us in private," Alli replied sarcastically.

"Alli, I think we should follow Hunter," said Hannah. She placed her arm around her friend's shoulder. "Maybe the Lord is leading us to safety with the help of this animal."

The two girls walked slowly behind the boys. They watched as Hunter jumped up and grabbed hold of the windowsill. Then he peeked inside the dark bungalow.

Several anxious seconds passed as he searched inside the house. Hunter was shocked as the cat placed its head in the window and stared directly into Hunter's eyes. His heart pounding, he let go of the window, snapping several dry vines as he landed.

"Nothing is inside the house besides the cat," Hunter called. Unable to keep his balance he quickly fell to his knees. He jumped to his feet and brushed off his hands and knees. "I think this will be a good place to hide for the rest of the night," he said.

"After you," replied Alli, still nervous about entering the house.

Hunter walked to the door where the cat had just entered. He carefully pushed it open, barely enough that he could slip his body in through the opening. Then Hayden entered, followed by Hannah and a nervous Alli.

"This bungalow is so cool!" exclaimed Hannah. Attempting to see her surroundings in the dark.

"All I know is that I am exhausted!" replied Hunter. "I'm gonna find something to lie down on and go to sleep."

"Do you think it's safe for all of us to sleep?" questioned Alli. "Shouldn't one of us stay awake and keep watch, in case someone comes?"

"We have the cat to keep watch for us," replied Hunter.

He sat down on the floor and slipped off his shoes, then rubbed the cat's head, under its chin, and stroked its back. The cat purred with delight from Hunter's touch.

Alli watched as Hunter took a small blanket that was draped over a chair. He scrunched it into a ball, laid his head on the blanket next to the cat and was asleep in seconds.

"Oh, great!" she exclaimed. "What are we going to do now? Our fearless leader has decided to sleep. Meanwhile, we are in a strange place, with a strange animal, under very strange circumstances."

"Hunter has been right so far," said Hayden. "I think I'm going to follow his example and sleep while we have a minute before the sun comes up."

"Hannah," called Alli, as she looked at her friend. "Don't you think we could be in trouble if one of us doesn't keep watch?"

"Come on, Alli. We didn't get a lot of sleep last night. I'm totally exhausted. I can barely keep my eyes open. Let's rest for a few hours while we can, 'cause who knows when we'll have the chance again," replied Hannah. "Besides, if the cat tries to eat us now, we hopefully won't feel anything—we'll already be asleep!"

"Oh, that's really comforting!" Alli exclaimed. She watched her friend retrieve a blanket from the back of the chair and lie down in the corner.

"If you want to keep watch, you can, Alli," Hunter said sleepily. "That might be a good idea. But, I really think this cat was sent by the Lord to bring us to a safe place."

Outnumbered, Alli watched her friends lie down and start to fall asleep. Not sure she really wanted to keep watch, and barely able to keep her eyes open, she reluctantly found a small blanket on the chair. And within seconds, she was fast asleep on the hardwood floor.

CHAPTER SIXTEEN

HANNAH AWOKE to a melodious chorus of animals singing and chirping relentlessly outside. She was sure she heard several types of birds, monkeys and possibly frogs or crickets combining to form an unusual band. She sat up slowly, yawned and rubbed her tired eyes.

"Mom, what CD are you playing?" she called. "I don't think I've ever heard you play this music before."

"Mom?" called Hannah. "Where are you? And where are we now? Are we getting close to this trip being over?"

Hearing no immediate response, Hannah opened her eyes and looked around. Suddenly, she remembered the events of the last two days. As the memories flooded back to her mind, she worriedly scanned the room. She gasped when she saw the large cat, still cuddled up next to Hunter on the wood floor.

"Well, I guess Hunter didn't get eaten last night," she thought to herself, chuckling.

She watched as the cat lifted its head and looked at

her. Then laid its head back down on the floor and closed its eyes.

"If everything we're doing wasn't so scary, this trip might actually be great!" she thought to herself. "Not many people get to travel to mysterious lands."

Looking around the small bungalow, she was surprised that no one had come home. Clothes were hanging neatly near the wall and adobe bowls and vases were tucked on a shelf over the sink. There was not a faucet, however, a small tube, that led out the window to the top of the house, lay in a basin.

"I wonder if whoever lives here catches water in a tub or something on the top of the house, and then channels it into the kitchen through this tube," she thought, as she carefully peered at the tube through the window.

Still scanning the interior of the house, cautious not to walk in front of the windows, she noticed several metal tablets sitting on the floor.

Intrigued, she picked them up and gazed at the amazing characters and symbols engraved into the metal, completely covering the page. She thought they had to be very similar to the golden plates from which the Book of Mormon had been translated.

As her stomach started to growl loudly, Hannah thought, "I wish I would've picked some extra fruit from the trees outside before we came in here last night."

She found that the bungalow rocked slightly as she walked, and she noticed a small door covered with a beautiful tapestry. Suspicious that someone could be hiding inside, she tiptoed softly toward the blanket and slowly peeled back one side, praying no one would jump out at her.

As she peered around the corner into the sectioned-off room, she was shocked at what she saw. Carved into the stone and adobe of the house wall, was the most amazing picture of a man. As she stared at the man, a thought flashed through her mind.

"This has to be a picture of Christ! I wonder why it is hidden in this room!" she thought to herself.

She released the tapestry and watched as it fell back into place. She turned and continued to scan the remainder of the interior of the bungalow. Hannah saw a small table and three chairs, as well as a bed against the wall. She noticed a small bowl of fruit sitting in the center of another tiny table, in what she assumed was the kitchen area. Starving, she ran to the table, causing the bungalow to rock softly back and forth.

"Hunter, are we having an earthquake?" called Alli, in a sleepy voice.

"I hope not," he replied, in a rough, scratchy voice.

"It's only me," Hannah replied, through a mouth full of food. "I was walking too fast."

"What are you doing?" questioned Hunter, with his eyes still closed. "What time is it?"

"Morning," she replied. "That's why I'm eating."

"Where did you get the food?" demanded Hunter. He sat up quickly, opened his eyes and looked directly at Hannah. "You better not have gone outside in the light!"

"Nope, I didn't. The food was in here on the table," she replied, as she stuffed another piece of an orange into her mouth.

"Well, don't eat it all. I'm hungry, too," squealed Alli. At the mention of food, she crawled on her hands and knees toward Hannah.

"Have you been up very long, Hannah?" asked Hayden, still lying motionless with his eyes closed.

"Only a few minutes, but long enough to see that this bungalow does belongs to someone. They could come home at any moment," she replied, still stuffing food into her mouth. "And whoever lives here must be the owner of the cat, because I bet that bowl on the ground is for its food or water."

"What?" squawked Hunter, sitting up quickly and looking at their surroundings. "You mean the cat I dreamed about all night is real?"

Hunter smiled as he stood. He stretched his arms, back, and neck, then reached down to tussle the cat's long, soft hair. He quickly scanned the inside of the bungalow, and then rushed to where Hannah was eating breakfast.

"I'm famished!" exclaimed Hunter, as he sat down next to Hannah and took half of her fruit.

"Hey, get your own," she cried, as she tried to grab back her fruit.

"So, did you check anything out in the city yet?" he asked, as he held her arms away from the food.

Giving up, she sat back down and replied, "I told you, I didn't go outside."

"What about the window? Did you look out the window?" he questioned again.

"No, not really. I didn't want to be seen," she replied.

She stood up and walked to one of the diamond-shaped windows. Standing by the edge, she peered through the window into the city outside.

"I can see a huge, very ornate building in the center of the city," Hannah described.

"Probably a temple, don't you think?" asked Hunter, listening to her while he finished eating.

"Yes, probably. The stones are a beautiful, soft-white color and the building is at least fifty feet tall. Next to the temple is a magnificent courtyard filled with many kinds of trees and flowers. And there is a smaller wall that forms a circle around the yard."

"Are there any other buildings that big around the city at all?" interrupted Hunter.

Hannah scanned the city and replied, "No, that is the biggest, but there are several other buildings by the temple that are fairly big and beautifully decorated."

"What else?" questioned Hunter, as the cat started to circle around his feet again.

"I don't think the cat has had anything to eat in a while," said Hannah, as she watched.

Hunter stood from the table and started to search the bungalow for something the cat could eat. "You keep describing while I find something for Sunny to eat," he insisted.

"Sunny?" questioned Hannah.

"Yep. She is a beautiful cat, her color is bright and sunny and she saved us until the sun came up," he replied, smiling. So I named her Sunny!"

"Well, Sunny sure likes you," commented Hannah, as

she watched the cat stay close by Hunter.

"Describe the city," insisted Hunter, as he searched through the house.

"Beyond the temple, there is a marketplace, I think. Colorful cloths that resemble tarps are everywhere, and people seem to be wandering through the area."

"Now, if we only had some money, we could buy more food, clothes and anything else we need to move around the city unnoticed," replied Hunter.

"Like a toothbrush?" asked Hannah, as she tried to clean her teeth with her shirt sleeve.

"Well, that's not exactly what I had in mind. But if that is what you need, then yes—a toothbrush, too," replied Hunter.

"Do you think the people here are righteous? Do you think they know we're coming and will they want to leave with us? Or are we going to have to convince them that we have been sent here by the Lord?" asked Hannah, still staring into the city.

"You know, Hannah, until you asked that, I hadn't really thought about how we're going to get two people from each tribe to leave their homes and go back with us. But, if you think about it, we're not doing anything different than the missionaries back home are doing. They travel to far off, unknown places, and they try to teach people they don't know the ways of the Lord and bring them into the light. That's all we're doing here," replied Hunter.

"Yeah, I guess we just got called on our missions earlier than most," she replied, chuckling.

"Hey," yelled Hunter. "I think I found the cat's food."

"Hunter, you can't yell like that! I thought something was wrong," Hannah snapped, holding her chest in fear.

"Oh, sorry," replied Hunter. "Just excited to find something for Sunny."

Hannah shook her head as she watched Hunter rub the cat's belly and chin, and enjoy the cat's happy purring from the attention.

"Finish telling me what else you can see out there," insisted Hunter, sitting on the floor with Sunny in his lap.

"Okay, I can't see everything, though. After the marketplace, there are bungalows everywhere. They are different shapes and sizes depending on the areas, but they are all very similar. Some are round, some are more oval, some are kinda fat and others are kinda skinny. They all seem to be hanging—suspended from the trees. And each one, regardless of its size, has a small, red adobe plaque that hangs over the door."

"Did you see a plaque when we crawled into this bungalow last night?" asked Hunter.

"No, I couldn't see anything through the clouds last night. And besides, we crawled into darkness, remember?" asked Hannah.

"Can you see a lot of people?" asked Hunter, curious as to what they looked like.

"I can see a few in the marketplace and a few out and about around their houses. There seems to be a group of men gathering near the temple courtyard, and several women are near one of the three waterfalls that I can see around the area," replied Hannah.

"What are the women doing at the waterfalls?" asked Hunter.

"They look like they're washing clothes," replied Hannah.

"I know what is happening at the marketplace, but what is happening with the men near the temple?" asked Hunter.

"They all seem to have weapons of some kind. One man is standing on the edge of the pool waving his arms in the air, like he is speaking," said Hannah.

"What kind of weapons? Can you tell?" questioned Hunter.

"Yeah, some have swords, and others have bows, arrows and spears. There is one type of weapon that I don't recognize," replied Hannah.

"I wonder if they know we are here," said Hunter.

"How could they know?" asked Hannah. "No one saw us come in, and we were able to hide before we were spotted," replied Hannah.

"That's true, but I still think it's a good idea to keep an eye on them," suggested Hunter.

"I think Alli fell back asleep and Hayden's not awake yet. Should I get them up?" asked Hannah. "If we have to leave in a hurry, I think leaving would be easier if they were awake first," giggled Hannah.

"Yeah, we better," replied Hunter.

"Oh, I'm already awake," said Hayden, opening his eyes. "How could anybody sleep with the two of you talking your heads off?"

"And I'm awake, too," added Alli. "I was trying to

pretend that all of this was a dream!"

"You know what? I woke up asking Mom what CD she was listening to," chuckled Hannah. "And Hunter dreamed about a cat all night long."

"Have you figured out what to do yet?" questioned Hayden.

"We've been getting our bearings in the city so far this morning. But I did see that whoever lives here has clothes that all of us could wear. Pants are neatly folded on the shelves over there, and shirts and dresses are hanging in the small closet," replied Hunter, pointing to the corner.

"I think if we looked a little more like the people in the city, we could possibly mingle and find out what tribe lives here in this city," interjected Alli.

"Yeah, I was thinking the same thing," agreed Hannah.

"What do the people out there look like?" asked Hayden.

"Well, I haven't seen very many people. But those I've seen look like people from back home, only dressed in robes and sashes. The women's robes are about calf-length and have three-quarter length sleeves. The men's robes, believe it or not, are shorter. They are about knee-length with three quarter length sleeves as well," described Hannah. "Oh, and all of them have different colored sashes."

"Do the colors of the sashes mean anything?" asked Hayden.

"I haven't looked closely enough to know. Before any of us go out, we'll have to get a better look," replied Hannah.

"I think we need to get changed and head out as soon as possible," suggested Hunter. His new friend, the cat, suddenly started to growl.

"Hey, some people are headed this way!" exclaimed Hannah, quickly ducking out of sight.

"Is there any place to hide in here?" asked Hayden, jumping quickly to his feet.

"I only saw one small area," replied Hannah, rushing toward the room full of paintings. "Quick, everybody get in here."

Hunter left the cat and ran toward Hannah, as Hayden and Alli quickly followed.

"There's not a lot of room," whispered Hannah.

"That's alright. I'm more worried about being found in here. We have no escape if someone pulls back the tapestry and finds us!" exclaimed Hunter. The kids suddenly heard a squeak as the front door swing open.

"Sunshine, are you in here?" called a sweet voice. "Sunshine, where are you, you silly cat?"

CHAPTER SEVENTEEN

"Your Highness!" shouted a soldier, as he raced inside the great temple in the center of the city. "Your Highness, I need to speak with you."

The temple guards dropped their swords to their sides as the soldier tried to race through the great room to the prophet's throne.

"I've got to speak to the prophet. Let me pass," demanded the soldier.

"You know the new rules, Bashan," replied the soldier. "No one can enter to see Tantua without permission. And you know he does not like to be called the prophet."

"I have to see him now," shouted Bashan. "We have a problem in the city."

Much to Bashan's dismay, the guard walked slowly toward the prophet, his Highness, Tantua. He watched as the soldier whispered into Tantua's ear. Then they looked back at Bashan, and Tantua laughed.

The soldier then sauntered his way through the great room, to where Bashan was waiting with the guard.

"Did you tell him?" Bashan asked anxiously. "I must speak to him, right now!"

"Yes, I told him," chuckled the soldier.

"And?" demanded Bashan.

"And," replied the soldier. "You may enter when you have calmed down."

"Move your swords," Bashan said. He pushed through the crossed swords in front of him and stomped toward the Prophet.

"Tantua, Tantua, I need to speak with you!" shouted Bashan. "Right now!"

"Not until you bow," replied Tantua.

He reluctantly bowed his head toward the prophet. "Tantua, I am the captain of your security. Would I come to you unless we have a problem?" asked Bashan.

"Is there a problem?" asked Tantua, sitting up straight in his throne.

"Yes, I think so," replied Bashan.

"You think so, or yes, there is a problem?" questioned Tantua.

"Your Highness, yesterday, the men reported an irregular grass pattern as they patrolled around the perimeter of the wall on the land. And this morning, my men reported that the stone tower was not returned to the ground properly after someone entered the city. I am afraid that a stranger could be here," Bashan explained.

"Why weren't they reported to me already?" screamed Tantua. "We could have solved this problem yesterday!"

"I'm sorry, Sir," replied Bashan. "I did not feel their report was important enough to trouble you. My men felt the trampled grass was caused by animals."

"Do you feel what they saw is important enough to trouble me now?" screamed Tantua. He stood from his throne and paced back and forth. "Have there been any reports of someone in the city?"

"No, Sir," Bashan replied.

"And you say the stone tower was left up during a storm?" asked Tantua.

"That is correct, Sir," he replied.

"This should be easy then. Whoever has entered our city knows nothing about us or how we live. They will look and act out of place. I want you to take every man you have available, and search every building, shop, market and bungalow in the city. Search every square inch. If any of the people so much as ask why, then I want them arrested and thrown into jail!" shrieked Tantua. "Do you understand me?"

"Yes, Sir. I understand," replied Bashan.

"Good, then get moving. I want a full report every hour until whoever is here is captured," added Tantua. "Oh and Bashan, there is a reason I have the soldiers guard the walls, next time report the problem or you will end up in prison. Do you understand?"

"Yes, Sir. I understand," he replied. "Sir, could these intruders be fulfilling the prophecy written on the stones of the temple by the great prophets?" asked Bashan.

"No, this cannot be about the prophecy. And if it is, then I will rid myself of the four, before anyone is the city learns of them. Do you understand me?" he yelled, at the top of his lungs.

"Yes, Sir. I understand," replied Bashan.

"Nothing will stop my reign—nothing! Especially some dumb prophecy written by prophets, whom I don't believe in!" bellowed Tantua.

Bashan bowed his head and backed out of the room, turning only after he had reached the entrance to the great room. He looked at the two soldiers and said, "Gid, you will remain on your post and protect our prophet. Heth, assemble every man that we have. Tell the men to meet in the temple courtyard in fifteen minutes or Tantua himself will be the one to punish them. Do you understand?"

"Yes, Captain," Heth replied, pausing momentarily. "Is there a problem, Captain?"

"Heth, assemble the men," shouted Bashan. "Quickly!"

"Yes, Captain," he replied, moving slowly toward the door.

"Then move!" Bashan screamed, frightening Heth.

Bashan watched as Heth ran into the entry of the Temple. Then he turned to Gid and said, "No one is to see Tantua today without my permission. No exceptions. Is that understood?"

"Yes, Captain," replied Gid.

"Remember, Tantua's safety is in your hands today. No one, no matter what the situation, is to see him without my consent," Bashan added.

"Yes, Captain. I will make sure!" replied Gid, taking his post in the middle of the doorway.

Bashan stormed off in the direction of the temple courtyard, slamming his sword into the wall as he passed through the door. Once he reached the courtyard, he quickly unlocked several tall cabinets. He pulled the doors open to reveal all sorts of weapons—swords, spears, cimeters, bows and arrows. As the men started to filter into the courtyard, Bashan pointed to the open cupboards. "Find a weapon, and then sit on the ground until I give you further instructions," he yelled.

Bashan watched as the men moved slowly to retrieve their weapons. "Hurry, men! We have a lot to do today," he ordered.

"What's so important that you have to bring me in on my day off?" questioned Zerin.

"Men, gather around so I only have to answer Zerin's question once!" yelled Bashan, motioning for the men to move closer.

Bashan watched as a few more men entered the courtyard, followed by Heth. Bashan stood on the edge of a huge stone water fountain and yelled, "Heth, is that everyone?"

Heth nodded his head and waved to Bashan, indicating that all of the soldiers were present.

"Men, we have bad news in our city," started Bashan. "More than two thousand years have passed since the Lord led us here to our safe valley to wait for his call to return. Never in those two-thousand years have we had a breech in our security, until last night."

"We have visitors in our city?" questioned one of the soldiers.

"More like spies in our city, sent here to destroy our prophet," said another.

"Wait men, wait. We are not certain that someone has entered our city. This is why you have been called here this morning. I am sorry for those of you who have to work an extra day. However for the good of the city, we need your help," Bashan explained.

"What does the intruder look like?" called a soldier from the group. "Do we know if there is more than one?"

"I do not know," replied Bashan. "Didn't you listen when I said I'm not sure if someone entered the city?"

"Then you do not know if anyone has even entered our city?" called another soldier.

"As Laish and Midian kept watch on the main land by the great stone wall yesterday, they found something they felt was suspicious. They reported their findings to me. However, I felt their findings to be unimportant. Then this morning, Midian found the stone that lifts us to our city, had been left out of place during the storm. I believe that an intruder used the stone to reach the city and that person is currently hiding somewhere in our city. But, again I remind you that I do not know that for sure."

"How will we ever find this person? There are those in our city that are not loyal to the Prophet Tantua, and they could help the stranger," Zerin said.

"Tantua has commanded that every inch of the city be searched, including buildings, the market place and every bungalow. Those people will have no choice but to do as we say, or they will go to the dungeon with the others who have not done as Tantua has commanded."

"Do we have the authority to arrest them if they do not cooperate with us?" questioned Heth.

"Yes," answered Bashan.

"Hundreds of people may be arrested today," commented one of the soldiers. "Do we have enough space in the dungeons for that many?"

"Bring them to the courtyard, and we will deal with them after we find the intruders," commanded Bashan.

"Where do we start?" asked Laish.

Bashan thought for a moment before he replied. "Laish, I want you to take a group of men and search the areas of Reuben, Simeon and Levi. Heth, I want you to take a group of men and search the areas of Dan, Naphtali and Judah. Another group of men follow Midian to the areas of Gad, Asher, Issachar and Zebulun. Everyone will report back here to me if anything is found. Do you understand?"

The men in the group nodded, and then separated into groups. Heth's group was the first to leave the courtyard, followed by Laish's and then Midian's.

Bashan watched the men quickly file out of the courtyard. Then he cautiously walked to the prophecy inscribed into the temple wall, and read the words written hundreds of years ago by the prophets of old.

"'In the year that Tantua, son of Tarshia of the tribe of Reuben, is pronounced prophet of the great and powerful city of the lost tribes, a great falling out of men will occur. As Tantua becomes hardened in his heart to the ways of the Lord and begins to preach false doctrines to the Lord's choice people, men's faith will fail, if they do not wax strong in the ways of the Lord. Do not harden your hearts to the ways of the Lord. Watch for the signs He will send to return the faithful tribes to the land of their inheritance. Remember, that these things are not written that they must come to pass, but only that they could come to pass. If Tantua falls to the temptations that are placed in his path, four will come with the strength of the Lion, through the direction of the Lord, to return you home to live with your Father once again. Stay always in righteousness. Your friend and prophet of the Lord, Judah.'"

Bashan reread the prophecy several times before he turned away angrily. He mumbled under his breath and headed for the great room to report the progress of the search for the intruders. As he reached the opening to the great room, he pushed passed Gid and marched angrily toward Tantua.

"Have you found them?" questioned Tantua.

"Not yet, your Highness. The men have just begun to search. I have placed my best men as leaders to conduct the search. I will report to you as soon as we have an update," replied Bashan.

"If the intruder is not found and I fall from the throne, you, my friend, will fall with me," warned Tantua. "It will be in your best interest that whoever has entered our city is found as quickly as possible. I would hate for you to end up in the dungeon."

"We will find this person, Sir. And when we do, I would like the pleasure of throwing him into the dungeon myself!" Bashan replied angrily.

CHAPTER EIGHTEEN

NEARLY THIRTY MINUTES passed while the girl with the sweet voice played and cuddled with the wild cat she called Sunshine. Tired of waiting, Hunter carefully pulled an edge of the rug to the side. He spotted the girl with the sweet voice. She had beautiful, long brown hair, was sitting on the ground with the cat in her lap. Hunter noticed the skins from the fruit he had eaten earlier still sitting on the table, and the blankets they had used as pillows still wadded up and scattered all over the floor.

"What's been going on around here, Sunshine? Only two days have passed since I was here last, and the place is a disaster. Have you had friends over or something, girl?" asked the girl. She picked up the cat and slowly crawled to the blankets. She shook each blanket out and laid it over the chairs, then noticed the fruit peelings on the kitchen table.

"So, you have had company," she said. She picked up the peelings and smelled the fruit. "And your company

has not been gone very long," she added, carefully looking around the room.

"Oh man, we're dead now," whispered Hunter. He
slowly let the tapestry fall back into place. "She knows
we're here!"

"Well, Sunshine, tell me—did you see anyone here last
night or this morning?" she asked, suspiciously looking
around the room.

Sunshine pretended that she had not heard a word the
girl had said. The cat casually walked to her food dish and
started eating.

"Well, that answers it for sure. I knew you would be
completely out of food, Sunshine, because I have been
gone for two days! Your dish is full, so you better tell me
who has been feeding you!" the girl demanded.

Sunshine did not even look up. She just lapped at the
water and continued to eat.

"Like a cat is really going to answer me," the girl whispered to herself, as she started scanning the area.

"Is someone in here?" she called, as she looked around
nervously. "Come on, show yourself!"

"What do we do?" whispered Hannah.

Hunter shrugged his shoulder and held his finger to
his mouth, signaling Hannah to be quiet. He again pulled
a small edge of the tapestry back so he could see the main
room in the bungalow. Unable to spot the girl, he pulled
the tapestry back further to see more of the room.

Suddenly, she took hold of the rug and hastily pulled
it open, revealing Hannah, Hunter, Hayden and Alli.

"Who are you?" screamed the girl, frightened by the

unexpected visitors. What are you doing in my father's home?"

"We are travelers from another city," Hannah replied calmly.

"And why have you broken into my father's home?" she demanded again loudly.

"We needed a place to rest for the night," Alli replied, walking out of the small closet like area into the open room.

Frightened, the girl backed away as Alli walked toward her. "Why did you come here? There are many other bungalows in the city," she said nervously. "Why here?"

"Your cat led us here," replied Hunter.

"Sunshine led you here?" questioned the girl, as she looked angrily at the cat.

"We were on the other side of the city. She saw us through the clouds, and led us here before we were seen," replied Hayden.

"Have you been seen by anyone?" asked the girl, looking nervously out the window.

"No, I don't think so," replied Hunter. "Only Sunny," he said smiling, as he pointed to the cat.

"The city is not safe for visitors. If you are found, we will all be thrown in the dungeons!" she exclaimed.

"Why isn't your city safe for us to go wherever we need to?" asked Hannah. "I thought we were coming to return one of the lost tribes back home."

"You are the four?" questioned the girl, with a shocked look on her face, surprised by Hannah's comments. "Four kids have come to save us?"

257

"What are you talking about?" asked Hunter. "Save who?"

Sunny stopped eating, looked up at Hunter and growled softly.

"I don't understand what you are talking about," said Hunter.

"The prophecy written by the prophet Judah of old," she replied quietly. "Are you the four from the prophecy?"

"What prophecy?" asked Alli, confused by her comments. "We don't know what you are talking about."

"The soldiers back down on the land talked about a prophecy yesterday, too," added Hunter.

"There is a prophecy written on the stones of the temple. The prophecy states that the Lord will send four to return the lost tribes home," she answered. "Can the prophecy be true? Are you the four the prophecy speaks of?"

"There is no such prophecy that we have ever seen," said Hannah, confused by the girls comments.

"Then why is it you are here to return the tribes home," asked the girl.

"One of our prophets left us a note that said we were to travel in the cave, find the tribes and bring them home," answered Hayden.

"If you have been told by a prophet of God to return the tribes, then I will help you!" she exclaimed excitedly. "Maybe you will be able to free my father before we go!"

"Where is your father?" asked Hunter.

"The new prophet, Tantua, has thrown my father in the dungeon," she replied sadly.

"Why?" asked Alli.

"My father is the head of the house of Dan. If Tantua could get him to say the prophets of old weren't the voice of God, then many would believe what Tantua is saying. My father refused, so he was taken," she replied tearfully. "Tantua is challenging the truthfulness of the prophecy. Anyone who believes in it is being thrown into the dungeons."

"Is that why so many of the bungalows were dark last night?" asked Hayden.

"Yes," she replied.

"Where are you staying? Why weren't you here last night?" asked Alli.

"My mother died several years ago. When my father was taken, I went to stay with my mother's sister," she answered.

"Why didn't you take Sunny?" questioned Hunter, as the cat wandered around his legs.

"My aunt is afraid of Sunny. I leave her here and try to return and take care of her every day or two," the girl replied softly. "She seems to like all of you."

"Who are the men leaving the temple in the center of the city?" asked Hannah, as she pointed out the window.

As the girl walked to the window to see, fear instantly spread across her face.

"Those are Tantua's soldiers!" she exclaimed. "They must know you are here. Quick, you must change."

"Change into what?" cried Hannah. "This is all we have."

The girl moved swiftly, gathering several articles of

clothing and shoes. She handed everything to them, and then said, "Change quickly. We must leave at once. Our lives are in great danger."

"Will Tantua not meet with us?" asked Hunter. "If he met with us, wouldn't he believe in the prophecies of the prophets of old?"

"Tantua will see you and then throw you in the dungeon," she sharply replied. "He does not want to give up his seat as a prophet. He wants complete power over the people. Now hurry and change!"

Everyone quickly changed, using the small room they had hidden in earlier. Once they were finished, the girl took their other clothes and put them in a small hiding place in the wall.

"Sunshine, do not allow anyone to find these things or others like Auntie will be in danger as well." She released the cat's face. She turned toward the kids, and quickly fixed and straightened their clothes where needed, then said. "Stay with me at all times. Do not speak to anyone. They will not understand you."

"How do you understand us?" asked Hannah.

"You speak a language that my father taught to me— an ancient language not spoken anywhere that I know of," she replied. "You must be sent by God."

"Does Sunshine understand you?" questioned Alli, looking at the cat.

"I think she does, but she can't talk to me and let me know for sure," the girl replied, smiling for the first time.

She carefully looked through the window and located the guards, not far in the distance. She pulled open the door and motioned for the kids to follow. Winding quickly through the area, they dodged in and out of bungalows and trees for several minutes.

"Where are we going? Where are you taking us?" Hunter finally asked.

"You know as well as I, that the best place to hide is in plain sight. We are headed to the mountainside above the waterfall ahead of us. I will show you the city and then take you to the marketplace in the middle of town. I think you should know something about the city first. When the time is right, you will know where you are in the city and what to do. Then we can rescue those thrown into the dungeons, before you return a few of our people back to the world we were taken from."

"The center of town?" asked Hayden anxiously. "Isn't that kind of dangerous?"

"We will see," she replied, smiling. "How is it that you found your way to our city?" questioned the girl. "No strangers have ever been here before."

"Let me tell you, it wasn't easy," replied Hayden, shaking his head back and forth. "We had to solve some clues, follow maps, dodge kidnappers, all sorts of stuff.

"Yeah, and without the help of the Lord, we never would have made it this far," added Hannah. "It's been a very long, hard journey."

"None of the people of the city, for thousands of years, except the prophets I'm sure, have ever been able to find a way in or out of the city. So I believe the four of you finding your way into our city is only by the Lord's hand," said the girl.

CHAPTER NINETEEN

THE GROUP TRAVELED in silence for several minutes. The terrain was rough and in some places, almost impassable. The girl jumped from rock to rock, using the vines that hung from the trees throughout the area, to help her maneuver faster over the terrain. Unfamiliar with the vines, Hunter took a hold of one and tried to jump as the girl did. The vine gave way under his weight and he crashed into a heap on the ground.

"Can I help you?" the girl called, trying not to laugh.

"No, thanks. I got it," replied Hunter, as he faked a smile. Muttering under his breath, he said, "You've helped me enough. I'm wearing a dress that I can barely move in, and I just smacked my head on the base of a tree. Boy, I can hardly wait to see what's next! I bet someone is going to jump out any minute and say—Smile, you're on Candid Camera!"

"Did you say something, Hunter?" asked Hannah. She reached out her hand to help pull Hunter to his feet.

"No, I was just talking to myself," he replied, still rubbing the knot on his head.

"You know, talking to yourself, isn't a good sign," teased Alli.

"And neither is having a vine snap and send you hurling to the ground," Hunter replied.

"Are we almost there?" called Hayden, tired of climbing up the hill.

"Almost," the girl replied, looking back at the four weary teens.

"I'm starving," called Hayden. "I didn't get anything to eat before we left."

"You should have gotten up when we did," replied Hannah.

"There's plenty of food around!" called the girl. She reached up and snapped a small piece of fruit from a nearby tree. She threw the fruit in Hayden's direction, then turned and said, "This will have to do until we can get back into the city."

"What kind of fruit is this?" asked Hayden, snatching it out of the air.

"This is called passion fruit. Do you have fruit like this where you are from?" she asked.

"We do, but I don't think I have ever tried one," he replied. He looked at the fruit, unsure whether or not to eat it.

"They taste good, Hayden," replied Hannah. "In fact, they're probably one of my favorite tropical fruits."

Hayden shrugged his shoulders and sank his teeth into the soft, juicy center.

"So, do you have names?" the girl asked, as she continued to scurry quickly up moss and vine-covered rock walls.

"I'm Hayden," he replied, holding up his passion fruit.

"My name is Hannah," she said, waving her hand at the girl.

"And I'm Alli."

"And what is your name?" the girl asked, looking over at Hunter.

"My name is Hunter," he replied in a deep voice, trying to impress the girl.

"Nice to meet all of you," she replied, as she finally reached the top of a small cliff.

"What is your name?" asked Hannah.

"My name is Kirakakash," she replied proudly. "I am the oldest daughter of Leif, who is head of the house of Dan."

"Kiraka...how did you say your name again?" Alli asked.

"Kirakakash," she repeated again. "But everyone calls me Kira."

"Kira, I can say that," replied Hannah, smiling. "That is a pretty name."

"Thank you," replied Kira. She brushed her long, brown hair away from her face, revealing beautiful green eyes. They were almost as intense as Sunshine's.

"Where are we going?" asked Hunter, still a little suspicious of the girl.

"I am taking you to the tallest point in our city so that I can show you where everything is," she replied.

"Hey, I just thought of something," interrupted Hayden.

"What is it?" asked Hunter.

"Kira, is Sunshine a lion?" asked Hayden.

"Actually, she is a mix between a lion and an ocelot. That is why she is so small, but has the features of a lion," Kira replied. "Why?"

"Well," he started.

"I hadn't thought about that," interjected Hannah, looking at Hayden. "Good thinking!!"

"Thought about what? Let us in on the secret," demanded Hunter.

"The symbol on the lamp, which started us looking for the Legend, and the reference to the lion in the letter from Joseph Smith," said Hannah. "I bet they are both referring to Kira's cat, or one like it."

"You're right. Sunny doesn't look like a domestic cat—she looks more like a wild animal," agreed Alli.

"Yep. Maybe she represents the lion that is spoken of in the letter and the lion on the lamp," said Hayden. "That's what I was thinking."

"You know, we're getting to be pretty good sleuths with all this Legend stuff," said Hunter. "I bet Sunny was sent by the Lord to help keep us safe last night."

"I agree," added Hannah.

"And I'll bet she is keeping your clothes and things safe as the soldiers are tearing apart my father's house right now," said Kira as she pointed toward the bungalow back down in the city. "It is good we left when we did."

"What?" exclaimed Hunter. "You've got to be kidding me."

"Look down at my father's bungalow," Kira replied. She crouched down behind a gigantic Elephant Ear plant and motioned for everyone to do the same. Then she pointed into the distance and continued. "We need to be very careful. Tantua has loyal men all over the city, and they do not necessarily dress like the other soldiers."

"Is Sunny alright?" asked Hunter, worried about the animal. "We left her inside."

"She can hold her own," Kira replied, grinning slightly. "Can you see her through the window?" she asked.

"Yes, I can," Hunter replied.

"Watch what she does as they get close to her," said Kira pointing. "My father trained her very well."

They watched as several soldiers started pulling Kira's family's belongings out of the house. The soldiers tore through everything inside, and they even threw the bowl of fruit on the floor. Every time they moved within three feet of Sunny, she would give them a warning growl and throw her grapefruit-sized paw out toward their feet.

"They won't kill her, will they?" asked Hunter, worried about the swords and spears the soldiers were brandishing.

"Only if they want the wrath of God to be upon them," she replied assuredly. "The lion is protected here, they cannot touch her."

The kids watched as a soldier suddenly lunged at Sunny. Sunny angrily reared back. She stood on her back feet and held her front claws in the air, growling ferociously.

"Now they've done it," said Kira. She held her hand over her mouth to conceal the large grin.

Sunny walked on her back legs for several steps, swinging her large front paws wildly in the air as she growled. The soldiers in the bungalow were so frightened, they stopped searching and ran out of the house. They checked every few seconds over their shoulders to make sure the angry cat was not following them.

"Isn't she great?" chuckled Kira, as she fell back and laughed at the soldiers' response to the cat. "See, I told you she would keep your belongings safe. She is the best lion."

"Why are they searching through all the houses?" questioned Alli. "What are they looking for?"

"They are looking for you!" Kira replied mockingly. "Somehow they know someone has come into the city."

"Well, I didn't tell anyone," said Alli.

"None of us did, Alli," replied Hunter.

"Who could know we are here then?" asked Hayden.

"You didn't have to tell anyone that you were here," replied Kira. "I'm sure you left several clues as you traveled around the city."

Suddenly, one of the soldiers reached inside the bungalow, grabbed something on the table and returned holding up the fruit peels from breakfast and screamed.

"What does he have?" asked Hayden.

"Breakfast," replied Hunter.

"What's so interesting about breakfast?" questioned Hayden.

"They know someone has been there," replied Kira. "I can only assume they believe it is the intruders they suspect to be inside the city."

"Why would they think it's us and not you?" Alli asked confused. "They know you live there."

"The soldiers know that I live with my Aunt and they know my father is in the dungeon. With fresh fruit peelings there, they must believe that someone has been there."

"So what now?" questioned Hunter.

"You are in a lot of danger. And now, because of you, so am I," she softly replied, as she watched the soldiers. "I hope I have done the right thing by helping you."

The kids watched in silence as the men moved from bungalow to bungalow, tearing them apart as they searched. They watched people get pushed out of their homes and babies cry as they were awakened. Then, without any thought as to what they had just done, the soldiers would move onto the next house to do the same thing all over again.

"This is not right!" exclaimed Alli. "We can't let them do this!"

"There is nothing you can do to stop them, except turn yourselves over to Tantua," Kira replied. "And because you are the only hope that my father will ever be released from that terrible dungeon, I will not let them find you. That is why I brought you here. You will need to know where everything is in the city, including all the escape routes to the land below the city and the safe hiding spots that the soldiers do not know about."

"Hey, everyone. We are a lot higher than I thought we were," interrupted Hayden, as he pointed to the cloud covered ground below. "We've got to be at least fifty feet or more above the ground. I didn't think we had climbed that high!" he exclaimed.

Alli glanced over the edge of the rocks and then quickly scooted back a few feet from the edge. "Don't tell me to look over the edge, Hayden," Alli complained, holding her stomach. "Now I'm gonna be sick!"

"I didn't make you look over," Hayden replied defensively.

Alli shot a quick smile at her friend. Then she laid back in the thick grass and held her spinning head.

"We will not be safe here for long, I need for you to watch while I point to safe places in the city. I will also point out the homes of the people that will help you if you get into trouble," Kira began.

The group looked down at the beautiful city as Kira started to describe places.

"If we start from the river that feeds the waterfall pouring over the edge of the valley into the lava below, you can see three men fishing. These men spend their entire day near the crystal blue waters, searching for food to feed the city. All three of these men are trustworthy. They are from the tribe of Zebulun. On the docks you will see two more men. They are tariff collectors for Tantua and are loyal to him. Do not trust them, or anyone with a bright orange sash tied around his waist. At the edge of the jungle, where the water ends and the trees and greenery begin, you will see women in the river washing their clothes. The women here are always loyal to their husbands. Right now, the women who are there, are the wives of Tantua's soldiers. I would not trust them. There are more women about thirty feet closer to the city, weaving baskets. Can you see them?" Kira asked, hoping Hunter was paying attention to her.

"Yes, I can. They are sitting in the lush, green meadows using reed leaves to weave with, is that right?" he replied, as he looked over at Kida.

"Yes," said Kira. "Those women are usually trustworthy. The wives of the soldiers don't weave baskets very often."

"You talked earlier about a prophecy," said Hunter. "Can you tell me where I can read it for myself?"

"There are two places that I know of. One is engraved on the courtyard wall inside the temple grounds. But, I don't think you are going to have any possibility of seeing that one, due to the activity around the temple."

"And the other?" asked Hunter, impatiently waiting for her reply.

"Well, the other is in the cave below the mountain we are standing on," she said nervously.

"Good, let's go there to see the prophecy," suggested Alli.

"We can, but it is very dangerous inside," warned Kira. "There's a good possibility we could be seen, attacked by animals or even burned in lava."

"What?" asked Hunter.

"Remember the lava that you saw flowing outside the mountain?" Kira asked.

"Yes, what about it?" questioned Hannah.

"The lava has to start somewhere, right?" asked Kira.

"Yes," Hunter replied.

"The lava that you saw flows through the mountain where the prophecy is written," she replied.

"Oh!" exclaimed Hayden. "The black ash that I am standing on, and can see all over the ground, is from the lava flowing throughout the area. I can only hope it's from a dormant volcano. Is that right?" asked Hayden.

"I'm not sure if the volcano is dormant or not," Kira replied. "I don't know what that means."

"Dormant means it doesn't ever erupt and explode," answered Hunter. "Do you understand?"

"Yes, I understand," she replied, quietly thinking for a moment. "I do not know if this makes the volcano active, but occasionally the lava does boil and rumble loudly. Then it fills the mountain and flows from the top up there," she said, pointing. "Down the sides of the hill, and then throughout the city," she replied, still pointing. "And as you can see, we have several small streams of lava that flow all the time."

"What was the loud blast that we heard yesterday?" asked Hannah. "Was that the volcano?"

"Yes, about every three or four months, the volcano builds with great pressure and then releases a loud blast. That usually happens within a day or so of the lava filling the cave where the prophecy is engraved, then flowing dangerously through the city," answered Kira.

"So, does anyone ever get hurt from the lava?" asked Alli nervously.

"Yes, every time the lava spills from the mountain and caves, many are hurt, sometimes even killed. That is why we've got to free my father," Kira said in a tearful voice.

"Why?" asked Hannah.

"The dungeons are the lowest place in the city, when the lava overflows it sometimes reaches the dungeon and fills it with lava, leaving the prisoners no way to escape," she replied.

"Then I guess we better save your father before that happens," replied Hunter.

Kira smiled and softly replied. "Thank you."

"I want to go see the prophecy engraved in the cave, but first, finish telling us about the city before we leave," insisted Hannah. "I want to know where we can go to be safe. What are all those colorful tarps and canopies down there?" she asked, pointing toward the city.

"Hannah, stay behind the bushes," Kira said as she grabbed Hannah's arm and pulled her back. "You can be seen from all over the valley up here."

"Sorry, I forgot," she replied nervously.

"Hannah is right. I do need to tell you about a few other parts of the city," said Kira. "And quickly, before the soldiers find us."

As they crouched down next to the large base of a Banyan Tree, with hundreds of vines falling from the braches and dense greenery from bushes and shrubs, Kira quickly pointed out another part of the city.

"Can you see the bungalows on the edge of the city, hanging from the Banyan trees?" she asked, pointing.

"Yes, those homes all have different shapes than the others," replied Hayden. "Don't they?"

"That is correct. Those are the homes from the tribe of Reuben. Because my father was arrested before he could talk to the leader of the tribe of Reuben, I do not know where their loyalties are. So, you need to stay away. Okay?" she asked nervously.

Everyone nodded in agreement, then Kira quickly continued.

"There, in the middle of the city, just to the south of the great temple, is the city marketplace. All of the tribes bring their different wares there, like clothes, shoes, jewelry, food, everything you can think of. They sell their goods everyday in the market," said Kira.

"Is it safe in the market?" asked Alli. "I would really like to see it before we leave."

"The marketplace is an area where, if you keep your heads down and don't bring any attention to yourselves, it is possible to wander through unnoticed. However, we are running a huge risk by going there. Some of Tantua's soldiers patrol the city everyday," she replied.

"Is there anyplace in the market that is safe for us hide in an emergency?" asked Hayden. "Somewhere we could go if we got separated from you? Or is there someone that might help us?"

"Yes, there is a lady in the center of the marketplace. You can't miss her. She sells beautiful jewelry and hand-made masks. Her name is Miaha. She is a good friend to my father, and she brings him food when the soldiers allow her to enter the dungeon. Because the guards trust her, they allow her to take food to the prisoners, without an escort. Occasionally when that happens, we can get messages to and from him. I know she will help us, if we need her to."

"How will we know what she looks like? Does she have a certain colored canopy or something?" questioned Hannah, unsure which woman Kira was pointing to.

"Her canopy has several beautiful colors. There is blue, red, green, yellow and purple along with the silhouette of my lion, Sunshine, or as you call her, Sunny, in the center. Can you see the canopy?" Kira asked, pointing.

"Hannah nodded her head and replied, "Yes, I think I can see the colorful canopy."

"Kira, how long has it been since you've seen your father?" asked Hayden.

"Quite a while now," Kira replied.

"How long exactly?" asked Hunter.

"Tantua had my father thrown into the dungeon before he was named the new prophet," Kira replied sadly.

"And how long ago was that?" asked Alli.

"Tantua has been prophet for more than three months," she replied.

"You haven't seen your father for more than three months?" shrieked Hannah.

"Actually, I haven't seen my father in almost a year," replied Kira.

"A year?" yelled Hunter.

"Yes, almost a full year," she replied.

"You've got to be kidding!" said Hayden. "No wonder you want to get him out of there so bad."

Kira nodded, wiped a tear from her eye, took a deep breath and said, "There are several more things that I need to tell you about before we leave for the cave. On top of several buildings, including the temple, are secret tunnels. Most of the buildings have easy access, so if you find your-self caught, you can enter one of those buildings and find your way to the top. There are several fire pits on the roofs. The fire pits are used to light the city at night. Not only do they provide light, but, they also, unbeknownst to Tantua, serve a righteous purpose. With the help of the white crystals, given to all tribe members to wear around their necks, even the babies, the fire pits can be used as an escape route from any dangerous situation.

On each of the fire pits, located about waist high, there is a small opening. When the crystal is placed into the opening and turned one-quarter turn to the right and then one-half turn to the left, followed by a complete turn to the right, a small hatch opens. The hatch is an opening to a secret tunnel that was built hundreds of years ago. The prophets back then knew one day they would be needed to ensure the safety of the righteous. They built secret open-ings from the top of the buildings to underneath the city. When you climb through the hatch, the opening allows you to escape from where you are. And, if you follow the tunnel, it leads to a safer part of town."

"And they are only found at those eleven pillars of fire, Kira?" asked Hayden, scanning the building tops for them.

"That is correct," answered Alli. "They were built by my father's tribe for the time when Tantua was made ruler."

"Your father sounds like a very smart man," said Alli, smiling at Kira. "I'm sure we will be able to find him and return him to your people."

"Kira, I don't understand. You keep talking about multiple tribes here in the city. Can you tell me exactly which tribes are here, so that we know how many more different cities we still have to find before we can complete our mission?" asked Hunter.

"Hunter, all the lost tribes of Israel are here in the city. We have been co-existing for as long as I can remember," she replied.

"Are you serious?" questioned Hunter.

"All the lost tribes are in one place?" asked Hannah, shocked by Kira's response.

"Yes! When you look over the city at the bungalows, you will notice that in several of the areas the houses are slightly different. Some are small, some are bigger. Some have different shapes, and some are built on the ground or are suspended from the Banyan Trees. Each different area represents a different tribe. Can you see what I mean?" asked Kira, pointing to the different bungalows.

Hunter nodded, and then looked up at her a bit bewildered. "The letter from the prophet back home told us that we needed to bring a member of each tribe back to the cave with us."

"That should be easier if they all truly live here, right?" asked Alli.

"I don't know," replied Hunter.

"I don't know how we will determine who is from which tribe, and if we have at least two from each," he said, as he rubbed his forehead. "I can't tell you how bad I wish I had an aspirin right now. My head is killing me."

"Determining who is from each tribe will not be

hard," said Kira. "What will be hard, is convincing a member from each tribe to go with you."

"How can we determine who is from which tribe?" asked Alli.

"The sash worn on each person's waists represents which tribe they are from," Kira replied, smiling. "The tribe of Dan, which is the tribe that I come from, wears blue sashes, like the sashes you are wearing right now. The tribe of Gad wears yellow sashes, and the tribe of Judah wears green. The only time this differs is for Tantua's soldiers. Remember, they all wear orange sashes," explained Kira.

"Really?" Hayden asked excitedly.

"Yes," Kira replied, smiling.

"Alright, something's going to be easy after all!" said Hannah, jumping to her feet.

"Careful, Hannah. Remember, you can be seen from the entire valley up here," said Kira, as she grabbed Hannah's hand and pulled her to the ground.

"Is that Tantua, the man you keep talking about?" asked Alli, pointing toward the temple doors.

Kira turned quickly to look and gasped when she saw the man. "Yes!" she exclaimed. "Make sure you cannot be seen!"

"Where? Where are you looking?" asked Hayden, frantically scanning the area.

"Can you see the great temple doors with all the writings and engravings on them?" asked Hannah.

"Yeah," replied Hayden.

"He is walking in the courtyard next to the red flowers. He is wearing a white robe with a gold tie around his waist. He has a band around his upper arm and one tied in his black hair," said Hannah.

"Hey," interrupted Alli. "Look, on the temple doors. There is an engraving of the lion! Can you see it?" Alli asked excitedly.

"Wait!" screeched Hannah. "Hayden, can you see Prophet Tantua?"

"Is he holding a staff with strings and feathers dangling from it?" asked Hayden.

"Yes," replied Kira.

"Then, yep, I can see him," Hayden answered.

"Good, then you know who to stay away from," said Kira. "We need to get moving. I've got to speak with my brother so we can get a message to my father that you are here," insisted Kira, as she cautiously stood up behind the tree.

"Before we find your brother, do we have time to see the prophecy written in the cave you spoke about?" asked Hunter.

"Yes, but we better hurry. Follow me," she insisted, as she hurried into the twisted, tangled vines and trees of the forest.

CHAPTER TWENTY

MANEUVERING AS FAST as they could down the hill, the kids struggled to maintain their footing on the steep terrain and the smooth, slippery rocks covered with ash. Their footing became more questionable with each step they took as the ash formed a layer of soot on their shoes.

Kira observed her new friends try to keep up with her. She saw a tear trickle down Alli's cheek as she fell for the third time on the rocks, tearing her robe.

Concerned Alli might give up, Kira called, "We don't have much further. We only have to make it another fifty yards or so to the small waterfall. We're almost there."

Alli looked up, relieved to be close and asked, "When we get inside the cave, can we sit for a minute? My legs are burning!"

"Yes, Alli," replied Kira. "There is a small waterfall just inside where we can stop for a drink and rest. But only for a moment, okay?"

Alli, somewhat relieved, smiled and continued following Kira down the steep hill toward the entrance to the cave. As they reached the bottom of the hill, Kira quickly located the small, inconspicuous cave entrance, hidden behind a small waterfall and several large bushes and trees. "We'll enter on this side of the mountain and then follow the pathways through the cave and exit on the other side," she explained.

"Whatever you think is best," replied Hunter.

Kira quickly started crawling through a narrow opening, barely big enough to squeeze through.

"Watch your head," she warned, as she wiggled her body through the opening.

Several feet inside, the tunnel started to widen. As Kira reached the area, she called, "Not much further and you can crawl on your hands and knees."

"How far?" called Alli, feeling a little claustrophobic.

"Only about ten or twelve feet," replied Kira. "Hang in there."

The cave was so dark, Hannah, Hunter, Hayden and Alli could not see anything. They reluctantly followed the sound of Kira's voice.

Alli breathed a little easier with every step. As the cave widened, continuing on her hands and knees, unable to stand up through the winding and descending tunnel. She prayed, as they moved deeper and deeper, for a feeling of peace to help her through her claustrophobia.

The group finally emerged from the small tunnel into a larger area.

"I can't see a thing!" complained Hannah.

"Me neither," added Hayden. "Kira, I know that you know where you're going, but I don't have any idea where I am, and I can't see a thing."

"Don't worry," she replied. She took the small, green, glowing crystal from around her neck, grasped the top and bottom, and quickly snapped it in half. Carefully reaching inside, she removed a small white object.

"Hey, the other night I saw men doing the same thing you just did. What do you have?" asked Hunter, watching intently.

"These are fire bugs," she replied, holding out her hand and smiling. "They provide most of the light for the entire city. It is said that the Lord provided us a way to have light wherever we needed it when the lost tribes were first brought here. With the fire bugs in our crystals, we have the Lord's strength and light," she replied, smiling. "This fire bug is my strength and light from the Lord. We are all given one when we are born."

"Fire flies?" asked Hunter, with an odd expression on his face.

"Everything here is symbolic, Hunter. The light of the fire bugs is symbolic of the light of Christ," she replied.

"I get it. I understand. I'm just surprised," he replied. He watched her release the bug, and the cave softly lit up.

"How far do we need to travel into the cave before we can see the prophecy?" asked Hannah.

"Not far," Kira replied. "But we need to be careful. We will be walking on a two-to-three foot wide pathway that leads us through several waterfalls, as well as small rivers of lava. These pathways are slippery at times, and they can be very dangerous. As you follow me, stay close and pay attention."

"Rivers of lava?" squeaked Hannah, looking around nervously.

"Yes. And because of the ash and cinders, everything in here is slippery," Kira said.

"You said there was a place to sit and get a drink for a moment?" Alli asked.

"Yes, just ahead of us about fifteen feet. The path that we walk on goes directly behind the waterfall. We can get a drink there, is that alright?" Kira asked.

Alli nodded, and they all maneuvered quickly to the water for a drink.

"This is really cool!" exclaimed Hannah, as she looked through the water toward the orange glow of lava in the distance.

"What's cool?" shrieked Alli. "Burning lava every-where, the tears in my robes, the bruises all over my body, or running from soldiers? What is cool about any of that?"

"Come on, Alli. You have to admit, that everything about this place is kinda cool," responded Hayden.

"You know what's really cool? That the Lord picked us to come and bring home the lost tribes," added Hunter.

"You know what would be even cooler?" asked Hannah. She reached under the waterfall and retrieved a handful of water.

"Cooler?" teased Hunter, as he dunked his head in the water to cool down.

"Yes, cooler," exclaimed Hannah.

"Okay, what would be cooler?" asked Hunter.

"Having Grandpa here with us would be cooler," she said.

"You know, I forgot. I have my cell phone," exclaimed Hunter excitedly. "I wonder if it would work from here?"

Hunter reached for his pocket and suddenly remembered his cell phone was in his pant's pocket back at Kira's house.

"So, do you have a signal?" Alli asked hopefully.

"I don't even have the phone," Hunter replied, as he slapped his hands against his leg. "It's in my pants back at Kira's house!"

Alli ginned widely and chuckled at Hunter's actions.

"Wow, Alli, I haven't seen you smile like that in days!" exclaimed Hunter.

"I'm sorry to interrupt, but we cannot stay here much longer. We have to keep moving. Everything in the cave can change in minutes," Kira insisted.

Alli splashed a little water onto her face and said, "Thank you. I feel much better now."

Kira turned cautiously and headed further into the cave.

"The prophecy is on the wall, closer to the other side of the cave. We will not take very long to get there. We just need to be careful," said Kira. She followed the small light fluttering a few feet in the distance. "The edge of the trail is windy in some places and meanders up and down."

The group followed Kira, amazed at the scenery that surrounded them. They wandered past several beautiful waterfalls, with their sparkling blue water and shiny white sand. A few steps further the scenery rapidly changed to smoldering embers of orange and black.

'I've never seen anything like this," said Hunter, astonished by the sight. "This is truly amazing."

"I'm surprised we're not burning up in here," replied Hayden. "You know that lava is over two thousand degrees."

"I think the only reason we're not is because of the waterfalls. They're adding just enough air and moisture around the area that the temperatures are staying relatively comfortable," reasoned Hannah.

"You're probably right, but wow! This is amazing," replied Hayden, still in awe at his surroundings.

"I really can't wait to tell Grandpa about all of this," said Hannah, smiling. "You know, I wish I had my camera!"

"We're here," interrupted Kira, pointing to a cave directly behind a waterfall.

Hunter hurried to see the engravings and stared at them for several seconds before he said, "I can't read a thing! This is written in a language I can't read."

Kira smiled, walked to the engravings and started reading.

"'In the year that Tantua, son of Tarshia of the tribe of Reuben, is pronounced Prophet of the great and powerful city of the lost tribes, a great falling out of men will occur. As Tantua becomes hardened in his heart to the ways of the Lord, and he begins to preach false doctrines to the Lord's choice people, men's faith will fail, if they do not wax strong in the ways of the Lord. Do not harden your hearts to the ways of the Lord. Watch for the signs He will send to return the faithful tribes to the land of their inheritance. Remember, that these things arc not written that they must come to pass, but only that they could come to pass. If Tantua falls to the temptations that are placed in his path, four will come with the strength of the Lion, through the direction of the Lord, to return you home to live with your Father once again. Stay always in righteousness. Your friend and prophet of the Lord, Judah.'"

"Wow! Judah, a prophet of the Lord, foretold the future, and again the Lord's people discount his writings and say they are not so," Alli said meekly.

"A lot like the events that happen over and over again in the Book of Mormon," added Hannah.

"You know, you'd think after a while of seeing the same pattern over and over, people would be smart enough to learn and not do it again," said Hayden, shaking his head.

"One of the major reasons Jesus gave his life for us, was so that we could repent of the dumb things we do," said Hunter.

"Yeah, but isn't the idea to learn so that we don't have to repent over and over?" joked Hayden.

"I do not understand everything you are talking about, but we need to start moving, we have a lot to do today before the storms come tonight," interrupted Kira.

"Storms? Do they come every night?" asked Hannah.

"Yes, most nights they do," Kira replied. "So, we must hurry. We need to get you all to the marketplace so that we can get a message to my father."

"You're right," replied Hunter. "Lead the way," he said, pointing down the trail.

"Is it very much farther until we reach the opening?" asked Alli, ready to take another break.

"No, not far at all," Kira answered as she hurried through the dirty black ashes that seemed to be getting thicker and thicker with every step they took.

"The cave is getting hotter," said Hannah. "Really humid or something."

"The last waterfall is nearly one hundred fifty feet away," answered Kira. "We need to move through this area quickly. There are no more waterfalls between here and the cave's opening. If the lava is high, not only is it hot, but it gets very hard to breathe in here."

"Then we better move faster," Alli agreed.

She hurried along the path's edge, hoping the ash was not quite as thick on the outside edge of the trail. As she quickly moved, Alli struggled with the heat. Suddenly, she slipped on the ash, falling forward toward the two thousand degree lava. Her small body slipped through the sharp chards of ash down toward the lava. Clawing for anything she could find to stop her plunge toward the fiery river below, she screamed in terror. Struggling to breath in the hot, humid air, and frantic with fear, she passed out.

"Alli! Alli!" screamed Hannah. She fell to her knees and scrambled to catch Alli's foot.

Hunter raced to help. He slid his long body over the edge and reached for his friend. It seemed like forever before he finally caught hold of Alli's ankle, stopping her fall, inches before she tumbled into the lava.

"Alli, Alli are you okay?" called Hannah, as Hunter slowly pulled her over the sharp cinders to the safety of the small ledge.

"Alli?" called Hayden, as he looked at her cut and bleeding arms and legs.

Hunter pulled Alli onto the ledge and laid her softy on the ground. Carefully, he pulled her long hair out of her face and gently wiped the black ash from her nose and mouth. He quickly placed two fingers on her neck to feel for a pulse and breathed a cautious sigh of relief when he finally found one.

"Is she alright?" asked Kira, nervously peering over Hunter's shoulder.

"She is still alive," replied Hunter. He motioned for Hayden to stop the bleeding from several cuts.

"We've got to get her somewhere that we can take care of her," insisted Hunter, as he looked up into Kira's warm, green eyes.

"If we get her to the marketplace, Miaha can help her. I'm sure of it," she replied.

"Then we better get moving!" insisted Hayden. He reached out and tapped Alli on the cheek. "Alli, come on. Wake up!"

"Come on, Alli. Wake up," called Hannah, as she held Alli's hand for comfort.

Hunter softly shook Alli's shoulder and again called,

"Alli, Alli, wake up!"

Alli's eyes twitched back and forth rapidly as though she was having a terrible dream, then suddenly opened. Unsure where she was or what had just happened, the silence in the cave was shattered as she started to scream.

"Aaaaaaaaaaaaaaaaaaaaaaaaaaaaaaaahhhhhhhhhhhhhhh-hhhhhhhhhhhhhhhhhh,aaaaaaaaaaaaaaaaaaaaaaaaaaaaaaaa hhhhhhhhhhhhhhhhhhhh!"

"Alli, it's Hunter. We've got you, Alli," he said, trying to comfort her.

Alli jerked her head from side to side. She looked around the area, desperately trying to remember what had just happened.

"Alli, relax. You're all right. It's okay," said Hannah, in a calming voice.

"Where am I?" she screamed frantically.

"We're in a cave, remember?" replied Hayden.

"We're with our new friend, Kira. We're looking for the lost tribes," Hannah calmly said.

Alli looked over her shoulder and spotted the long brown hair of her new friend.

"Are you hurt?" asked Hunter, as he helped Alli sit up.

"I hurt everywhere," snapped Alli, holding up her throbbing, aching arms.

"No, I mean is anything broken?" clarified Hunter, steadying her back with his arm.

Alli took a deep breath and coughed because of the ash in her mouth. Several hard, gut-wrenching coughs later, she finally replied, "I don't think anything's broken."

"Do you think you can stand up?" asked Kira.

"I don't know. I can try," she softly replied, as she grimaced from the pain.

"Help her, Hunter!" begged Hannah, as she watched Alli begin to cry from the pain.

As Alli reached her feet, she looked up at Hunter and said, "Thank you for saving me!"

Hunter smiled and replied, "I was glad to do it! Now, no more slipping, tripping, falling or trying to be killed, okay?"

"Okay," Alli replied as a small smile started to cross her face.

"Come, we need to get moving! We don't want to be trapped inside this cave," called Kira.

Hayden and Hunter helped Alli to walk for several minutes before Kira called, "Hunter, can you come here for a moment?"

Hunter let go of Alli's arm and whispered, "Hayden will take care of you. I'll be right back."

Alli nodded, and Hunter hurried twenty feet ahead to where Kira was standing.

"Look at the entrance to the cave," she said, as she pointed.

"What? I can't see anything," Hunter replied.

"I can see a shadow moving. Can you?" Kira asked nervously.

Hunter, searched the opening for any shadows, but he was unable to see anything. "I can't. Are you sure you saw something?" he asked.

"Maybe my mind is playing tricks on me," she replied,

shrugging her shoulders.

Suddenly, the quiet of the cave was shattered by the commands of several soldiers coming from behind the group.

"You were right! Let's get out of here, fast!" shouted Hunter. He shoved Hannah and Kira through the cave.

"Hunter!" yelled Hayden. "Help me. I can't carry Alli alone."

Hunter turned around to see Hayden struggling to help Alli. She cried in pain every time Hayden tried to move faster, and Hunter could see the soldiers gaining ground.

"Come on, Alli. You've got to walk faster," demanded Hunter, as he raced back toward them.

"She can't move. I think she's frozen in fear!" Hayden exclaimed. "Either that, or she's passed out with her eyes open!"

As Hunter reached Hayden, he frantically took hold of Alli's arm. He picked her up and threw her over his shoulder. "Get the other girls to safety. I am depending on you. I will meet you as soon as I can back at Kira's father's bungalow."

"But, Hunter, let me help!" Hayden protested. "We can make it faster if I help!" he said.

"Maybe so, but I really need you to catch up with the other girls and make sure they are not in any danger," insisted Hunter as he struggled with the extra weight and tried desperately to keep his balance.

"Hunter, please!" cried Hayden, afraid to leave his brother's side.

"I said, move it!" I need you to take care of those two. GO!" he screamed. "You're in charge until I get back."

Hunter watched as Hayden sadly turned and ran toward the girls.

"Okay, no worries, Alli. I got ya," whispered Hunter. He moved her as quickly as he could through the small cave.

As Hannah saw Hayden running toward them, she turned and ran as fast as she could toward the cave's entrance, with Kira close on her heels.

As they reached the edge of the cave, Kira anxiously called, "Wait, Hannah! I don't feel good about this. I think someone is out there."

Hannah was not listening. So anxious to get away from the soldiers, she flew through the opening into the light. Straight ahead of her stood a heavyset man, well over six feet tall. He had large, muscular arms and a well-defined chest. His long jet-black hair was pulled into a ponytail. He wore a blue leather headband, covered in black Egyptian symbols, and had a smaller band around his arm with the same symbols. He wore a white robe and had a blue sash tied around his waist, and he wore leather sandals on his feet.

"Hannah, wait!" called Kira, as she saw the soldier in the distance. "I knew a soldier was out here. Don't let him catch you."

"Stop, girl!" demanded the soldier. "The Prophet Tantua would like to see you. Why are you running?"

Hannah, afraid of what Kira had said about the Prophet Tantua, and not wanting to be thrown into prison, instinctively made her move. As she scanned the area for something to protect herself with, she noticed a huge vine hanging from the cave. She grabbed the vine and swung her legs and feet up and over the small lava canal and dropped them solidly on a huge rock on the other side.

"You will not escape from me, girl!" called the large soldier. He searched for a vine strong enough to lift him over the canal.

Sure the soldier would follow her, Hannah grabbed another vine from the mountain wall and swung her feet and legs again, this time over the lava. They landed solidly on the muscular man's right shoulder.

The solid impact broke her hold on the vine and sent her slamming roughly to the ground. Dazed from the jolt, she scrambled to her knees, and then quickly jumped to her feet. Her opponent, although skilled, was not as lucky as she was. As he flew backwards from the force of the impact, he tripped, lost his balance, and crashed into the mountain next to the waterfall, hitting his head on a rock.

"That was lucky, and really dumb, Hannah!" yelled Hayden, as he grabbed her arm. "Come on. We've got to get out of here, right now!"

"Yes, look!" exclaimed Kira. "There are several soldiers coming through the cave's opening." She pointed anxiously toward the base of the small hill they had climbed earlier during the day and said. "We must go. Our lives are in serious danger."

"We can't leave without Hunter and Alli," protested

Hannah. "We've got to find them and save them!"

"We have no choice. Hunter said he would meet us back at Kira's house. Now, come on. We've got to go!" ordered Hayden.

Hannah looked over at the soldier lying on the ground. Not sure why, she leaned over and grabbed the leather band tied around his arm. Then she turned and followed Hayden and Kira into the dense trees and bushes.

"Where can we hide, Kira?" asked Hayden, as he panted for breath.

"I don't think the soldier saw my face. But if he did, then my father's home is not safe anymore," she replied. "We must get word to my brother, before the soldiers return to the temple.

"Hunter is going to meet us at your home with Alli!" exclaimed Hannah. "How are going to warn him that it's not safe to go there?"

"We don't have to," replied Hayden, as he pointed back toward the cave.

"What do you mean?" asked Hannah, quickly turning to see where Hayden was pointing.

Hannah was petrified at the number of soldiers she saw moving toward her.

"Hurry," insisted Kira. "We must get word to my brother quickly."

CHAPTER TWENTY-ONE

"WHAT ARE WE going to do now?" cried Hannah. She watched in horror as the soldiers marched Hunter, and a still unconscious, Alli outside the cave.

"At least Hunter can understand what they are saying," said Hayden.

"No one but Hunter can understand the language here, Kida," said Hannah,

"I should have stayed and helped Hunter," said Hayden, upset he had not stayed with his brother.

"If you would have stayed, you would have been captured, too," replied Kira.

"But I feel guilty that I didn't stay. Things could have been different," replied Hayden.

"We'll figure out a way to save them," replied Kira. "I know my father will know what to do."

"But what if they are killed before we get to your father?" Hannah asked through sobs.

"Tantua will not kill them—at least not right away. He

will want to show the city his great power. He will want to show them that the prophecy was not true, and the four will not be able to return the tribes to the land of their inheritance," replied Kira.

Hayden, Hannah and Kida watched momentarily as the soldiers tied a rope around Hunter's waist and forced him to carry Alli without any help. With the point of a spear placed firmly in his back, the soldiers started to walk toward the city.

"Where should we start?" asked Hannah, ready to get moving.

"In the market. We need to get to Miaha as quickly as possible," replied Kira.

"That might be a good idea," added Hayden. "And we probably should start sooner, rather than later, 'cause we're about to have company. Look! Several soldiers are moving this way," Hayden frantically announced. "There is nothing we can do for Hunter right now. Come on. Let's go!"

Kira nodded her head. Hayden and Hannah quickly followed her, leaving Hunter and Alli alone with their captors.

"Bashan?" called Midian, as he entered the courtyard of the temple. "Captain, Bashan? Are you in here?"

"Yes, over here," answered Bashan, still staring at the engravings on the stone wall. "Have you found an intruder?"

"Yes, two of them," Midian replied.

"Were there others?" asked Bashan, carefully eyeing Hunter, who was still carrying Alli on his shoulders.

"I believe so. Laish and Heth stayed to search the area," Midian replied.

"Nice work, men," said Bashan, nodding his head and answering in an approving tone.

"Where do you want me to take them?" asked Midian.

"We will take them straight to Tantua. He demanded to see whoever had entered the city," said Bashan.

"Would you like my group to stay and help you, or return and continue searching for the others?" asked Midian.

"Stay. If Tantua has questions, you will be able to answer better than I," answered Bashan.

"Before we take them to Tantua, I have one question, Bashan. May I ask you something?" questioned Midian.

"Sure," Bashan replied, anxious to hear his question.

"Do you believe there is any truth to the prophecy engraved on the wall," he asked.

"I'm sure there is some truth in it," Bashan replied evasively.

"How much?" asked one of the soldiers.

"Well, that I do not know," Bashan answered, staring through the courtyard to the far wall of the temple.

"Have you ever thought that we are stopping the plan of the Lord?" asked Midian.

"No!" Bashan replied boldly.

"Then what do you think?" asked Midian, hoping for Bashan to give him some answers.

"I think that the Lord's will is done in all things. If he did not want this boy to be captured and brought before Tantua, then they would have been able to evade their capture," he replied.

"I hadn't thought about that," replied Midian, deep in thought over the words his Captain had just spoken.

"Could the Lord's will be for the boy to be caught, in the hope that when Tantua meets him, he would see the way of the Lord and change?" asked Midian innocently.

"Are you saying that the Prophet Tantua is not right-eous?" Bashan asked, acting shocked.

"No! No, Captain. I was not thinking that. Please don't say anything to Tantua," he begged.

Bashan glared at Midian for several moments before he replied. "Your loyalty better be to Tantua."

"It is, Captain," he nervously insisted. "It is!"

Bashan turned, looked at his soldiers and called. "Men, stand up straight, be attentive to Tantua and do as he says, I do not want anymore of you to end up in the dungeons."

Bashan pushed the beautifully ornate white doors open to the great room where Tantua was waiting for information. Continuing to talk to the soldiers, Bashan said, "Tantua will want to know where the rest of the intruders are. Be ready to answer when he asks, Midian," instructed Bashan. He slapped his friend on the shoulder and pushed him inside the room.

"Greetings, Your Highness. I have brought the intruders," said Bashan, as he knelt at the base of stairs that rose to the throne.

"You know the law, Bashan. No outsiders may see the city and live!" shouted the man sitting on the throne. "You need to go put them to death."

"Before I did, I wanted to check with you," replied Bashan.

"That is a good idea," said Tantua.

"Maybe you should question them and see where the others have gone," suggested Midian.

"Good idea, Midian. Now tell me, prisoners, where have the others that were with you gone?" yelled Tantua, trying to intimidate Hunter.

"What others? What are you talking about?" asked Hunter.

"Don't play with me, boy!" yelled Tantua angrily. "Bashan, were there any others?"

Bashan turned to Midian and whispered, "Tell him what you saw."

"Your Highness," started Midian. He bent down on one knee and bowed to the prophet. "As we searched the city, we heard screaming in the tunnels of lava and decided to investigate."

"Yes, yes. Did you see any others?" Tantua snapped abruptly.

"Yes, Sir, we saw three others—two girls and one boy," Midian replied.

"Five total? Not four?" questioned Tantua.

"Yes, Your Highness," Midian replied.

"Then the prophecy in not correct," he said, breathing a deep sigh of relief.

"Not unless one of the people seen with them is from our city," replied Bashan.

Tantua frowned at the thought that the prophecy could still be true. He abruptly demanded, "Then get out there and help the other soldiers find them. This search does not stop until we have captured everyone involved."

"Yes, Sir," replied Midian, bowing again before he moved away.

"Your Highness," interrupted Kish. "Do you think these visitors are the ones the prophecy engraved upon our temple speaks of? And if they are, could they possibly return us to our Lord?" Kish asked. "Without their help, we may never be able to return."

"We do not need their help to return to our Lord!" snapped Tantua. "The Lord has given us all that we need to return on our own, when we feel the time is right."

"You mean, when you feel the time is right," snapped a strong voice from the shadows of the room.

"Who is there?" called Tantua, as he squinted his eyes tightly and stared into the shadows.

"You should know my voice by now, son," replied the confident woman. She entered the great room in a beautiful white gown, adorned with fine jewelry, which hung on her ears, neck, hands and ankles.

"Mother, what are you doing here?" snapped Tantua, irritated by her presence.

"You know the ways of the Lord, Tantua. You were taught to make righteous choices, like your father," she started. "Has the power of the throne driven you to behave like this, or are you so selfish that you will not give your services to this great city or to the Lord. Do you remember that this throne never was owed you? But was given as a way for you to serve others, showing them guidance and direction in the hope of helping them someday return to their Father in heaven. And by doing so you would be serving your Lord and Savior as the many righteous prophets before you have done. How dare you let them down! How dare you let me down!"

"Mother, this is no place for you to be. You know that I am the prophet, whether I want to be or not and as such, you know that you are not allowed to speak to me this way," Tantua warned.

"Remember, son, what the Lord gives, He may also take away," she replied.

"Mother, I don't care who you are. You may not speak to me that way," Tantua insisted.

"I'm sorry, son. However, I believe that it is every mother's right and duty to teach her children the right things to do," she replied, her voice never wavering.

As she turned to leave, Tantua called, "Mother, I think you forgot something. I think you better remember that I have spared you and other members of our family from the dungeon. Kindness can only last so long before I do to you as I have done to others!"

"Tantua, I do not take well to threats. When you begin to act as a prophet of the Lord, then I will begin to treat you as one. Until that time, I will only drop to my knee when I am praying to my Heavenly Father," she replied bluntly.

Tantua watched as his mother left the great room, slamming the door closed when she exited.

"Your Highness, what about the prophecy?" asked Bashan. "Is there anything to it?"

"That is enough about that stupid prophecy. We will discuss this later," he said angrily. He rose to his feet, grasping a tall spear. "The penalty for entering our city uninvited is death! Until I can speak with my counsel, I want these two thrown into the dungeon. And when the other intruders are found, throw them in the dungeon with them."

Hunter understood every word that had been spoken.

"Your Majesty," interrupted Hunter. "May I say, it is an honor for us to come to your city and show you the way home."

"What is this boy babbling about?" Tantua shouted angrily. "He does not even speak our language. How are we to know that he has been sent from God? He must be one of the false prophets spoken of by our prophets of old."

"No, I'm not a false prophet. I have been sent from God to help you return," replied Hunter.

"Keep him quiet. I do not wish to hear his voice!" screamed Tantua as he pointed his bright gold spear at Hunter's throat.

"What are they taking about, Hunter? Why does he keep yelling at you?" questioned Alli. "Please, whatever you're saying, stop! You're just making him more upset."

"Now, the girl I can understand," declared Tantua. "Beautiful sounds are coming from the mouth of such a pretty young woman."

"He can understand you, Alli!" whispered Hunter. "But he can't understand me. He thinks you're pretty."

"But I can't understand him," she whispered to Hunter.

"You better address him before he gets upset again," insisted Hunter, as he watched Tantua.

Alli looked at Hunter with sheer fear on her face. She looked up to the man on the throne, smiled slightly, brushed her hair away from her face and replied, "Thank you, Your Highness."

"I will translate what he says, and then you can reply. Okay?" whispered Hunter,

"Tell him it is an honor for us to be here," said Hunter, whispering in Alli's ear.

"Your Highness, it is an honor for the four of us to be here in your great city. We are grateful to be welcomed here by your people," Alli said nervously. "We have only come to help your people."

"You presume much to think you are welcome here," Tantua replied sharply. "And why would you think that we need your help. We are a very self-reliant people. You must receive punishment for sneaking into our city. But, before I make a decision, I will pray to my God, and counsel with my advisors. Guards, take them to the dungeon."

"But, Your Highness, we have come a long way looking for..." started Alli.

"I know what you seek, and you will not find it here. Your journey has been in vain and will probably cost you your lives," Tantua barked.

"But, Sir, we really are here to help you. We have been directed here through the help of the Lord," Alli insisted as Hunter had whispered into her ear.

"And yet, I can see that only you speak the language?" he replied. "How are we to know that you are not a false prophet yourself, sent here by Satan to lead us astray?" he snarled angrily. "I will not be convinced until I have spoken with my counsel. Then we will know, for the Lord speaks to me."

"Your Highness," interrupted Kish. "They seem like good people, truly sent here by the Lord to help our people return and be freed."

"Be freed from what? You are not held here in bondage," barked Tantua.

"I did not mean freed from bondage, I meant freed to return and live with the Lord," insisted Kish.

"Kish, I've told you and others today that I am not to be spoken to so freely!" screamed Tantua. "Guards, he can spend the next three days in the dungeon with these imposters. Take them away now, they have upset me," he said, as he turned his back to the group.

Hunter and Alli were nervous when the soldiers pointed their spears toward the two and led them out of the great room.

"Hunter, what is going on?" cried Alli.

"They don't believe we are here to help them," replied Hunter. "We are being thrown into the dungeon until he can decide whether we are to live or die."

"What?" cried Alli, still bloody and weak from the fall earlier in the cave. "Hunter, please don't let me die here," she begged.

"Everything will be fine, Alli," consoled Hunter, steadying her as they walked. "The Lord will protect us. He sent us here to do a job, and He will provide a way for us to complete the mission. Have faith!"

"Have faith? Then tell the prophet again," Alli demanded, as she felt the sharp tip of the spear push the back of her arm. "Tell them we are here to help!"

"Ouch!" she screamed, as the soldiers pushed the tip of his spear into her shoulder. "You're hurting me!" she shrieked, as a drop of blood formed on her shoulder.

"Quit fighting with them, Alli," warned Hunter. "The prophet is not going to talk to us any more right now."

"Yes, he will," she insisted. She pushed past the guard with the spear and moved toward the prophet.

"Your Highness. Your Highness," called Alli. The soldier forcefully grabbed her arm and started to pull her out of the room. "May I tell you one thing before you send us away?" she pleaded. "Please?"

"Stop!" demanded Tantua. "One thing. You may tell me one thing before you are thrown in the dungeon permanently."

"The Lord sent us here not only return your tribe, but all of the lost tribes of Israel. We were told that the journey would be dangerous, and that at times our lives would be in danger. But until the tribes were returned, the Lord could not return. Would you allow us to take just two members from each of your tribes and return them to the Lord?" she questioned.

"People of the lost tribes who are here in this room! You know the prophecy written in the cave and on the wall at the temple. 'Four will return here to take us back to our land and the return of our Savior and King.' Tantua is trying to stop that from happening. If we are thrown in jail, then you must release us so that prophecy from the prophets of old may come true," yelled Kish angrily. "You know the prophecy states that Tantua does not want the prophecy to be true because he will lose the throne!"

"Be quiet, Kish," Tantua ordered. "I will decide if these children are those written about in the prophecy of old, not you. Guards, take them to the dungeon, now! I have heard enough."

"Are you afraid to find out for sure if they are sent from the Lord?" pressed Kish.

"That is enough!" yelled Tantua. "If they are truly on a mission from God, then they will know the answer to a question written of by the prophets of old."

"What did he say, Hunter?" screeched Alli.

"If we are truly sent from God, then we will know the answer to a question left by the prophets of old," Hunter replied, trying to listen to the two men.

"Ask us anything!" shouted Alli. She ripped her arm away from the soldier and took several steps back toward the prophet.

"I will give you three days to prepare before I ask you the question. If you are correct, you may leave our city and never return. If you are wrong, you will be thrown into the lava outside the city. I suggest you pray for the next three days to your God for His help. Your very lives depend on it. Guards, take them and Kish to the dungeon. Kish, you are blessed to be my friend. Your sentence would be greater if not!" snapped Tantua, as he pounded his spear on the ground.

CHAPTER TWENTY-TWO

HUNTER STUMBLED as the soldier pushed him into the dark, cold, stone cave, the soldiers called the dungeon. The air was musty and smelled as though they were standing in a swamp. Moss covered the walls and felt slimy as Hunter put his hand against the wall for support.

A quiet sniffle echoed through the cave as Alli, afraid of being in the dark, afraid of bugs, and especially afraid of the unknown, started to cry.

"Do not worry, girl," consoled Kish. "I have spoken to Kira. She and your two friends sent me here with a message for our father. Now don't worry. All will be well!"

"How can you speak our language?" questioned Hunter.

"I, like my sister, was taught your language by our father. He was given the language from the Lord for the very time that you arrived," he explained.

"Where are we going to find your father?" asked Alli. "I don't want to stay in this stale, yucky place any longer than I have to."

"The caves are large, and there are many prisoners. We will have to start searching," he replied. "If he is still alive?"

"What do you mean?" asked Hunter.

"It has been several months since our contact, Miaha, has been able to find my father," he replied. "But if he is still alive, he will know what to do."

"Kira said Miaha talks to him often," said Alli nervously.

"I know, I didn't want to upset Kira, so I tell her every week that father sends his love," Kish replied.

"I had hope when I thought your father was alive," said Alli worriedly. "But, I don't know now."

"There will be others that can help us if my father has already returned home," said Kish, trying to reassure Alli.

"Where do we start looking?" asked Alli. "If he's alive, I want to find him right now!"

"We start searching here," Kish replied smiling. "These caves are big and every time they fill with lava they get bigger and bigger. There are many trails and caves."

"How are we going to search? We can't see anything in here, and I have no idea what your father looks like," she said, in a tearful, whiney voice.

"Did Kira give you a crystal necklace to wear?" Kish asked, looking for the magnificent stone around their necks.

"No. We were on our way to the market when we were caught by the soldiers," replied Hunter. "Kira wasn't able to get them to us before then."

Kish shook his head and asked, "Did she take you to the mountain to examine the city before she stopped to see the city?"

"Yes," cried Alli.

"We have been over this plan a thousand times. I don't understand why she couldn't follow it!" he mumbled to himself.

"We will search together and use my light for now. It will take us a little longer, but we'll be okay," Kish said, puckering his lips.

"By the way, my name is Hunter," he said, reaching out to shake hands.

Kish, unsure what Hunter was doing, replied, "As you have heard, my name is Kish." He reached out his hand, making the same motion as Hunter.

Hunter smiled, as he realized Kish did not know what he was doing. "I'm sorry," started Hunter. "Where we come from, this is called shaking hands. It is a gesture we make when we meet someone."

Hunter reached out to Kish's hand, grasping it firmly and shaking it up and down.

"This is nice," Kish said, smiling at Alli and Hunter. "In our land, the gesture we make is like this."

Kish made a fist with his left hand and lifted his arm. He brought his fist to his right shoulder, and then took his fist back to his left side.

Excited to show Kish the gesture, Alli made a fist with her left hand, and said, "My name is Alli." She pulled her fist from her shoulder, holding it at her side as Kish had done.

"It is very nice to meet two of the four sent from God. What chosen spirits you must be, to be in such great favor of the Lord!" exclaimed Kish. "I only hope to be able to earn the trust of the Lord like you have!"

Hunter smiled at Kish's remarks. He looked down to the ground, unable to say a word, as he did not feel that he was worthy to be on such a special mission for the Lord.

"We must start searching. We have a lot to do," insisted Kish. He pulled the crystal from his neck, just as Kira had done earlier, and snapped it open. He carefully and removed one firebug and released it above his head about a foot to the right.

"How do you get the firebugs to stay ahead of you, and in the same position you release it?" asked Hunter.

"We train them," replied Kish. "They represent the Light of Christ. In order to light your path to return to Him, you must work hard, study and train yourself to always choose the right. We do the same with the fire-bugs. We work hard to train them, which is why they represent the Light of Christ to us. That is also why they stay right where we need them to."

"I didn't know you could train a bug," replied Hunter, amazed at the small insect.

"What do you use for light where you come from?" questioned Kish.

"We have a thing called electricity back home," Hunter replied vaguely. "It's a little hard to describe, so I will just have to show you when we get you to come back with us."

Kish nodded his head in agreement and said, "We must hurry. Follow me. Let's start looking for my father."

Kish wandered through the cave, following a small tunnel back and forth, descending gradually the farther they walked. The light from the firebug was soft and cast an eerie glow in the musty cave. As they walked, the walls of the cave occasionally sparkled as the light from the firebug shone on the small flecks of gold in the cave.

"Kish, the small flecks in the wall, are they gold?" asked Hunter.

"I do not know if it is gold, but it is the material that the prophets use to keep their records," Kish replied. "That is why Tantua sends his prisoners to this dungeon. Their job is to remove the small pieces from the walls, so that Tantua's men can melt them down and hammer it into plates."

"Are we far from where the prisoners are?" asked Alli, as they walked into a large opening in the cave.

This area of the cave was filled with greenery of every kind. There was grass on the ground, and moss on the trees and walls. Small green vines even hung from the branches of the trees.

"This doesn't look like what I would have pictured a dungeon to look like," Alli commented.

"I guess prison is anything that keeps you from doing the things you like, right?" teased Hunter. "You and Hannah would die if you couldn't lay out and get a tan!"

"No we wouldn't," replied Alli, as she made a face at Hunter.

"Any sign of your father, Kish?" asked Hunter.

"I am looking," he replied as he walked further into the large room. He paused for a moment, looked at Alli and Hunter and said. "Stay here, I will run through this cave and see if I can find him. This will help our search go faster."

"Stay here? In the dark?" questioned Alli.

"I will only be gone a minute," Kish replied, as he ran off calling for his father.

"This is spooky," said Alli as she reached out in the darkness and took hold of Hunter's arm.

"Oh, come on, Alli. You can kinda see in here once your eyes get used to the dark," teased Hunter.

"I know. It's just eerie being a prisoner in a dungeon with who knows what kind of bugs!" she exclaimed.

Suddenly, a branch from a Banyan Tree snapped as it was stepped on. Not able to see who caused the noise, Hunter called, "Who's there?"

A soft, but deep and soothing, commanding voice startled Hunter when it responded, "I knew the Lord would send you to come for us."

Hunter spun around nervously, unsure who was behind them.

"Hello?" Alli called softly. Hoping her imagination was running wild. "Who is there?"

"Well, hello to you, too. I am surprised to hear the voice of a young girl," the voice replied, still hiding in the darkness. "So, you can speak our language."

"Yes, Sir. Where are you?" asked Alli, hopelessly scanning the darkness for the stranger. "Show yourself. You have no reason to hide from us."

"I'm right here," called the deep, soothing voice. The

man stepped from the darkness into the shadowy mist of the cave.

Alli watched as a large man appeared. He was taller than Hunter by three or four inches, making him at least six-foot-five or six and approximately two hundred and thirty or forty pounds.

"Why are you here?" asked the man.

Hunter quickly whispered to Hannah what the man said.

"You should know already, if you think we are here to save you," replied Alli.

The man moved closer, staring quietly at the two teenagers. As he moved closer to Alli, she gripped Hunter's arm tightly, digging her fingernails into his skin.

"Careful, Alli, that hurts!" he exclaimed.

This distracted Alli's attention away from the stranger long enough for him to move within inches of her face.

Alli looked up, startled at how close he was to her and screamed in fright. As she looked at the man, she was almost hypnotized by his piercing blue eyes. They sparkled brightly above a long, unruly, salt-and-pepper beard and shaggy, dirty, shoulder-length, brown hair. His clothes were torn and tattered. And it was easy to see that, even though he was large, he was starving.

"I'm sorry. I've probably frightened you," he exclaimed, stepping back from the Alli.

"No, we're not frightened," insisted Alli, trying to control her shaking legs.

"Well, you are stronger than I am then. Any time Tantua speaks, I get scared," the man replied, smiling and revealing surprisingly white teeth.

"Who are you?" asked Alli.

"I am the same as you—a prisoner," the man replied evasively.

"Do you have a name?" asked Alli.

"I do, and I will tell you after you tell me what you are doing here in Tantua's dungeon," insisted the man.

"We've been sent here by your prophet, Tantua," replied Hunter.

"He is not my prophet!" the man exclaimed angrily.

"You were about to tell us your name," said Alli, smiling cautiously at the man.

"That's right. I am ..." he started, suddenly interrupted by Kish.

"Hey, whoever you are, get away from them," he screamed, racing to their aid.

The man quickly moved into the cover of the trees, disappearing in the darkness.

"Who was that?" Kish asked breathlessly.

"I don't know—a prisoner here," replied Alli. "He was about to tell us his name when you scared him."

"Did you find your father?" questioned Hunter.

"No, and I searched the entire dungeon," Kish replied nervously. "I hope he is still alive. I hope Tantua did not have him killed when he wouldn't deny Christ."

"That's a dreadful thought," declared Alli. "What are we going to do now? Without your father all hope of returning home may be gone. We are stuck in a dungeon, Hannah and Kira are alone in the city, and we will never get the lost tribes back home!"

"Don't give up all hope yet," declared Kish. "Until

CHAPTER TWENTY-TWO

I am sure he is gone, I will never give up."

"I agree, we have only been searching a short time," said Hunter. "Let's keep looking, at least a little while longer."

Alli wiped the nervous tears from her eyes, took hold of Hunter's arm and said, "I won't give up, unless you do."

"Good Alli. Kish do you know, are Kira, Hannah, and Hayden, alright?" asked Hunter worriedly.

"They are safe for now," Kish replied. "But they will need help soon."

"Should we continue to search for your father?" asked Alli.

"I can't see how that would hurt until Miaha comes," answered Kish, squinting into the foliage against the wall.

"The man that was talking to you, I think I can see him. Maybe I will try to catch him and see if he knows where my father is," whispered Kish.

Like a cat, Kish pounced on the man, knocking him face first into the wet, gooey moss. He took the man's arm and twisted it quickly up behind his back, causing the man to moan in pain.

"Who are you, and why are you spying on us?" demanded Kish, as he twisted the man's arm a little tighter.

The man remained quiet while Kish again demanded an answer.

"Get off me, and I will tell you," replied the man.

Kish, sure he recognized the voice, released the man's arm and helped him to his feet. After brushing the grass, dirt and moss from his robe, the man turned around and looked at Kish.

As he stared at Kish for several uncomfortable seconds, he finally said, "Kish? Kish, is that you?"

Staring into the man's intense blue eyes, Kish suddenly recognized the man.

"Father!" he screamed. He threw his arms around the weak man, smothering him with a hug. "Father, you're alive. I was so worried, I thought you were dead. I was so afraid without you. I wasn't sure I could do as you asked if you were gone. This is the best day of my life."

Kish rattled on for several seconds before he released his father from the bear hug he had been giving him and yelled, "Oh father, have I got a lot to tell you!"

Can the kids free Kira's father and escape the dungeon undetected? Will they be able to sneak through the mysterious city and find safety before Tantua's soldiers find them? Could they possibly convince members from each tribe, not loyal to the prophet, to return with them to New York? Can they even find a way to return home with the bridge now destroyed? How can all of this possibly happen?

Join Hannah, Hunter, Hayden, Alli and their new found friends on their final adventure as they attempt to escape the clutches of the soldiers, steer clear of the exploding mountain of lava, and stay one step ahead of the evil prophet determined to keep them imprisoned forever!

ABOUT THE AUTHOR

Although born in Provo, Utah, Tina spent most of her life in San Diego, California. Her writing is strongly influenced by her hometown experiences and her large family whose flair for story telling never ends.

As a direct descendent of Heber C. Kimball and Orson Pratt, the stories told to her by her parents about them encouraged a fascination with the Book of Mormon, Church History, and the adventures of the early saints.

Tina is the author of *The Liahona Legacies,* a Book of Mormon adventure series for youth.

Tina Storrs Monson currently lives in Draper UT, a suburb of Salt Lake City. She attended Brigham Young University where she met her husband, Kreg. They have been married for seventeen years and have four children.